I KEPT SITTING WITH DAVID AND HIS TABLE AT LUNCH. The guys were all fine with it. And the girls who'd been my friends? I didn't have much in common with them anymore.

I wasn't stuck-up. I'm not stuck-up. I'm just not interested in the same things as other girls. I don't know their code. And, honestly, I don't want to. I have more in common with David and his friends than with a bunch of girls. Or, at least, more in common with David. I don't actually hang out with the other guys, except at lunch. David's my friend. My best friend.

Or he was, until Luke came along.

THAT'S WHAT FRIENDS DO

CATHLEEN BARNHART

Quill Tree Books
An Imprint of HarperCollinsPublishers

Quill Tree Books is an imprint of HarperCollins Publishers.

That's What Friends Do
Copyright © 2020 by Cathleen Barnhart
All rights reserved. Printed in the United States of America.
No part of this book may be used or reproduced in any manner whatsoever
without written permission except in the case of brief quotations embodied
in critical articles and reviews. For information address HarperCollins
Children's Books, a division of HarperCollins Publishers, 195 Broadway,
New York, NY 10007.
www.harpercollinschildrens.com

Library of Congress Cataloging-in-Publication Data

Names: Barnhart, Cathleen, author.
Title: That's what friends do / Cathleen Barnhart.
Other titles: That is what friends do
Description: First edition. | New York, NY : Harper, [2020] | Audience:
  Ages 8-12 | Audience: Grades 4-6 | Summary: Told in two voices,
  middle-schoolers Sammie and David's long-term friendship is endangered
  when new student Luke begins flirting with Sammie just when David
  decides to confess his crush on her.
Identifiers: LCCN 2019026617 | ISBN 978-0-06-288894-5 (paperback)
Subjects: CYAC: Best friends—Fiction. | Friendship—Fiction. | Middle
  schools—Fiction. | Schools—Fiction. | Family life—Fiction.
Classification: LCC PZ7.1.B371273 Th 2020 | DDC [Fic]—dc23
LC record available at https://lccn.loc.gov/2019026617

Typography by Catherine San Juan
21 22 23 24 25   BRR   10 9 8 7 6 5 4 3 2 1
❖
First trade paperback edition, 2021

MY MOM, SUZANNE WARNER, WAS MY FIRST STORYTELLER,
AND THE STORIES SHE TOLD HELPED ME TO KNOW
THE WORLD AND FIND MY PLACE IN IT.
MOM, THIS IS FOR YOU.

FRIDAY, DECEMBER 19

DAVID

I slide into my seat on the bus—fourth row from the back—and a beat later Sammie slides into hers, on the other side of the aisle from me.

Her cheeks are pink, like she's been running. A couple of locks of her springy, dark hair have escaped from her ponytail, and they boing around her face. She pushes them back, but they immediately spring forward again.

She shrugs out of her backpack, which is so full that the zipper won't close at the top.

"What's with the backpack on steroids?" I ask. "Did you empty out your locker?"

"No," Sammie says, with that tone she uses when I'm supposed to already know something. "Books, silly. We have to read *The Giver* over break, you know."

"*The Giver* is *book*," I say. "Not *books*. And it's a pretty thin one, as books go. Your backpack is not begging for mercy because of *The Giver*."

"You know me. I like to have a plan," Sammie says, and she's right on both counts. "My plan for winter break is to read *The Giver* and the other three books in the series. And after that, I'm reading the Dark Is Rising series."

"Sammie," I say, "as your friend—"

"Your *best* friend," Sammie interrupts.

"As your *best* friend, I'm begging you to take a chill pill. It's *vacation*."

"I know," Sammie says, holding up one hand to stop me. "But I like to read."

"How many books total?" I ask.

Sammie looks off into space, counting them up. She squints, and her lips move a little as she does the math. "Nine, total," she says. "That's my goal." She grins at me, her dark brown eyes shining.

"You're such a nerd," I say. "That's more than half a book a day. I'm just hoping to get through *The Giver*, which I got as an audiobook so I can listen while I'm restocking shelves."

Sammie leans back in her seat and stretches her legs out in front of her. "Would you rather listen to *one* book while working, all day long, at your dad's store, or read *nine* books while lounging in front of a fire, drinking hot chocolate—with marshmallows—and eating homemade chocolate chip—"

"Not fair," I groan.

"I know," she says, smiling. "But that's my plan: fire, hot chocolate, yummy baked goods, and books."

She pushes a curl of hair off her face, again, and looks right at me, waiting. I have a winter break plan too, but I don't say anything.

Because my plan is to tell Sammie Goldstein my real, true feelings for her.

SAMMIE

David Fischer is my best friend for a lot of reasons. First, of course, he's not a girl. Okay, maybe that's not the best *first* reason because it makes me sound like I like him *just* because he's not a girl. So scratch that.

First, because I've known him since kindergarten, when we were on the same Little League team. But I've known lots of other kids since even before then, like Carli Martin and Sarah Canavan. They're *not* my best friends. Anymore.

So, first because he's funny. But also because he's nice. Funny *and* nice.

Okay, scratch all of that. David Fischer is my best friend because five minutes after I walk into my dark, silent house on the first day of a very long winter vacation, he texts me and asks, *Want to come over? You can tell me more about your goals for vacation and I can make fun of you.*

I look at the clock on the microwave. Dad's still at the office and won't be home for hours. My mother's probably showing houses, so who knows when she'll appear. And Rachel and Becca, aka the Peas, are guaranteed to be MIA until after dinner because they're in high school, and presidents of half the student clubs.

Sure, I text back.

When? David asks.

Leaving in 15. Then I have a great idea: *Meet me at the fort! I'll bring snacks.*

I wait, watching my phone. After a minute, David texts back, *OK. I'll bring flashlights & hand warmers*

& feet warmers

& butt warmers

I fill the kettle and turn it on, then carry my backpack upstairs and dump out all my school stuff onto my bed. I take the bag back down to the kitchen and fill it with snacks: Chex Mix, pretzels, and some brownies the Peas made last night. When the water boils, I make a thermos of hot chocolate. Then I grab a deck of cards and a stadium blanket from the back of the family room couch and head out through the sliding glass doors, across the backyard and up onto the Greenway.

It's deserted. No surprise, with the sun setting in less than an hour and the temperature only slightly north of freezing.

David's house and mine are in different neighborhoods, but they both back up to the Greenway. A long time ago, before my whole neighborhood was even built, the Greenway used to be railroad tracks. Dad told me that there were a bunch of railroads that ran between New York City and the Westchester suburbs, and each one had its own tracks and terminal. This railroad went broke, and the tracks were abandoned. They got covered over with dirt and grass, and then someone had the idea to turn the whole thing into a walking trail. Which I walk on all the time to go to David's house. Then, last summer, we found the fort.

DAVID

Meet me at the fort! Sammie says. With an exclamation point.

"Ugh," I say out loud. The Fort is our special place,

our secret, so I get why Sammie wants to meet there. But it's not a *real* fort, just a giant cement drainage tunnel underneath the Greenway. In the summer, it's always cooler than outside, which is nice. In the summer. Today, when the weather app says forty degrees, the Fort will be freezing, and probably dark, but we'll be alone there. And maybe we'll have to huddle together for warmth, and maybe—

I text back and say okay to Sammie's crazy Fort idea.

Then I head to the bathroom, brush my teeth, and spritz some of Pop's Binaca breath spray in my mouth just in case.

I stare at myself in the mirror, focusing on my eyes, which are at least green and are the least embarrassing part of my face. "Sammie," I say, pretending the green eyes in the mirror are her brown ones. "There's something I want to tell you, about my feelings for—blech!" I shake my head no and try again, pretending I'm holding a cup of hot chocolate. "Mmm, this hot chocolate is sweet and creamy, just like you." No way. I try again, putting one hand on a hip to look cool and relaxed. "Hey, Sammie, there's something I want to tell you—"

"Who're you talking to?"

I jump, startled, and bite my tongue.

Inez, my babysitter, is standing at the bathroom

door, holding a bunch of folded towels. "Who's in here with you?" she asks.

"Inezzz," I whine. "You made me bite my tongue."

Inez makes a *pfft* sound. "*I* didn't make you do anything. The door was open. I was heading to put away these clean towels, which I just washed and dried and folded, thank you very much, and I hear you in here, talking. Who're you talking to?"

"Not you," I say, my tongue throbbing.

Inez steps further into the bathroom and looks around. "Who, then?"

"No one," I say. "I was just . . . practicing."

"Uh-huh," Inez says, nodding like she knows exactly what I mean, which she probably does.

In my pocket, my phone buzzes. "Gotta run."

"All righty," Inez says. "Practice makes perfect. Good luck."

"Thanks," I shout back at her from the hallway.

SAMMIE

As soon as I see David walking toward me on the Greenway, I cup my hands around my mouth and shout, "Race you!" Then I start running. My backpack is so full that it bumps hard against my back with every step. It hurts, but David's running too, so I can't stop because whoever gets into the Fort first wins.

We run from opposite directions, jumping over the low wooden rails that edge the side of the Greenway, almost at the same time, then tumble and slide down the embankment. There's no snow yet, but luckily the ground is frozen, so I don't end up smeared with mud. I pick myself up and get one foot into the fort.

"I win!" I shout, pumping my fists.

David staggers into the tunnel and collapses, groaning and panting.

"Oh, stop being so dramatic," I say. "You ran fifty yards, max."

"But I had to go all out," he protests, "to beat you."

"You didn't," I say, holding out a hand to help him up. "*I* beat *you*."

He grabs my hand and pulls himself up to sitting. "What'd you bring to eat?"

"Where are the hand warmers?"

He grimaces. "I kind of forgot them. Inez distracted me."

"Don't blame Inez. You're the one who forgot. But that's okay because I made hot chocolate."

"Hot chocolate," David says, sounding disappointed. "That's it?"

"Of course not." I toss him the folded-up stadium blanket. He shakes it out and spreads it on the cold cement.

"Chips?" he asks hopefully.

I shake my head no, and reach into the backpack. "Pretzels," I say, pulling them out and tossing the bag to David.

"Anything else?" he asks.

"Remind me again, what did you bring?" I put one hand on my hip and tip my head a little to one side, trying to look serious. But David knows me.

"Nothing," he says, grinning. "But I'm me and you're you."

"True. Which is why I also brought Chex Mix," I say, pulling it out.

"My favorite," he says.

"I know. And brownies." I toss that bag down onto the blanket. "The Peas made them, but you know they'll never actually eat them." I sit down and pour the hot chocolate into two cups. "This would be so perfect if we had flashlights and hand warmers."

"Sorry," David says through a mouthful of Chex Mix and brownie. He picks up a cup, blows on it, and takes a drink. "Mmm. You can use the flashlight on your phone."

"It runs down the battery too quickly." I hold out my hot chocolate, and we clink our cups together, then drink.

David pulls out his cell phone and puts the flashlight on, illuminating our picnic feast scattered around the blanket.

"Too bad there's not a hand warmer app," I say, pulling my mittens on.

"Would you rather have hand warmers or hot chocolate?"

"I'd rather have both," I say.

David finishes his hot chocolate, picks up the thermos, and pours another cup. "Would you rather drink hot chocolate while sitting on a giant ice cube or drink a fruit smoothie while sitting on a heating pad?"

"What flavor is the fruit smoothie?"

"Orange mango."

"No contest, because I hate mango, so I'd definitely go for the hot chocolate–ice cube combo."

"What if it was a strawberry-banana smoothie?"

I grab a handful of Chex Mix, and inspect it to make sure there are at least two nuts. "That's harder," I say. I pop the Chex Mix in my mouth and chew. "I guess it would depend on the time of year. Smoothies taste like summer to me."

"Smoothies taste delicious to me," David says. "But hot chocolate is definitely the right choice for now." He holds up his cup. I take mine and touch it to his, then drink down a delicious mouthful of warm, chocolaty goodness.

We sit and talk and eat until we've finished the hot chocolate and most of the snacks and it's so dark in the Fort that I can't even make out David's face, three feet from mine.

I pull out my phone and check the time. Four fifteen.

"Sunset is at four thirty," David says. "Want to come hang at my place for a while?"

"I should go home. We're leaving to go skiing tomorrow morning." I sigh.

"You make it sound like it's a pair of itchy wool socks that your grandma gave you for Chanukah," David says. "It's a week of vacation. You'll survive. Cheer up."

"The Peas will be there," I say gloomily.

"They *are* your sisters," David says.

"But they're annoying," I say. "They'll want to go get facials or something instead of skiing. With my mother, of course, and she'll try to talk me into going too. Who could possibly think it's fun to have to lie still in a chair with smelly gunk smeared all over your face? Then she'll buy me makeup and other stuff I don't want. I don't even wear makeup, which my mother doesn't seem to notice."

David rubs his thumb and index finger together. "Poor, poor Sammie. Getting stuff bought for you. The world's smallest violin is playing sad songs for your suffering."

"Plus, skiing cuts into my reading time."

"Let me remind you what I'll be doing all week."

I grin. "Unpaid labor at L. H. Fischer Sporting Goods?"

David nods. "From tomorrow morning until like nine p.m. on December twenty-fourth, I will be working at good old L. H. Fischer because it's the Christmas season! And 'a third of our profits for the year are made during the Christmas season,' according to Pop." He groans. "I won't even have you to complain to. When will you be back?"

"On the twenty-sixth." I stand up and start to put the leftover snacks in my backpack. David grabs one last brownie.

"While you're schussing down the mountain, think of me slaving away at the store."

"I definitely will," I say. "Now get off my blanket so I can fold it up."

David stands and steps off the blanket, then helps me

fold it up. I tuck it under my arm, then head out of the Fort and up the embankment. Back on the Greenway, we stand for a minute, not sure how to say good-bye. David stamps his feet, then crosses his arms and tucks his hands into his armpits.

"See you in a week," I say.

"Not if I see you first," David says, pulling one hand out of an armpit and giving me a good-bye wave.

DAVID

I was five years old when I met Sammie Goldstein. It was the first day of Little League, which Pop had been waiting to sign me up for since the day I was born. He bought me my first glove practically before I could walk, and gave me a batting tee for my fourth birthday, which, PS, I used all the time, as a microphone.

I never minded having a catch with Pop, or even watching part of a game on TV, but I was just as happy to draw or play with Legos or pretend to be a really cool rock star with my batting-tee-microphone.

It was a super-cold Saturday morning in March, but of course Pop wouldn't let me wear my winter coat to practice. He said I'd be fine in a long-sleeved shirt and sweatshirt. I was *not* fine. I was already freezing in the car, and I kept trying to convince him that I *really* didn't want to play Little League, but he wasn't even listening to me because he'd decided we were doing this. That's my pop.

We got there, and Pop was dragging me across the outfield, and there was a baseball rolling toward me across the grass, and I looked up to see this *girl*—wild, curly black hair—running like mad toward the ball, which was headed right for my feet. Pop was deep into his crap lecture about being part of a team and trying new things blah blah blah, so he didn't see the ball or the girl running after it.

The ball knocked against my toes, and I tried to bend down to pick it up, but Pop had a death grip on my arm. I guess he thought I'd make a break for it if he even loosened his hold.

"Pop," I said, trying to interrupt his pep talk. "Pop. The ball." He looked down and let go of my arm, and I bent and picked the ball up.

The girl reached us at that moment. Her cheeks were pink, and she was panting a little.

"That's mine," she said. "My dad threw it right to me, but I missed the catch."

I held the ball out for her and she took it.

"Thanks," she said, and then she was running again, but this time away from me.

During that first practice, I learned Sammie's name, and how to catch a ball rolling toward you on the ground (you have to stand in the path of the ball, so that if you don't catch it in your glove, supposedly you'll stop it with your body). I learned that I was decent at catching balls, thanks to Pop's "Hey, sport, let's go have a game of catch!" but that I stunk at hitting, even off a tee, which was what we did. I learned that even though she was the only girl on the team, Sammie was a better hitter than anyone else, and that she was Jewish like me, and that she lived in the neighborhood next to ours but went to a different elementary school, which was why I had never seen her before.

By the end of the day, I also knew this: Pop wasn't going to have to drag me to any more practices. I was going to be at every single practice *and* game, because Sammie Goldstein would be there too.

That one season could have been the only time Sammie was on my team. She could have been just a girl I crushed on in kindergarten. But Pop and Dr. Goldstein felt about Little League the way I felt about Sammie, so by the end of the season, they'd signed on to coach a team together, which meant that Sammie and I would be together too, on the same team, every spring. Then our two families started doing other stuff together—a summer barbecue, New Year's Eve, a trip to Harbor Yard one time to see the Bridgeport Blue-fish—and Sammie and I were thrown together, not friends exactly, but something more than teammates.

Then middle school started, and for the first time I was in the same school as Sammie. I saw her every day, on the bus, and in the halls and in the cafeteria. I was happy just to see her, but in the middle of last year, she started sitting at my lunch table. And then started saying I was her best friend. I liked being Sammie's best friend because it meant I got to be with her more.

I've never told her how I feel, but I will. Someday. When the time is right, when everything is perfect.

SATURDAY, DECEMBER 27

SAMMIE

David Fischer is my best friend for a lot of reasons, including that when I text him and say, *Can I come over?*, because we're finally back from skiing, David will text me right back and say, *Sure.*

Except today, when he texts, *Later?*

How much later? I ask. Because Dad is seeing patients all day, and the Peas are out shopping for expensive stuff they don't need, and my wannabe-Pea mother is moping because they didn't include her. Any minute she's going to turn on me and want to pluck my eyebrows or take *me* shopping for stuff I don't need.

IDK, David texts back. *Have someone coming over.*

Who? I text back, because I know every someone David does.

Luke

"Who?" I say out loud, because we don't know anyone named Luke.

But before I can text and ask, David texts, *New kid.* And then there's radio silence from him for an entire hour.

DAVID

I'm doing Shrinky Dinks with Allie when the doorbell rings.

Mom shouts from upstairs, "Answer that. It's probably Luke."

She's the one who set up this Meet the New Kid thing when I was supposed to be hanging out with Sammie, who's finally back from her family vacation. So couldn't she just come downstairs, open the door, and do a Mom thing, with cookies and a "let me introduce you to my son, David, who's in seventh grade too"? Nope. I push my colored pencils and Shrinky Dinks over to Allie's side of the table, and turn on the TV to ESPN so it will look like I've been watching sports, not dorking out doing arts and crafts with my little sister.

I open the front door, and think: *twelve minutes*. Because that's how long Luke Sullivan will be my friend.

He's already started his growth spurt, and has hair on his upper lip, enough to maybe even shave. Me? My upper lip looks like a baby's butt: smooth and soft. And freckled. I'm rocking the freckles.

The only person who would think that I have anything in common with Luke Sullivan is my mother.

"Thanks for inviting me over," he says.

"Come on in," I say. He steps through the door and walks past me, back toward the family room, where Allie is still sitting.

"Hey," he says to Allie. He smiles, which activates a dimple.

Even Allie understands the coolness of Luke Sullivan, because she takes one look at him and his dimples, makes a strange kind of squeaking noise, and bolts upstairs to her bedroom.

"That's my weird sister, Allie," I say. "She's in fourth grade, but she acts like a baby sometimes."

Luke laughs. "My sister *is* a baby. She poops in a diaper. At least yours is toilet trained."

"Yours is adopted, right?"

"Yep. From China."

Mom knows Luke's mom from when they went to

law school together, and she gave me all the facts ahead of time: the adoption, his mom quitting her lawyer job, and the family needing to move to a new house, even though it was the middle of the school year. I felt sorry for him until I saw him.

Luke looks around at the family room: Shrinky Dinks sheets and colored pencils are spread all over the table, and the Knicks are on TV. There's an awkward silence when I figure he's calculating how long he has to stay to be polite, but then he says quietly, nodding at the table, "I used to love that stuff when I was a little kid. My babysitter, Bronia, was really into arts and crafts."

"You should see Allie's room," I say. "It's full of stuff she made, and all of it's pink and glittery."

Luke laughs. "Sounds like my little sister's room, except my mom did the decorating. She painted flowers all along the bottom of the wall, if you can believe it." He shakes his head. "She never did any of that stuff for me or Matt when we were little."

There's an awkward silence while I try to think of something to say. "How about a game of Ping-Pong? We have a table in the basement."

"Sure," Luke says. "I'm pretty good. I used to play all the time at my friend Ty's house."

My basement has *everything*, thanks to Pop, proud owner of L. H. Fischer Sporting Goods. We've got a Ping-Pong table, foosball, pogo sticks, a couple pairs of stilts, a magnetic dartboard, two Nerf basketball hoops, a *real* pinball machine, and a life-sized boxing dummy. There's also an Xbox, but Pop keeps the controllers in his room and has a whole list of crazy rules about days I can play, and even though it's winter vacation *and* a Saturday, today's not one of them.

Luke walks to the Ping-Pong table, picks up a blue paddle, grabs a ball, bounces it a couple of times, and serves.

Of course, he isn't "pretty good" at Ping-Pong; he kills it, beating me three games in a row.

"Best four out of seven?" I say. I manage to win games four and five, but then Luke comes back and wins game six, and it's over.

He sets the paddle down on the table and turns to check out the rest of the rec room. He turns the boxing dummy on and takes a swing at its chest. "You're so lucky, having a dad who owns a sports store. Getting first dibs on the coolest stuff."

"Most of the time I get the stuff that doesn't sell. Or returns that can't go back out on the shelf."

"Do you ever get to hang out there? At the store?"

"I *work* there sometimes," I say. "Free labor, when the paid employees don't show."

Right then, Luke spots the framed, autographed Carmelo Anthony jersey. "Wow," he says.

"That was a twelfth birthday present from my parents." The truth is, I wanted a vintage Percy the Penguin doll, from the *Northern Province* comic series, which is my favorite. It was even autographed by the cartoonist, Melvin Marbury. I found it on eBay, and showed Mom and Pop, but they got the jersey instead. I know every other guy my age thinks that jersey's the coolest thing in the world, but I really wanted Percy.

Luke wanders over to the wall of my Little League team photos, Pop's shrine to the father-son bonding experience of baseball. There's a bookcase below the shrine, where I keep part of my comic book collection and some of my own drawings and paintings, including two displayed in picture frames on the top of the bookcase, but Luke doesn't notice any of that. He's focused on the Little League photos. He reaches out and touches the team picture from last spring. "You play baseball?"

"Spring Little League. Yeah."

"What position?"

The position that I like to play—every year—is benchwarmer, with a little bit of Powerade distributor and Dorito bag finisher thrown in, but I say, "Outfield, mostly. I can throw."

"Cool," Luke says. He takes the photo off the wall to look more closely at it. "I play catcher. Three seasons. I was on the Diamondbacks in the fall." He mentions the name of his team casually, but I know exactly what it means: the Diamondbacks were the county champs.

"Who's the girl?" he asks, pointing right at Sammie in the photo. She's in the back row, and even though we're all wearing caps and her dark hair is pulled into a ponytail, she stands out.

I grab on to the photo frame because I kind of want to take it away from Luke. I don't. I just hold on to the bottom left corner while he holds on to the bottom right corner.

"Her name's Sammie." I try to sound kind of bored.

"What's a girl doing on a boys' team anyway?"

"She likes to play baseball. And she's really good."

"Hey," Luke says, still holding the photo. "I think I might have played against her. Does she play fall ball? I remember a girl catcher. She was hot."

I pull the photo away from him.

Upstairs, the doorbell rings. I hear Mom clomp down from the second floor and open the door.

"David," she hollers. "Sammie's here."

"The hot girl?" Luke says. "She's here? Right now? No way."

"Sammie," I say. "Her name is Sammie."

SAMMIE

I wait an hour, then text David *Coming over now okay?* and walk to his house along the Greenway.

But when Mrs. Fischer answers the door, she looks surprised to see me. "Hello, Sammie," she says. "I didn't know you were coming over. David has a new friend here."

"Luke," I say, like I know all about him.

"They're in the basement."

"Great," I say, taking off my boots and coat and heading for the basement door. When I open it, the two of them are standing at the bottom of the stairs, looking up. The Luke kid has at least four inches on David. He looks kind of familiar.

"Hey, David," I say, walking down the stairs.

"I know you," Luke says.

"Really?" I say. "I don't know you."

He holds out his hand like he wants to shake. "Luke Sullivan. Nice to meet you."

I curl mine into a fist and wait for him to do the same. We bump knuckles. "Sammie Goldstein."

"We played each other," he says. "Last fall. I was on the Diamondbacks."

"Oh," I say. "You beat us."

He grins. "We beat everybody. County champs."

"What've you guys been doing?" I ask David, wandering over to the bookcase, where there are a couple of his drawings, framed. I pick up the one that's a copy of the cover of his favorite *Northern Province* comic book, *Oliver Shoots a Biscuit in the Basket.*

"We played Ping-Pong," David says, watching me and starting to blush. "Luke won."

"Sounds fun," I say, setting the drawing back down. David relaxes. He hides his artistic side from his guy friends. They know he can draw cars and spaceships and guns with flames shooting out of them. They ask him to draw that stuff, like it's a party trick.

I'm the only one who knows about his *Northern Province* comic book obsession. And that he'd rather draw a cross-eyed moose or a chubby dog than cars and spaceships and flaming guns. And that he *can* draw all of those things. I don't understand why he doesn't want the other guys to know, but I keep his secret. That's what best friends do: keep each other's secrets.

"Who would you rather play against?" I ask. "Luke? Or me?"

David picks up the little white ball and bounces it

on the Ping-Pong table. It makes a *pock-pock-pock*ing sound. "Here's a better question," he says. "Would you rather play Ping-Pong against a zombie or an alien?"

"Wait," Luke says. "You didn't answer her question."

"How many arms does the alien have?" I ask, holding out my hands so David will throw me the ball.

"Two," he says, tossing it right to me.

I catch it with my left hand and ask, "Eyes?"

"Yep. And ears."

"What are you guys talking about?" Luke says. "Aliens don't exist."

"How tall is it?" I ask David, sending the ball up in a high arc and catching it with my right hand. "If it's a little alien who can't see over the top of the table—"

"Six feet tall. But no more questions. It's an alien that looks kind of human and is six feet tall, with the same number of eyes and arms and legs as us, but we don't know if it has X-ray vision or super-fast reflexes or a killer headache from the change in air pressure on Earth or what."

"Does it want to eat me?"

"Unknown."

"Hmm," I say, thinking. I lob the ball back to David and he catches it. "An alien with unspecified strengths and weaknesses. And we don't even know why it's here in your basement, right? It could be the Ping-Pong champion of the universe."

"Could be," David agrees, bouncing the Ping-Pong ball on the table.

"Or it could be like E.T.—"

"But six feet tall," David reminds me.

"Right. A six-foot-tall alien who got lost and is scared of everything."

"Could be."

I sigh. "I gotta go with the zombie."

"That's stupid," Luke says. "It's a *zombie*."

"It's not stupid. I *know* the zombie wants to eat my brains, right? Which gives me a huge advantage. He'll be all distracted, thinking 'Brains! Brains!' so I just have to keep my focus on the game. I can totally win against a zombie."

"And then he'll eat you!" Luke says.

"I'm confident I can avoid being eaten by the zombie," I say, "*after* I whoop him in Ping-Pong."

"Do you guys always do this?" Luke asks. "Talk about made-up stuff?"

"Not always," David says.

"Yep," I say at the same time.

"I like talking about real things," Luke says. "Like

the Knicks. Or Little League." He turns toward me. "Or *you*."

He stares right at me, his eyes open too wide, like he's daring me to blink.

"That's weird," I say, trying to look right at him, into his wide-open eyes. I feel exposed, and hold my paddle up in front of my body like it's a shield. "I'm right here. We can't talk about *me*."

"We did before," Luke says.

"We did not," David says, dropping the Ping-Pong ball onto the table. It bounces once, then rolls off the side.

"When you weren't here," Luke says to me.

"We talked about *baseball*," David protests, looking down at the ball as it rolls away from the table.

Luke smiles at me, a wide, toothy grin. "We talked about *you* playing baseball."

I don't like his smile.

"I'm going out for our school team," I say. "David too."

"Me three," Luke says.

"What school do you go to?"

"Yours," Luke says. "Starting after break." He grins, showing his white teeth.

For a moment I'm sure he's going to start laughing

and say, 'Gotcha!' Or maybe I hope that's what he'll do. But he doesn't. Instead he ducks down beneath the Ping-Pong table, then pops back up holding the ball. He tosses it to David and says, "Maybe I'll be in some of your classes."

David catches the ball and tosses it to me.

"It's a pretty big grade," I say. "Unless you're in honors—"

"Duh," Luke says. "Of course I'm in honors."

"Of course," I say.

David and Luke both hold out their hands for me to toss the ball to them. I look back and forth, then set the ball on the table and turn away from them. "C'mon, let's do something else. What can we all play together?"

NEW YEAR'S EVE

SAMMIE

I'm eating breakfast when David texts me, *Sullivans r coming 2nite.*

The Luke Sullivans.

I groan.

"Bad news?" Dad asks. He's at the stove, making himself an egg-white omelet.

"Kind of. Do you know the Sullivans?"

"Is that the new family? Your mother mentioned them. They have a son your age, right? He plays baseball."

"Yeah," I say. "They're coming tonight. To the Fischers'."

Every year, the Fischers have a New Year's Eve party, and every year the same people come. It's my favorite holiday, better than Rosh Hashanah or Passover, which are really just long, boring meals. And waaay better than Yom Kippur, which shouldn't even be called a holiday.

"How nice," Dad says. "Someone new for you and David to hang out with."

It's not nice. It's ruining the best day of the year. But I don't say that.

Instead, I finish my cereal and clear my place, load the dishes into the dishwasher, then head to my room, where I try to read *Greenwitch*. But I keep hearing Luke say, *We talked about you*, and when I look at the clock it's one thirty and I've only read twenty pages.

I do *not* want Luke getting to the party before me, so I text David. *Can I come over?*

Forty-five minutes later he texts back, *Now? Party starts at 7.*

I look at the clock: 2:17 p.m.

I'm bored, I text.

Sure

When I get there, David's in the family room with Allie, working on a picture book. It's probably their hundredth book. She writes the story and David draws

31

the pictures. Allie keeps them all in her room.

I spy half a sandwich on the kitchen counter, which I pick up and inspect: peanut butter and jelly, with no bites taken out of it. Score!

"Can I have this?" I ask, holding up the sandwich.

David barely looks up from the page he's working on. "What? Yeah, sure. But it's from like four hours ago. You can make a fresh one."

"I will," I say. "But I'm gonna eat this one first. I'm starving. I forgot to have lunch."

I polish off the half sandwich, then make another whole one and pour myself a glass of OJ. Then I sit down at the table between David and Allie. I reach out to pick up a drawing, but Allie says, "Wait! Don't take that one. You'll mess up the order."

"Sorry," I say.

She hands me a stack of pages. "They're numbered. Be careful."

I take the pages and ask, "What's this one about?"

"A little kitten who gets lost and a girl finds her and brings her home."

David turns his head so Allie can't see and rolls his eyes.

"Wasn't your last book about a kitten?" I ask.

"Yes, but that was a city kitten who got lost in Central

Park. This is a country kitten who's born in a barn and gets lost when she wanders into the cow pasture."

"Good thing you're a natural at drawing kittens," I say to David.

"And aliens," David says. "But Allie never wants to write stories about them."

"They're scary," Allie protests. "And ugly."

"What about a kitten who gets abducted by aliens?" I ask Allie.

"Too scary," she says.

"What if the aliens think the kitten is a god?" David says.

"And they start to worship it," I add.

Allie taps her cheek, thinking. "I guess that wouldn't be so scary," she says. "If the aliens were kind of cute. Like R2-D2."

"He's a robot, not an alien," David says.

"It could be funny," I say. "Maybe the aliens don't understand the kitten."

"Right," David says. "Like they think 'Meow' means 'Me out,' and they keep taking the kitten to different places, but the kitten says 'Meow.'"

"What if they build a giant gold throne for the kitten, but it thinks it's a litter box?"

"And poops on it!" David says, grinning.

"You guys are gross," Allie says.

"I could draw great poop," David says.

I grin at David. "C'mon. Can't you take a break from your illustration duties and challenge me to a game of Nerf hoops?"

He grins back. "I guess I can tear myself away from the kittens."

Four hours later, we're sitting at the dining room table—with Luke—playing Blokus when Mr. Fischer calls out from the kitchen, "Who wants a frozen mudslide?"

"What's a frozen mudslide?" Luke asks.

Allie and her two friends, who are sitting at the other end of the table, start to giggle.

David, who's been studying the Blokus board for two full minutes, sets down his piece.

"What's a frozen mudslide?" Luke asks again, setting his piece on the board to block David. The girls giggle again.

Every time he says anything, they do that. It's really annoying.

"It's a drink with ice cream and Kahlua and vodka," David says.

"Me," Luke calls out. "I want one."

David laughs. "Pop's not asking the kids. After he makes the adults' frozen mudslide, he'll make us some with ice cream and coffee syrup."

"My parents are okay with me having a little alcohol," Luke says.

"Yeah, but mine aren't," David says, sounding embarrassed.

"Next year," Luke says with a grin. "I'll get my dad to work on yours."

Next year? I think to myself. I was hoping the Sullivans were a one-time thing. I sigh, apparently loudly, because David asks, "You okay?"

"Fine," I say.

When I was little, the Peas even came to New Year's Eve at the Fischers'. We'd all play Guesstures—adults and kids, with everyone divided into boys against girls. I would be teamed up with one of the Peas because I couldn't read well enough yet. The whole rest of the year, I never did *anything* with the Peas. But on New Year's Eve, I was included, and I felt so grown up.

Back then, I wasn't allowed to stay up until midnight. I would go to bed on an air mattress on the floor in David's room. The two of us would whisper together and try to stay awake to hear the adults cheer when the ball dropped, but we never made it. I'd fall asleep at David's and wake up in my own bed in a brand-new year. It was magic.

Then the Peas and all the older kids stopped coming.

They got too cool for New Year's Eve at the Fischers'.

That will never be me. I will never stop coming here on New Year's Eve, no matter how grown-up I get. It's our tradition.

After I win Blokus and David wins Trouble twice and we drink virgin frozen mudslides until we can't drink any more, David says, "How about a game of Ping-Pong?"

"Sure," Luke says. "I'm kind of sick of board games."

Luke's really good at Ping-Pong, so he beats David in three games. Then it's my turn.

He serves and I hit it back, and then we volley, with me keeping my eye on the ball and Luke acting like he's not even trying. I win the first point. As Luke starts his second serve, he says, "How come you don't play softball?"

"Why should I?" I say, sending the serve back to him.

"It's a girls' sport."

"So?"

"You're a girl."

I nod. "I'm a girl who plays baseball."

"What position?"

"Catcher," I say, sending the ball over to his side as hard as I can.

He hits it back to me. "I play catcher too. I was the starter on my fall team. During playoffs, I stayed in almost the whole game."

"Me too," I say. "I was the starting catcher spring, summer, and fall."

"I was on the Diamondbacks."

"I know," I say. "You told me already."

"So if I'm going out for the school team this year, I guess I'll be your competition."

The ball hits the very left corner of my side of the table. I try to get it with a backhand but miss, and it goes flying off somewhere in the room. Point for Luke. I glance at David, who's watching from the side, not saying anything. He lobs me another ball so I can serve.

I bounce it and send it over to Luke's side. "David's trying out too." I glance at David, wanting him to be part of this conversation. "Right?"

He shrugs. "I guess so."

"We should practice together, dude," Luke says, looking at David as he hits the ball back toward me. All of a sudden, I'm not even here.

"The first meeting's in March," I say. "You've got eight weeks to try to get better than me."

"What if I'm already better than you?" Luke says, smiling as he sends the ball back to my side. "Maybe you're the one who needs the practice."

I want David to say something, to tell Luke how good I am, but he doesn't.

I manage to win the first game, but then Luke wins three in a row. He sets his paddle down and says, "Losers play each other, right?" Just then, Mrs. Fischer calls, "Five minutes until the ball drops."

I set my paddle on the table and we head upstairs.

Mrs. Fischer hands out glasses of champagne to the adults and sparkling cider to us. We hold our glasses and wait, and then it's the last minute of the old year. We all count down together.

"Happy New Year!" everyone shouts when the big silver ball touches down. I clink my glass against David's. Dad is kissing Mom in that super-embarrassing way, and the Fischers are kissing, and the other parents too. I take a sip of my cider so I don't have to look at the adults, or at David and Luke, standing right in front of me. But as I'm drinking, Luke leans in, grabs my arm, and pulls me toward him.

"Happy New Year," he says right into my ear. His mouth is so close that I can feel his breath, hot and wet, on my face. Then his lips touch my cheek. They're squishy and warm, and they meet my skin for just a second. He backs away and smiles at me, but I can feel the spot where his lips touched. The spot where he kissed me.

I look at David. His eyes are wide, like he's surprised. Or confused.

"C'mon," I say, grabbing his arm and heading toward the basement, away from this weird, embarrassing situation. "We have a game to play."

"Right," David says.

We head back down to the basement. I can still feel the spot on my cheek where Luke's lips were. I want to rub at it, to erase it, but I don't.

NEW YEAR'S DAY

DAVID

He was so slick, the way he moved right in and kissed her, like it was nothing, like he'd done it a million times before.

Of course, that's what you're supposed to do when the ball drops: kiss the girl. Except I never have. I never even thought of it.

But last night, lying in bed after everyone left, it was all I could think of. I kept watching it happen over and over in my mind, wondering what Sammie thought, and what she felt, and whether I could possibly ever be as smooth as Luke.

I woke up this morning still thinking about it, and

even texted Sammie, *Want to hang out?* but she texted back, *Can't. Homework*

The only cheeks I've ever kissed are Mom's, Grandma Gert's, and Bubbie's. Does kissing a girl's cheek feel the same as kissing Bubbie's wrinkly, powdery cheek? I hope not. Pop kisses me all the time, on my cheek and my forehead and sometimes right on my eye, but I don't kiss him back. Besides, he's a dad and smells like Old Spice aftershave and has prickly man-beard hairs. I wonder how Luke learned to kiss a girl, and, more importantly, how *I* can learn. They don't teach that in health, or even in science class.

That's what I'm thinking about as I head down to breakfast, so when I glance through Allie's open bedroom door and see her giant SpongeBob SquarePants pillow sitting propped up against her regular pillows, it's like a light bulb switches on right inside my brain. I can hear the TV in the family room, tuned to *Dora the Explorer*, which means Allie's downstairs, watching it. Typical Allie. She's in fourth grade but she acts like she's four.

SpongeBob will be perfect practice, I think as I tiptoe into Allie's room and sit down quietly on her bed. I inspect him. His face is flat, not like a real face, but he has the right parts, including a mouth. He's smiling right at me, almost saying, *Go ahead, kiss me, you fool.*

I gaze into SpongeBob's eyes. "Hey," I say, "would it be all right if I . . . ?" Then I lick my lips, close my eyes, and lean in. But when I open my eyes, I'm kissing SpongeBob's nose. Note to self: keep the eyes open.

I sit back, take a breath, lean in—eyes open—and kiss him right on the mouth. Sort of where his two buck teeth are, because his mouth is open in a huge smile. I'm not sure what kissing real lips—or teeth— feels like, but I can say kissing SpongeBob's flat lips is nothing like kissing Bubbie Edith's cheek.

I sit back, take a breath, and try SpongeBob again, this time parting my lips a little and pushing my tongue out until it hits the fabric where SpongeBob's tongue is. I try moving my tongue around, but SpongeBob's tongue feels the same as his teeth: a little like I'm lick-ing someone's silk shirt.

I sit up, take a breath, and go in again.

"What are you doing?" Allie says from behind me.

I jump, startled, and quickly wipe my mouth with the back of my hand. "I . . . must have fallen asleep."

Allie puts her hands on her hips. "You were not asleep. You were licking my pillow." She walks over and bends down to inspect SpongeBob, and even I have to admit there's a wet spot right where his tongue is.

"It's wet!" Allie says.

"Okay, okay," I say, holding my hands up. "I was eating a marshmallow, and it got on my fingers, and I accidentally smeared it on your pillow, and I didn't want you to be all mad about it, so I . . . I licked it off."

Allie leans in and eyeballs SpongeBob's mouth. If she had a magnifying glass handy, I'm positive she'd whip it out.

"Where did you get a marshmallow from? And besides, it doesn't look like there's any marshmallow. It looks just wet."

"I licked the marshmallow off very thoroughly."

Allie sighs and steps back, putting her hands on her hips again. "Really?"

I open my eyes super wide in my best imitation of innocence and pull a finger across my chest, making an X. "Cross my heart, that's the truth," I say, thinking that I need to find something better than SpongeBob to use for practice, because I need a lot of it.

MONDAY, JANUARY 5

DAVID

I get on the bus the first day after winter break, and Luke waves at me like he wants me to sit next to him, so I do, even though he's two rows closer to the front than I usually sit. Two stops later, Sammie gets on and sits across from us. She's carrying a rolled-up poster, which she sets down on the seat beside her. I don't say anything about it because I know better.

Luke leans forward and flashes his white teeth and dimple at her. "How's it going?"

"Oh, hi, Luke," Sammie says. Then she turns to me. "Where's your extra credit science project?"

"We had extra credit for science?" Which, of course, I knew.

"Yes," she says impatiently. "It was super easy. All you had to do was calculate what you should be eating using MyPlate and keep a food diary for two days, and then match what you actually ate to the MyPlate recommendations."

"Bummer," I say, trying to sound super regretful. "I wish I'd remembered."

Sammie *always* does the extra credit, even if she has an A-plus in the class, and she *always* thinks everyone else does it too, even when they're me, a kid who's allergic to schoolwork generally and to extra credit specifically.

Behind her back, the guys call her "Snergir," which stands for "Super Nerd Girl," which she kind of is, but they mostly say it because they're jealous that she's a better athlete.

"That sounds boring," Luke says. Big mistake.

Sammie blinks, then blinks again, like she has something irritating in her eye. Then says to me, "It was totally cool." She shakes her head so her hair bounces all over the place. And then she's off and running. "I did it the first two days of vacation—"

"Wait," I interrupt. "While you were away skiing?"

"Yes," she says impatiently. "So I wouldn't forget. I learned so much. Did you know that nuts have a lot of fat in them? In fact, a *handful* of peanuts—"

"Hey, Sammie," I say, interrupting her, because in another thirty seconds she'll be pulling the rubber band off her rolled-up poster and showing us her "totally cool" extra credit science project. "We should tell Luke about E. C. Adams. About teachers and stuff." I turn to Luke. "Do you know what classes you're in?"

"Nah."

"You don't have your schedule?" Sammie asks.

"Nope," Luke says. "I'm supposed to pick it up from the guidance counselors' office."

"You couldn't get it before winter break?" Sammie asks.

"I probably could have, but what difference would it make? I wouldn't know any of the teachers' names or whether they're good or not."

"I would have wanted *my* schedule ahead of time," Sammie says. She looks at me, waiting for me to agree with her, which I normally would do, but I don't because of Luke.

He turns to Sammie and asks, "So who are the good teachers? And who do I have to watch out for? Tell me everything I need to know about E. C. Adams Middle School."

"The teachers are all nice," Sammie says, which is completely not true.

"Señora Alicea is not nice," I correct her.

"She's not deliberately mean," Sammie protests.

I turn to Luke. "Señora Alicea has a voice that is so high only dogs can hear her. She's always about three seconds away from completely losing it."

"Spanish teacher?" Luke asks.

"Yep." I pitch my voice as high as I can, stick my chest out, and clap my hands together. "*Clase, clase, escúchenme, por favor!*"

Luke laughs.

"She's not that bad," Sammie says.

"Yes she is," I say. But then I change the subject. "You'll definitely have Mr. Phillips. He teaches all the seventh-grade science classes."

"*He's* nice," Sammie says.

"He's a space case," I say. "A real hippie, from the nineteen sixties, with a ponytail and possibly the last VW bus on Earth. Always has a piece of chalk behind his ear—he's allergic to the whiteboard markers. Also can't remember anybody's name. He calls everyone 'you with the.' I'm 'you with the red hair.' And my friend Jefferson's 'you with the president's name.' He *knows* Jefferson's name, but he still doesn't *call* him by it."

Sammie pipes in. "Amanda Archer's in my class. He

calls her 'Queenie.' Like he *knows* she runs the grade."

"What about English?" Luke asks, leaning over, toward Sammie's side of the bus.

"I have Mr. Pachelo for English," she says, and then she stops, because even she can't bring herself to say Mr. Pachelo is nice.

"I had him last year," I say. "This year I was spared. Mr. P has some . . . digestive problems. His classroom smells like farts all the time." I do a cough-fart to imitate how he pretend coughs to cover up the fart sounds. "It doesn't fool anyone because one second after the cough-fart, there's a cloud of stink so bad your eyes start to water."

Sammie nods, pinching her nose shut like there's a real Pachelo fart in the air. "Some of the girls spray perfume on their hands right before class. I sit in the back of the room, where the smell's not as bad."

The bus pulls up in front of the school, and as we stand to get off, I feel kind of like when Mom and Pop take me to sleepaway camp in the summer, except this time I'm Pop and Luke's me. I'll watch him walk off the bus, spot the cool seventh graders, and wave good-bye to me, exactly the way Pop watches *me* as I walk through the gates of Camp Towanda and wave good-bye to *him*. Except *my* eyes won't be all red, and I won't be honking into a Kleenex.

Part of me also feels just a little bit relieved, because of Sammie.

But Luke waits for me to get off the bus and walks into school right next to me. We pass Corey Higgins and Markus Johnson and their crew, who always stand outside until the last possible minute, and I watch Luke size them up, and them size him up.

"Dude," Corey says, nodding at Luke.

"Word," Luke says, nodding back, but then he turns to me. "Can you go with me to the guidance office?"

"Sure," I say.

Together, we walk upstairs, past the music and drama and art rooms, to the counseling wing, and Mr. Lang, who's my guidance counselor, turns out to be Luke's counselor too. He hands Luke his schedule, says, "Welcome to E. C. Adams Middle School, Mr. Sullivan," and we're on our way out when a short woman with curly gray hair and purple eyeglasses stops us.

"Gentlemen," she says. "What luck."

She holds out one hand to Luke. "You must be Luke Sullivan. I'm Dr. Ginzburg, the school psychologist."

He nods, takes her hand, and shakes it.

"Tough time to start at a new school," she says, still smiling widely.

Luke shrugs, and she pats him sympathetically on one shoulder, then turns to me.

"David Fischer," she says, like she knows me. She holds out her arms kind of the way Pop does when he's about to hug me. I take a step back and she holds her hand out for me to shake, so I take it.

"*Thank you*," she says to me, "for helping Luke find his way around."

She starts to walk with us as we leave the guidance office, asking Luke about his favorite classes at his old school, his hobbies, the new baby. I half listen to them talk as we walk, but half of me is scanning the halls for familiar faces, because I don't want any of my friends to see me with the school psychologist.

We get as far as the art room and I'm beginning to get nervous because it seems like she's going to walk Luke all the way to his first-period class, and me along with him, and we'll definitely cross paths with some of my friends, which will mean an entire lunch period of the guys making jokes about my mental health, so I say, "I can take it from here. I know where I'm going."

Dr. Ginzburg smiles at me like she knows exactly what I've been thinking. "All righty," she says, patting my shoulder. Then she puts her hand on Luke's shoulder and says to him, "I'm here if you need me. Do me a favor: Stop by in a week or so and let me know how everything's going, okay?"

Luke nods.

When we're around the corner, I breathe a sigh of relief. "Whew. That could have been super embarrassing."

"What?" Luke asks.

"Being walked to class by Dr. Ginzburg."

"Why?"

"She's a psychologist, duh. Like if you're having a mental breakdown or something. My friends would have a field day with that."

"But she was walking with me," Luke says. "Because I'm new."

Technically, he's right. She was walking with him, and not because he's crazy, just because he's new. But my friends wouldn't care about technically. And all of the other kids who could have seen me walking down the hall with the school psychologist *really* wouldn't care about technically. It's not worth explaining to Luke, though, because it's moot.

"What's your first class?" I ask. "I'll walk you there."

It turns out Luke's in social studies with me, and Mrs. Russo puts him at the desk next to mine. And then he's in Spanish second period with Señora Alicea and me, and in English, and every single one of my classes. In every class, he gets a seat next to mine. Except in math, which is the only class I have with Sammie. She sits next to me, in the back row. Mrs.

Knell puts Luke on the other side of Sammie, so she's between the two of us.

At lunch, he even chooses to sit with my crew, the seventh-grade goofballs and second-string athletes. I figure it's because he's taking his time, seeing if the Corey-Markus table is really the top of the heap. But I kind of like having him at my table, even if it's only for a day.

As long as I can keep him away from Sammie.

FRIDAY, JANUARY 16

DAVID

On the second day of school, Luke sits with my crew again. And on the third day, and the fourth. He even asks the guys, and Sammie, for their cell numbers. It's almost like he doesn't know how to read the signs, like he's from Pakistan or Uzbekistan instead of Villemont.

By the middle of January, we're E. C. Adams Middle School's Calvin and Hobbes. Girls follow us in the halls. Of course, they're following Luke, but I'm always with him, so it's like they're following me.

We're walking from English to music, and Carli Martin and Sarah Canavan, two of the most popular girls in seventh grade, start walking behind us, even though they don't have music.

"Did you catch the Knicks game last night?" Carli says loudly to Sarah.

"I love the Knicks!" Sarah squeals. "When I get the rubber bands on my braces changed, I'm going to get Knicks colors."

Luke ignores them. "What are you doing this weekend?"

"*Not* going to Hebrew school," I say. "Three-day weekends are the best. Thank you, Dr. Martin Luther King."

Luke laughs. He thinks I'm funny all the time, even when I'm not trying to be, and he's obsessed with my word-burping talent. "Can you burp that? Martin Luther King?"

Instead, I burp, "Hey, hey, hey! MLK Day!"

"That's disgusting," Sarah says from behind us.

"And disrespectful," Carli adds.

I don't care what they think. Luke thinks I'm hilarious. I pull open the music room door and motion for Luke to go in.

"Don't you have somewhere to be?" I say to Carli and Sarah. "Like your own class?"

Carli runs one hand through her hair like she's trying to signal something. Looking past me, she flutters her eyelashes and calls, "Bye, Luke!"

Luke doesn't even hear her. He's got his backpack on the chair next to him, and he waves me over.

"I saved you a seat," he says.

"Thanks, Luke," I burp.

He cracks up laughing as Mrs. Baptiste claps her hands to start class.

SAMMIE

Carli Martin and Sarah Canavan come flying into English class just as the second bell rings. They slide into their seats, right in front of me, smirking and raising their eyebrows at each other like they're sharing some big secret, and I know, even before Carli opens her stupid mouth, exactly who they're giggling about.

"He's so cute," Carli whispers loudly to Sarah.

"He's delicious," Sarah says. She sighs and pulls her blond hair up into a giant messy bun on top of her head.

Marissa, sitting on the other side of Sarah, leans forward. "Who're you talking about?"

"Duh," Carli whispers. "Luke Sullivan. We were walking with him and David Fischer in the hall just now. *That's* why we were almost late."

Luke and my best friend.

The whispered conversation is interrupted by Mr.

Pachelo. "Everyone, take out *The Giver*. Let's talk about chapter five. What happens to Jonas?"

Even though I read the book weeks ago, at the beginning of winter break, I remember chapter five. A couple of kids giggle. Sarah leans over toward Carli and whispers, "*Stirrings*." She grins and shakes her head, making her messy bun bobble.

Normally, I would raise my hand to answer. I always raise my hand. But the whole stirrings thing is embarrassing. I don't want to be the one who says it. Amanda, Sarah, and two boys in the front all raise their hands.

Mr. P calls on Amanda.

"Jonas has a sexy dream about a girl," she says. Everyone starts giggling. Except me.

"That's right," Mr. Pachelo says. "But he doesn't use that word. In fact, Jonas doesn't seem to know how to think about his dream. What does his mother tell him is happening?"

"She says he's having stirrings," Andrew answers.

Carli leans over and whispers to Sarah, "I think I'm having some stirrings for you-know-who."

Mr. Pachelo puts his hand over his mouth and coughs. The kids in the front row all duck their heads and try to cover their noses with their hands. Sarah grabs a tissue from her backpack and holds it over her nose. "I sprayed it with Juicy Couture perfume," she whispers to Carli.

"What does Jonas's society do for stirrings?" Mr. Pachelo asks, pretending like he hasn't just stunk up the entire room.

No one raises their hand because they're all focused on not breathing in, so I do, and he calls on me. "They give him a pill to make the feelings stop. His parents take the pills too."

"Why do you think stirrings—or what we'd maybe call 'crushes'—are something Jonas's society is medicating away? What's dangerous about those kinds of feelings?"

"They could make people uncomfortable," I say. "Like, if someone has a crush on you, but you don't have a crush back."

Other kids start raising their hands. Mr. Pachelo calls on Max, then Raven, then Sarah. Everyone has opinions about why stirrings could be bad, although the class agrees that we wouldn't want anyone to give us a pill to make them go away.

Right before the bell rings, as we're putting our binders away, Carli says to Sarah, "Let's catch up with LukeandDavid. Mrs. Baptiste always goes past the bell."

I take my time getting to the cafeteria. I don't need

to catch up with LukeandDavid.

I'm the last one to sit down at our lunch table, and the only seat left is directly across from LukeandDavid. Andrew and Max are doing a blow-by-blow of how LukeandDavid got two burgers each from the lunch ladies.

"Anyone want to split my second one with me?" Luke asks. I do, but there's no way I'm going to say so.

"Me," Kai says.

Luke tears the burger in two and gives Kai half.

Then Jefferson tells a story about how LukeandDavid had to pretend to be animals in drama class, so they both pretended to be sloths and refused to move at all. I laugh when I'm supposed to and act like every story they tell is hilarious.

When the bell rings, LukeandDavid get up together, dump their trays in the trash together, and head out of the cafeteria together, with Carli and Sarah following them all the way to math class. I trail behind even though I'm in math with them and Carli and Sarah aren't.

By the time I get on the bus after school, I'm ready to lob a grenade at LukeandDavid. Anything to break them apart. They're sitting together, of course, in one seat, and David's talking as usual and Luke's laughing.

I want to remind David about *us*, so I swing into the seat across from them. "Glad it's Friday. You got any plans for MLK weekend, David?"

David shrugs. "Sleeping in on Saturday and Sunday. Maybe catch up on a little TV. That's it."

"No Hebrew school on Sunday?"

"Nope. Not on a three-day weekend."

"Why is Hebrew school on Sunday anyway?" Luke asks. "Don't you go to synagogue on Saturdays?"

Before David can answer, I say, "Remember at the beginning of winter break, when we met . . . you-know-where, and it was freezing cold, but we didn't care?"

"Where?" Luke says, but I pretend like I don't even hear him.

"We could meet there this weekend," I say.

"Where?" Luke asks again.

"It's not really a winter hangout," David says, sounding uncomfortable that we're even talking about it. It's our secret place. None of the other guys know the Fort exists.

"Where?" Luke asks. "And why isn't it a winter hangout?"

"Never mind," I say. "It's just a secret hideaway David and I found. But you wouldn't think it was fun.

It's kind of dorky actually." I turn to David. "And you *can* go there in the winter. We did, remember? It was fun."

"My butt froze, even with the blanket," David says, half smiling.

"Sounds cool," Luke says. "It needs a name."

"It has a name," I say. "Fort Maccabee."

Luke laughs. "Seriously? Where is this secret Fort Maccabee?"

But before David can tell him, I ask, "You working on anything new?"

"What are you talking about? Working on what?" Luke asks, leaning forward. "Why are you being so mysterious?"

"Never mind," I say.

"Nothing," David says. Then *he* changes the subject as fast as he can. "You got any MLK weekend plans, Sammie?"

"Nope," I say, but I actually do: I'm going to get my best friend back. That's *my* weekend plan.

SATURDAY, JANUARY 17

DAVID

I'm sitting at the kitchen table eating my second delicious bowl of Lucky Charms when Sammie texts me. *Want to hang out? Play Wii? I'll meet you at the fort with hot chocolate & then we can come here.*

Sammie hates playing Wii. The only reason the Goldsteins even have a Wii is because Sammie's sisters use it to exercise. And what's with her obsession with meeting at the fort? It was bad enough in December, when the temperature was at least above freezing. I check the weather app. High today of seventeen. What is Sammie thinking?

But I suddenly realize I haven't hung out with her in weeks.

I'll wear my warmest ski mittens and we won't stay at the Fort long, and Sammie makes great hot chocolate. I do want to show her the awesome drawing I did of Elwin the Moose. Plus, I'm always up for playing Wii.

Sure, I text back.

1 hour.

I pop another spoonful of sugary deliciousness into my mouth, and my phone pings again. It's a text from Luke: *Want to come over?*

Before I can text back, Mom's cell rings. She answers, "Hi," which means it's Pop on the other end.

"Oh dear," she says into her phone, shaking her head and making a *tsk*ing noise. "What a shame. And none of the others are available?" She *tsk*s again and her eyes land on me, then look away, and I know *exactly* what that means: Staffing Crisis at L. H. Fischer Sporting Goods. Yet another loser sixteen-year-old has bailed on his Saturday morning shift because he's suffering from an outbreak of flaming acne or explosive diarrhea. In one minute, Mom's going to hang up her cell, turn to me, and say, "David, honey, your father really needs you at the store today." I know how things go at L. H. Fischer Sporting Goods, and I know if I don't act fast, my entire Saturday will be shot, and saying I already made plans with Sammie won't count for squat. So I grab my phone and text Luke back, *Sure. Now?*

Whenever.

1 hour

OK. Don't ring the bell. Just knock.

So when Mom hangs up the phone, turns to me, and says, "David, honey," exactly as I predicted, I try to sound super sorry, like I'm stuck between a rock and a hard place.

"Gosh. I just made plans with Luke. He doesn't have any other real friends in New Roque yet, and I think he's having a really hard time, with the move and new school and all." I lay it on super thick, too thick probably, but Mom doesn't even notice.

She sighs and nods. "Wendy said the transition's been rougher than they expected. It's always hard to have to make new friends, and in the middle of the year in seventh grade—I wouldn't want you to let him down."

Which is how she ends up dropping Allie at a friend's and me at Luke's, and going herself to bail out Pop and the understaffed L. H. Fischer Sporting Goods. I kind of feel guilty about it, but she's the one who married Lewis Herschel and his store.

It's not until I'm standing on Luke's front porch that I remember I didn't tell Sammie about the change of plans. "Ugh," I groan, bummed about missing out on Sammie's hot chocolate, and on time with Sammie. I grab my phone and shoot her a text: *Have to bail. Sorry. Have to hang with Luke today.* I hit send just as Luke opens the door.

SAMMIE

I make a thermos of hot chocolate, pour the plate of homemade-by-the-Peas oatmeal raisin cookies into a bag, and head to the fort. Walking along the Greenway, in the sun, it feels almost warm. But when I get inside the fort, I remember how cold cement can be. I stand, not wanting to lean against the cold cement walls, and wait. I stamp my feet and wait. I drink a cup of hot chocolate. And wait. Drink another cup. Wish I'd thought to wear ski pants, and wait. When I've finished the entire thermos and my teeth are chattering, I figure I might as well walk to David's.

But as soon as I'm up on the Greenway, I discover something else about our tunnel fort: there's no cell service. Because David texted me a half an hour ago to tell me he was ditching me. For Luke. Again.

So I spend the morning alone in my room, doing homework and reading *The Book of Three.*

In the afternoon, the Peas actually come into my room, to check on me. They never come into my room. They never check on me. Most of the time, the Peas don't even *notice* me. Which is fine, because I never know what to say to them. Becca's a senior and Rachel's a junior, and they're all about school and clubs and varsity tennis and shopping. They have so much in common with each other that I'm not even a third wheel, I'm a wheel on a different car. But today, between their morning shopping outing and their afternoon trying-everything-on session, I catch their interest. I must look pretty pathetic because they come into my room together.

"Are you sick?" Rachel asks.

"Did you have a fight with David?" Becca asks.

"No," I assure them. "I just have a lot of homework."

"It's a three-day weekend. You'll have plenty of time to do homework," Becca says. "Even *you* need a break from homework now and then. How about some fro-yo? Our treat."

"Okay," I say, mostly so they won't go blabbing to my mother that something's wrong with me. "Sounds fun."

I change out of my pj's, and we head to Milly's Van-illi Yogurt Bar.

Becca drives, Rachel rides shotgun, and I sit in the back, trying to follow their conversation. Which is hard.

"That blue crop top only works with mom jeans," Rachel says.

"Why are you wearing Mom's jeans?" I ask.

"What about the Lululemon joggers?" Becca says to Rachel. "They're perfect with a crop top."

"To a party?" Rachel says doubtfully. "No way."

"It's a chill sesh," Becca says.

"It's a party," Rachel says. "Micah will be there."

"Hey," I say. "Who's Micah? And why are you wearing Mom's jeans?"

Becca laughs. "Not *Mom's* jeans, silly. Mom jeans. You know: high-waisted jeans. They're super in right now. And"—she wags her finger at Rachel—"they're perfect with crop tops." She glances in the mirror at me. "You would look adorable in mom jeans. Want us to take you shopping for some?"

"Umm, no," I say. "But thanks."

At Milly's, Becca and Rachel each get one kiddy-sized cup of sugar-free vanilla yogurt, which they each top with three blueberries and a walnut. I take a large cup and almost fill it with chocolate and peanut butter yogurt, leaving just enough room for some crushed Reese's Peanut Butter Cup candy and hot fudge topping.

Then we grab a table, and dig in. Or, I dig in, while the Peas take microscopic bites from their tiny treats. I'm almost enjoying myself, half listening to Becca and Rachel debate who should take photos for the school paper at the next basketball game—Becca is better with action shots but Rachel has an eye for artsy, unexpected pics—while I focus on getting just the right mix of cold yogurt, candy, and gooey hot fudge on my spoon.

Then the door opens, and Luke and David walk in, trailed by Luke's mom holding his baby sister.

"Hey, Sammie!" Luke says, giving me a huge smile.

"Oh, hey," I say.

Becca and Rachel interrupt their debate on each other's photography skills to turn and stare at Luke.

"What'd you get?" Luke asks, leaning over me until his nose is practically in my yogurt. David hasn't said anything. Not even hello.

"Fro-yo," I say.

"Duh. What flavor? What toppings?"

"Chocolate and peanut butter, swirled together," David says, his eyes not meeting mine. "With crushed-up Reese's Peanut Butter Cups and hot fudge on top." He looks at me, then at Luke. "It's what she always gets."

"Sounds awesome," Luke says. "Can I have a taste?" He opens his mouth, waiting. I clutch my little plastic spoon, loaded with a perfectly constructed mouthful of cold and warm sweetness, and I don't move.

"Who's this?" Becca asks.

"Luke," I say, still holding my spoon.

"C'mon," Luke says. "Lemme taste it."

I don't like to share my spoon with other people. Not even people I like, and Luke *isn't* one of those.

David comes to the rescue. "Here," he says, handing Luke a clean spoon. "Use this one."

Luke shoves his spoon into my cup, takes a huge spoonful, and pops it in his mouth. He rolls the fro-yo around in his mouth, making *mmm* sounds, then swallows. "Pretty good. But not creative enough. C'mon, David. Let's get our own."

They head off to the fro-yo machines. *LukeandDavid*, I think. Together. I wish I could think of something to say to David so he would remember us, remember me. But anything I say to David I'll be saying to Luke. I'm suddenly not hungry.

"Let's go," I say to Becca and Rachel, who have gone back to their photography debate.

"You didn't finish," Becca says.

"I took too much. I'm full." I hold out my giant, gooey, chocolaty cup. "You guys want it?"

Becca and Rachel shake their heads no.

David and Luke have their backs to me, checking out all the available flavors. I want to tell Luke that David will get cotton candy with rainbow sprinkles, chocolate chips, and gummy worms. But I don't. It doesn't matter.

As we're walking to the door, Becca says, "Aren't you going to say bye to your friends?"

"Nah," I say. "They're busy."

"That Luke kid is cute," Rachel says as she climbs into the car. "Why have I never seen him before?"

"He's new."

"I think he likes you," Becca says.

"Ugh," I say. "I *don't* like him."

Rachel and Becca laugh.

"Middle school," Rachel says, shaking her head. "It stinks."

SUNDAY, JANUARY 18

SAMMIE

"Sunday mornings are the best," Dad says, leaning back in his seat on the other side of the diner booth from me.

I smile. "The best."

It's our Sunday ritual. The two of us have breakfast at the diner, while my mother and the Peas are off getting their fingernails and toenails painted. Dad always jokes that he'd rather have his fingernails pulled out than painted. My mother doesn't think it's funny, but I do.

Candy, our waitress, sets down my stack of chocolate chip pancakes and Dad's Hungry Man breakfast. Dad folds his newspaper so it's open to the first page of the sports section while I start cutting up my first pancake into bite-sized pieces.

I pour a small puddle of syrup onto my plate, then spear a piece of pancake with my fork. I dip it into the puddle of syrup, and am just about to pop it in my mouth when I see Luke and Mr. Sullivan, walking straight toward us. Mr. Sullivan stops to say something to Candy, the waitress. He takes her arm and pulls her close, putting his mouth right next to her ear. Candy has her back to me, so I can't see her face, but her body goes stiff and I'm pretty sure she's not enjoying whatever Mr. Sullivan is saying. He steps back, lets go of her arm, and laughs.

I'm so focused on watching Luke's dad that I forget about Luke until he slides into my side of the booth and leans his whole body over my plate.

"What'd you get this time?" he asks. I scooch my butt away from him, toward the window, and pull my plate over. He laughs. "I promise not to eat any. I'm already stuffed." He leans back and pats his belly.

"Doc," Mr. Sullivan says to Dad, leaning over the table and holding out his hand. "Breakfast of champions, am I right?"

Dad puts his fork down and shakes Mr. Sullivan's hand. "Good to see you, Jim."

"And these two," Mr. Sullivan says, gesturing toward my side of the booth. "Look at them, two baseball stars." He leans both hands on the table, winks at me, and stage whispers to Dad, "Luke's gonna give your girl a run for her money, I guarantee you that."

Dad laughs. "Sammie? I'm not worried about her. She's tough. She'll hold her own." He winks at me. "Right, Buddy?"

I nod and look down at what's left of my pancakes because I don't like this conversation.

"Well, then," Mr. Sullivan says. "Enjoy the rest of your Sunday. C'mon, Luke."

"See you Tuesday," Luke says as he slides out of the booth.

"Yeah," I say. I watch Luke's reflection in the glass of the window until he walks out of the diner. I exhale, relieved.

"Are you worried about Luke?" Dad asks.

I shake my head no. "Not worried. But he keeps . . ." I don't know how to put Luke into words. Dad looks at me, waiting.

"He's in my space all the time," I try. "Like the way he sat down next to me just now. I didn't invite him to sit here."

"Hmm," Dad says. He takes a sip of his coffee. "He's

trying to psych you out. You're tougher than that, Buddy. Stand up to him."

Stand up to him. I nod.

As Dad's paying the check, he says, "How about the batting cages? Start working on your fighting form so you can hold your own with Luke."

"Sure," I say.

Thirty minutes later, I've got a bat in my hand and the pitching machine's loaded with a hundred balls. I'm swinging at the pitches, my arms and shoulders loosening up and getting warm as the machine spits out ball after ball.

"That's my girl!" Dad says from behind the mesh. "Remember to track the ball."

I already am, so I dip my head in a quick nod that tells him I heard. That's the thing about my dad: he gets me.

I love the sound of my bat connecting with a ball, and the way I can feel that moment in my hands, a sharp thrum like a bolt of lightning charging me up. Ball after ball comes at me, and I'm in the zone.

The machine runs out of balls and stops. I turn around and see Dad talking to some woman. She's waving her hands around, and Dad's just shaking his head no. *No, no, no.*

I take the bat back to the clerk at the desk. Dad's still talking to the woman, who, I realize, is Coach Wright, one of the PE teachers at school.

"Sammie's not interested," he says.

"Just think about it," Coach Wright says. "For high school and college. She could have a future."

"She's happy playing baseball," Dad says.

The woman holds out her hand and Dad shakes it. As she turns and walks away, I notice a crowd of girls from my school at the last batting cage. Some are in my grade, but they're not girls I was ever friends with. They're all clapping and singing some kind of chant. I can't quite make out the words.

Then I recognize Haley, who's new this year, and in three of my classes. Her long blond air is pulled back in a ponytail, which is how she usually has it in school. Today, she's wearing a baseball cap with the ponytail threaded through the hole in the back, and a bright green T-shirt that says "Police Athletic League." I'm pretty sure she's never worn either a cap or a sports T-shirt in school. I would have noticed. I watch her swing a white-and-gold baseball bat. I don't think I've ever spoken to her in school, except when we're doing group work. She taps the bat against her foot, looks up and sees me, and waves. I wave back.

"What did Coach Wright want?" I ask Dad as we leave.

"You. For the middle school girls' softball team. I explained that you play baseball. We're not interested in some girly version of the real thing. Right, Buddy?"

"Right," I say.

DAVID

On Sunday morning, Luke texts me again, and invites me to go to the diner, and I'm already starting to type *Yes what time*, because I love the diner, but when I ask Mom she says no. I look up from my phone, startled.

"But Luke—"

"I bought bagels and lox," Mom says. "Your father arranged for Jeanine to open the store this morning so we can have a nice family breakfast."

Sorry, can't, I text Luke. Then I ask, *But I could come over later, like 11?* because a nice family breakfast is sure to get Pop thinking about a nice father-son day at the store, and that is not how I want to spend any part of my three-day weekend, so I have to act fast.

Okay, Luke texts back as Mom puts out the breakfast.

At twelve thirty, I'm sitting in Luke's brother's bedroom with an Xbox controller in my hands. Luke's bedroom used to be the closet for his parents' room, so it's super small and we can't hang out in there, and also there's no playroom in the Sullivans' house. But his brother, Matt, is a high school senior and has Nintendo Wii and Xbox in his bedroom, plus some really cool games, and he said we could hang out in his room because he's working.

We're still playing video games at three thirty, when Mrs. Sullivan knocks on the bedroom door and tells us to go play outside because Lily, the baby, needs a nap. Luke's got a basketball hoop in the driveway, so we play HORSE for a while, but it's cold, and my nose starts to run, and I'm just about ready to say, "I think I should go home" when Luke asks, "Hey, you want to go to a movie? Have you seen the new Kevin Hart one yet?"

I was half planning to text Sammie and see if she wanted to hang out, but it's a three-day weekend, so I can hang with her tomorrow. I love going to the movies, especially when it involves popcorn and gummy worms. "Maybe," I say. I pull out my phone and check the movie times. "It's showing at four fifty-five and seven thirty. Let's do the seven thirty."

"Or we could go to the four fifty-five and get pizza after."

"At the seven thirty show I bet there'll be other kids we know," I say.

Luke's quiet for a minute. He bounces the basket-ball a few times, takes a shot and makes it, then says, "If we eat first, we'll have to eat here. My mom will make 'homemade' pizza, and she'll ruin it completely. She makes some kind of whole wheat crust that always tastes like it's not cooked enough, and she'll put stuff on top like broccoli and spinach."

Since I *did* have lunch at his house and his mom *did* serve us almond butter and banana sandwiches on some kind of dry brown bread that had crunchy pieces of uncooked grain in it, plus a side of raw carrots, I believe Luke about the pizza. "Okay, five o'clock it is."

There are only about a dozen people in the theater, so we get great seats. Luke's mom didn't give us any money for snacks, but I've got some cash so I spring for a giant tub of popcorn and a box of gummy worms, and Kevin Hart's hilarious, and we both laugh out loud at the bachelor party scene and the football game.

As we're walking out of the theater afterward, telling each other the funny parts, someone calls out, "Luke!"

Luke stops and turns around. I turn around too, and see three guys walking toward us, with a couple of girls trailing behind. The guys are all wearing Burton snow-boarding jackets, in different colors, and they all look like Luke. Not the same features, but the same feeling, like they're sure of themselves. Like they know they're cool. The tallest one, whose hair is long and blond and whose Burton jacket is black, holds up his hand and says, "Luke-ster, 'sup?"

"Hey, Paul," Luke says, high-fiving him.

"How's your baby sister? You getting to change any diapers?" He leans in and sniffs the air near Luke. "I think I smell baby poop. Unless that's your new cologne."

The three guys laugh. Luke sort of smiles. "Good one," he says. "What movie are you guys seeing?"

"Same as you, I'm sure," the kid in the blue plaid Burton jacket says. His skin is darker than the other two and his hair is black; when he smiles, he shows the same mouthful of straight, perfect white teeth. "The new Kevin Hart film."

"We already saw it," Luke says. "We came to the early show."

"Bummer," Paul says. "You coulda sat with us."

"Who's the ginger?" the third kid says, pointing his chin at me. He's a couple inches shorter than tall, blond Paul, and his jacket is black and lime green. He's wearing a gray knit cap that also says Burton on it so I can't tell what color his hair is, but I'm sure it's *not* red.

"This is David," Luke says. "He's from my new school. David, meet Paul and Sebastian and Tyler."

The three all nod at me and murmur sounds that might be "hello" or "hey" or "'sup," or might be "hurl" and "hay" and "snip."

"Hey," I say back, trying to look half as cool as they are.

"They're friends from Villemont," Luke says.

"Your *best* friends, bro," plaid jacket Sebastian says.

"Right," Luke says. "Best friends."

The two girls catch up. "Hey, Luke," the first one says. Her blond hair's up in a high ponytail that she tosses when she talks, and I catch a cloud of sweet perfume. The second girl hangs back, standing behind plaid Sebastian almost like she's trying to hide behind him. She doesn't say anything.

"Hey, Brittany," Luke says to the first girl.

"How's the new school?" she asks.

"Pretty much like the old one." Luke smiles. "Same song, different lyrics."

"Nice coat," Sebastian says to me. "Is it from Walmart or Kmart?" He looks at Paul and grins.

"Neither," I say. "It's from L. H. Fischer Sporting Goods."

"His dad owns that store," Luke says like it's something to be proud of. I decide I won't mention that the coat came off the sale rack two winters ago. Mom held it up to me and said, "In a couple of years this will be perfect."

"Do they carry Burton?" Sebastian asks me.

Before I can answer, Luke says, "Is that the brand? Or the name of the plaid? Because yours is really plaid."

"It's the brand," Sebastian says, like he doesn't even realize Luke's making fun of him. But then he reaches behind him and takes the silent girl's hand, and the way he does it is some kind of challenge to Luke.

"Hey, you should hang out with us sometime," lime-green Tyler says, stepping in between Luke and Sebastian.

"Definitely," Luke says.

Then we stand around for a long, awkward minute while no one can figure out what to say next. Finally, Luke pulls out his phone and looks at it. "Gotta run. My mom's here to pick us up outside." Which is not true at all, because we're going for pizza and then *my* mom is picking us up, but I nod and murmur, "Yeah, gotta run."

When we're out of hearing range, I say, "Your old friends seem cool."

Luke shrugs. "We moved almost a month ago. The only one who's even texted me is Ty."

I don't know what to say, so I change the subject,

sort of. "Who was that girl? The one who didn't say anything."

"Courtney."

"Yeah. Did you guys have some kind of fight? I mean, why was she hiding behind Sebastian like that? Did you mug her in a dark alley once? Or steal all her hair products?"

Luke laughs. "Nah. She was my girlfriend."

"Oh."

"For almost six months," he adds. He turns and gives me a quick smile. "She broke up with me the day before I moved to New Roque. By text. And started dating Sebastian the same day."

"Oh," I say again.

"Sammie would never do that. Right? Sammie's much more fun than Courtney too. Courtney would *never* want to hang out in a secret fort. You guys are so lucky, having your own fort."

I *know* our fort is not that great. But there are three things I also know with complete certainty. First, Luke understands exactly who the cool kids are at E. C. Adams, and could be part of their group if he wanted. Second, he has actual, real experience in the girlfriend department. And third, Luke really does like Sammie, which is *not* cool.

TUESDAY, JANUARY 27

SAMMIE

Except for the awful fro-yo incident, I didn't see David at all over MLK weekend. I thought about texting him on Sunday, but didn't feel like getting dissed again. Then he texted me on Monday afternoon, when the weekend was practically over, but we were skiing for the day anyway.

On the bus on Tuesday, I'm hoping he'll say something about being sorry for bailing on me, but he sits down next to Luke, then asks, "How was skiing?"

"Fine," I say.

He's silent for a moment, then turns to Luke and starts talking about the movie they saw, without me, on

Sunday. The two of them trade lines from the movie the whole bus ride, like I'm not even there.

On Wednesday, things get worse. In math class, Luke takes my pencil and won't give it back. I'm trying to grab it from him when Mrs. Knell says, "Samantha and Luke, what is going on back there?" The entire class turns around to look at us.

On Thursday, I end up next to Luke at the lunch table, and he eats half of my French fries. Right off my plate. Without asking.

On Friday, I'm next to him again in the cafeteria, and when I push his hand away from my tray, he drops it onto my chair, so it's almost brushing against my leg.

"Cut it out," I say, pushing the hand off my chair, but he just grins at me.

I look to David, who's sitting across from us, and wish he would tell Luke to stop being a jerk, but he doesn't even notice what's going on.

I don't see David all weekend, again, because my family goes skiing, but on Monday, I somehow get stuck next to Luke, again, in the cafeteria. After lunch, as we walk to math class, he keeps bumping into me. Like he actually doesn't know how to walk.

So today, I decide I'm not going to sit next to Luke

no matter what. Even if it means pulling up a chair from another table. I push through the cafeteria doors, busy plotting how I'll do it, when Haley steps in front of me. Her hair is pulled back into a ponytail, but no baseball cap today. And she's wearing an oversized blue sweater, with no writing on it.

"Hey," she says. "I saw you at the batting cages over MLK weekend."

"Right," I say. "I saw you too."

"You were killing those pitches. Great swing."

"Thanks," I say, kind of embarrassed that she was watching me. I wouldn't have even noticed her if Dad hadn't been talking to Coach Wright.

Some girl walks by us and Haley nods and smiles, then looks back at me. "How long have you been playing?"

"Baseball? I've been in Little League since I was in kindergarten, but I've been playing my whole life. My dad says my first word was 'ball.'"

"Me too," Haley says, smiling. "Not the first word thing, but playing ball. My mom played college softball. Now she's on a women's league. She was hoping I'd become an athlete, and lucky for both of us I did. You going to the cages again anytime soon? I didn't see you there this past weekend."

I shrug. "I dunno. Going was my dad's idea. To get ready for baseball season. I guess if he wants to go again . . ."

"We have time reserved every weekend until official practices start in March. Maybe you want to come practice with us?" She raises one eyebrow.

"Us who?"

"The girls' softball team. You know, you can go out for softball this year. There's a school team. You don't have to play on a boys' team."

I laugh. "I know I don't have to. I want to."

"Really? Why?" Haley asks, tipping her head to one side like she's studying me.

"Because baseball's challenging. It's hard and it takes skill to play."

"So does softball."

"But softball is for girls."

Haley crosses her arms. "What exactly are you?"

I start to answer, but there's nothing I can say that will sound right. I shift from one foot to the other. I want to explain about being serious about playing, and not worrying about how I look and what I'm wearing. "I'm a baseball player," I say. "It's a real sport."

Haley laughs. "So is softball. Have you ever even *seen* a girls' softball game?"

I'm sure I have, but when I start to think about it, I can't picture anything. Then I remember: cheering. "I heard a game once," I say. "It was on the field below where I was playing. A bunch of girls were doing these chants and things. They sounded—"

"Like people having fun?" Haley finishes my sentence. "Like teammates cheering each other on?"

I wanted to say "like girls," remembering the way Dad and I laughed about it in the car on the way home afterward. But I don't. Instead I say, "Silly. They sounded silly."

"Since when is cheering for your teammates silly?" Haley says, shaking her head like she can't believe me. "That's what being part of a team means—having a good time *together*. No wonder everyone says you're stuck-up."

Haley turns and walks away. I'm standing there like my feet are glued to the cafeteria floor, my hands gripping my tray. I stare after her, and I'm pretty sure my mouth is hanging open. Stuck-up? Me? Haley's got it all wrong.

DAVID

Knowing that Luke likes Sammie *and* he's experienced in the girlfriend department, I start to notice things.

Like the way he takes her pencil in math class and won't give it back. And how, every day at lunch, he ends up sitting next to her. She's always late because she comes from Mr. Pachelo's English class, so maybe it's just by coincidence that the last open chair is always next to Luke. But I decide to do a little experiment.

Our table fills up until there is just one empty chair—next to Luke, with his backpack on it. I pick up my tray and head to the salad bar. Just as I get there, Sammie comes through the cafeteria doors. I wave to her, and so does Luke. I'm just about to go over and invite her to our table, even though it's hers as much as anyone's and she doesn't need an invitation, when some girl walks up to her and they start talking. Haley something, her name is. She only started at E. C. Adams in the fall, and is the opposite of Sammie; where Sammie is small and quick and wild and dark, Haley is tall—as tall as Luke—and pale. She moves deliberately, like she's stalking something, like she's sure of herself. Her blond hair is always pulled back into a tight, neat ponytail. Even when Sammie puts her hair in a ponytail, there are pieces that can't be captured. Haley's pretty, I guess, but not as pretty as Sammie.

After a minute, Haley walks away, Sammie turns toward our table, and I spring into action. Well, not *spring*, exactly, but I wave and walk toward her, pretending like I don't even notice Luke hovering over his backpack, which is still on the chair.

I let Sammie get two steps ahead of me, and sure enough, right as she's at the table, Luke whips his backpack off the chair and says, "This seat's free."

"Great," I say, elbowing past Sammie and plopping my unwanted dough-boy butt right down next to Luke, feeling like I just hit a winning home run. Sammie walks around to the other side of the table and sits in my seat.

"Five weeks until the mandatory baseball meeting," I say, trying to shift attention away from the musical chairs event.

"Why is it mandatory anyway?" Luke asks.

"Coach's way of weeding out the guys who aren't serious," Jefferson explains. "He always makes it the first Tuesday in March because it's a totally random day."

"If you don't show up to that meeting, with all your paperwork complete, don't bother coming to tryouts," Max says.

Kai nods, wagging his finger at Luke like he wants to say something but he can't because his mouth is full of pasta. He chews and swallows. "You need a physical. I have mine next week, so I'm trying to bulk up." He leans over his tray and shovels another forkful of pasta into his mouth. Kai's shorter than me, and thin, sort of like a very short piece of human spaghetti, and no amount of pasta is ever going to make any difference.

"I had mine back in November," Andrew says, blinking twice. "I already printed and filled out the forms. I'm psyched to see how my new contacts do." He blinks quickly a dozen more times, his dark eyes sending out some kind of Morse code. Andrew is a better player than me, but not by much. He really loves the sport, though, and plays three seasons. For years, he wore glasses, which he insisted hurt his game. This past summer, he got contacts, which make him blink twice as often as anyone else. The jury's out on whether he'll play any better.

Sammie doesn't seem to be paying any attention to the conversation. She's sitting over her tray, holding her fork and staring at nothing.

"What about you, Sammie?"

"Huh? What?" She stares blankly across the table at me.

"You have your physical yet?"

Her eyes dart to Luke, then dart away.

"Of course," she says. "Dad set it up for me in the fall."

Sammie's not a person who bursts into tears when she's upset, but I can tell: she's upset. It suddenly occurs to me that maybe Sammie wanted to sit next to Luke just as much as he wanted her to.

Which is when I realize that Luke will make the team for sure, and Sammie too, but me? I'm a benchwarmer. How many of those does the E. C. Adams baseball team need? What will happen to Sammie and me, to our friendship, if I'm not even on the team? And worse: What will happen between Sammie and Luke if they're together all the time without me?

I try to remember the last time I hung out with Sammie alone, without Luke. It was New Year's Eve, before Luke and his family arrived. That was the night he kissed her, while I stood there and watched.

I realize I've been hanging with Luke so much that I kind of forgot about Sammie. Before it's too late, I need to get her alone, away from Luke, with just me.

SAMMIE

Before sixth grade, I had plenty of friends who were girls, and we did normal friend things. Then we started middle school, and something happened to my friends. They changed. All of a sudden, they turned cliquey and giggly and dumb. Sarah Canavan, who used to come over to my house and color and play board games, started wearing eyeliner and lip gloss, and flirting with boys. Carly Martin, who used to shoot baskets with me in my driveway, became this dramatic, weepy person who started straightening her curly brown hair and painting her fingernails a different color every single day. Then she began spelling her name "Carli"—with a heart instead of a dot over the "i." Suddenly, my friends were whispering about each other in the halls and crying in the bathrooms and passing notes and batting their eyelashes at boys—the same boys they used to complain about sitting next to because they might get cooties. When I teased them, or pointed out how silly they were being, my girl friends would look at me like I was the silly, crazy one.

Once, in the hall before school, Sarah was braiding Marissa's hair. I was doing homework, and only half listening to the conversation.

"Can you do pigtails?" Marissa asked Sarah.

"Not today, silly," Sarah said. "Amanda has pigtails."

"Why can't Marissa have pigtails too?" I asked.

Both girls looked at me like I was insane.

"The same as *Amanda*?" Sarah asked.

"Yeah. The same as Amanda. Why can't Marissa

have pigtails, the same as Amanda?"

"She just can't," Sarah said, like that explained anything. "She can't."

It was like they'd learned a code that I couldn't decipher.

Then, in November of sixth grade, I got sick. I missed three days of school. I texted all my friends to let them know, but no one texted me back, not even to ask how I was feeling. On the third day, when I started texting them to get the homework I'd missed, no one responded. It was like I didn't exist. I got so desperate that I finally tried calling. Sarah's cell rang and rang, until I got a message that her voice mailbox wasn't set up. Carli's went to voicemail after the second ring, and even though I left a message, she never called me back. I knew Raven's home phone number, from when we were little, so I tried that, but when her mom answered, she said Raven was in the shower. Mackenzie's mom answered her cell, said, "Hold on," then a minute later came back on the phone, all apologetic, and said Mackenzie was "indisposed." I was eleven. I had to look that word up.

Finally, after I'd texted and called every girl who'd ever been my friend, I texted David Fischer. We'd known each other for years from Little League and

New Year's Eve and summertime family barbecues. We were friends. The kind of friends you are when your families are friends. But he was in my half of my classes, and he texted me right back. He saved me. He made copies of the math handouts and his science notes and the vocabulary sheet for English. And he brought everything over to my house, along with some Brazilian candies that his babysitter made.

I told myself there was some kind of explanation for the girls. That when I got back to school, everything would be the same. But when I returned, after only three days out, none of my so-called friends would talk to me. Not in the halls, not in class. At lunchtime, I went to sit at our table—their table—and there were no empty chairs. I actually saw Raven pull an empty chair away right when I walked into the cafeteria. But I thought I had to be imagining things, so I grabbed a chair from another table, pulled it over, and sat down. No one said a single word to me. I was invisible. They didn't *pretend* I wasn't there; I *wasn't* there. I tried to act like everything was normal. I sat in my seat and choked down a couple bites of sandwich, and acted like I was part of the conversation, but my insides were turning to ashes.

The next day, I didn't know what to do. I couldn't

sit with those girls again. But I had nowhere else to go.

David Fischer saved me, again.

When the bell rang for lunch, I started gathering my books and things up as slowly as I could. I was stalling for time, trying to figure out where else I could go so I wouldn't have to face the girls. David was in my class, which was math, and he was still packing up too because his backpack and binder are always a disaster.

"Hey," I said. "Did you understand that last problem Mr. Johnson put up on the board?"

"I think so," he said.

"I totally didn't get it. Could you maybe go over it with me? At lunch?"

"Sure," he said. So we walked into the cafeteria together, and I stuck right next to him while we got our trays and our food, and sat down. I knew all the guys at his table—I'd played on Little League teams with most of them at some point. David showed me how to do the math problem, which I'd actually understood, of course. Then we talked about basketball and the Knicks' awesome win against the Suns, and how amazing Kristaps Porziņģis was.

That weekend, I called David and asked if he wanted to hang out, maybe shoot some hoops. He said sure.

The next week, something shifted, and I became visible to the girls again. In English, Sarah asked me if

I'd finished reading *The Midwife's Apprentice*. In science, Marissa and Raven wanted to be in my group for the volcano experiment.

But I kept sitting with David and his table at lunch. The guys were all fine with it. And the girls who'd been my friends? I didn't have much in common with them anymore.

I wasn't stuck-up. I'm not stuck-up. I'm just not interested in the same things as other girls. I don't know their code. And, honestly, I don't want to. I have more in common with David and his friends than with a bunch of girls. Or, at least, more in common with David. I don't actually hang out with the other guys, except at lunch. David's my friend. My best friend.

Or he was, until Luke came along.

DAVID

The bell rings, so we all stand up and dump our trays in the trash, and Luke of course is walking next to Sammie, but I have a plan.

"Hey, Sammie," I say, stepping up next to her on the other side. "Would you rather play baseball in a dress or a bathing suit?"

"What?" she asks.

I repeat my question.

"What kind of dress?" she asks.

"That's so stupid," Luke says. "That's never going to happen."

"Your bat mitzvah dress," I say. Sammie hated her bat mitzvah dress.

"One-piece or two-piece bathing suit?" she asks.

I slow down my pace, and Sammie slows with me.

Luke groans. "You guys and your 'would you rather.' Ugh." He runs to catch up with Andrew and Kai.

"A one-piece."

Sammie tips her head to one side, thinking. "I'd go for the dress. Better coverage for sliding."

"Me too," I say. "Definitely the dress."

"I'd like to see you in my bat mitzvah dress," Sammie says, flashing me a quick smile.

"Hey," I say, like I just thought of it. "Want to meet at the Fort sometime? Like we did during winter break? Maybe after school one day?"

Sammie looks at me, and I can tell she's surprised. "Just you and me?"

"Just you and me."

She shrugs. "Okay. Could you remember the hand warmers this time?"

I grin. "I'll try. But I'll probably forget."

THURSDAY, FEBRUARY 5

DAVID

I finally have a plan to hang out with Sammie, so of course God decides to prank me. The rest of the week is one of the coldest on record. The Channel 12 weatherman practically poops his pants with excitement about how cold it is. "And the high today will be a whopping twelve degrees!" he says on Friday. I hate the word *whopping*. I hate weathermen. And weatherwomen. And winter.

On Saturday it warms up into the mid-twenties, and we get a couple inches of snow. It's still in the twenties on Sunday, so I text Sammie *Fort?* then don't hear from her for almost two hours, when she finally texts back *Can't*.

Skiing. It drops down into single digits on Monday, and when a thaw finally sets in on Tuesday, it rains, so I still don't say anything to Sammie. Wednesday, it's warm and not raining, but the ground's muddy and gross, plus the weather app says it'll get up to fifty on Thursday. So I wait until Thursday because I want the Fort to be perfect.

When the last bell rings, Luke has to stay after to talk to the teacher, which I am pretty sure is a giant "go for it" sign from God.

"Meet you on the bus," I tell him, then race-walk out of class.

It's so warm out that kids are carrying their coats, and the sun is shining, and everything is going my way.

Sammie's in her seat, so I slide in next to her. "Fort in an hour?"

"I thought you forgot," she says. "Or were goofing on me."

"I didn't forget," I say.

Sammie nods. "Promise you'll be there?"

"I promise," I say, then move across the aisle to my regular seat. A couple of minutes later Luke gets on and sits down next to me.

Sammie gets off at her stop and waves good-bye, and then it's my stop.

"See you tomorrow," I say to Luke.

Mom is standing at the bus stop, and when I go to step off the bus, she's blocking the doorway.

"Tell Luke he needs to get off here," she shouts, like I'm deaf.

"Why?"

"The baby's sick. Wendy had to take her to the doctor, so there's no one home at his house."

"He's in seventh grade," I protest. "He can be home alone."

Mrs. Cataneo, the bus driver, interrupts. "Excuse me. We need to get a move-on here."

Mom pushes past me and steps into the bus, then hollers, "Luke! You're coming home with me."

Mom drives us the two blocks home, while I stare out the window trying not to curse at God, who is definitely laughing at me. Luke talks the whole time. I can't figure out what to do. *Promise you'll be there*, Sammie said. If I cancel, she'll think I'm mad, or worse, that I did it on purpose, to hurt her, again. But if I take Luke, it'll be his fort too. While Inez makes us lemonade and sets out pretzels and grapes for a snack, and Luke tells me all about last night's Knicks game, which I saw too, I try to figure a way out of this stupid situation.

Almost the whole hour passes, Luke beats me too many times to count at Ping-Pong, and I'm no closer to any brilliant solution. What it comes down to is this: I can't not show up. But I can't cancel. So finally, I text Sammie, *Change of plans. Luke's here. I'm bringing him 2 ok?*

Then I tell him we're going to the Fort.

SAMMIE

David slides into my seat on the bus and practically whispers, "Meet in an hour?" Like we're doing something secret. I say okay, then pull out the book I'm reading. When Luke gets on the bus, I pretend I'm totally focused on my book. I don't say anything.

At home, in the kitchen, I make a thermos of hot chocolate. Then I microwave a bag of popcorn. There's a plate of brownies on the counter that the Peas made. David's in luck. I fill a baggie with them.

I dump my school stuff out of my backpack. Then load in the food, a deck of cards, and a couple of packs of hand warmers, because David will probably forget, and head out the back door, across the yard and onto the Greenway.

I feel my phone vibrate in my pocket and pull it out.

A text from David: *Luke's here. I'm bringing him 2 ok?*

I stop walking and stare at the screen. It's *not* okay. The Fort is our special place. David's and mine. We've never brought anyone else there.

I stare at my phone, at David's question that I don't want to answer.

I type *Go without me*, but before I can hit send, I rethink it. David will take Luke there. It will become David and Luke's fort instead of David's and mine.

I change it to *I'm on my way* and hit send.

Cool, David texts. *I've got a wool blanket and hand warmers and a deck of cards.*

I shove my phone in my pocket and walk as fast as I can because I'm mad and because I want to get there first. But I hear Luke's laughter echoing from the Fort while I'm still on the Greenway.

I climb over the wooden rails that line the sides of the walk and jog down the embankment to the tunnel entrance, then stand, staring into darkness, trying to let my eyes adjust.

"Hey, Sammie!" Luke practically shouts. My name echoes around in the cold, empty tunnel while I stand there, blinded.

"Hey," I say into the still-dark tunnel, willing my eyes to see them, to see inside.

"Snacks," David says, his shape appearing out of the dark. "Awesome." He holds out his hand and I give him the snack-filled backpack. "You're the best, Sammie," he says, but his voice sounds flat. Tight. Like he's nervous.

"Thanks," I say, the inside of the tunnel finally becoming visible.

"Yeah," Luke says, moving toward me. He grabs my hand. "Come. Sit down. Let's eat!"

He pulls me into the tunnel like it's his, and I'm the one who's new.

"This place is so cool," Luke says. "Thanks for sharing it with me."

I don't know how to make him let go of my hand. Do I say something? Just pull away?

Then he sits down on David's blanket, still holding on to my hand, and I lose my balance and fall right on top of him.

DAVID

Luke takes her hand. He's holding her hand, and she doesn't stop him, and I see the whole thing: how he sits down and pulls her to him, and she collapses on top of him.

Luke laughs and Sammie pushes herself up to sitting and crosses her legs, wrapping her arms around them.

"It's freezing in here," she says, like she's asking for big, strong Luke to put his arms around her.

I keep setting out the snacks on the cement in front of the blanket like I don't even know what they're up to. We sit down and eat everything that Sammie brought and drink all the hot chocolate, except that Sammie only has one cup and a handful of popcorn, and Luke eats three brownies and a little popcorn, and I eat all the rest. The whole time, I keep eating and telling jokes like everything's fine, like it's just the same as always, and Luke laughs at everything I say, even when I'm not being funny.

But the whole time I'm thinking that I've known her forever, and she should be my girlfriend, not his, but whose fault is that? Mine, because I didn't ever make a move.

I have to show her how I feel, and fast, before it's too late.

FRIDAY, FEBRUARY 6

SAMMIE

I push through the girls' bathroom door, and almost right into a gang of them crowded around Sarah Canavan, who's leaning over the sink and studying herself in the mirror.

"Do you think this color lip gloss makes me look washed out?" she says.

"Not at all," Mackenzie says. "I love it! It's sexy but sweet."

"Very you," Marissa says. "Perfect."

Sarah, still looking at herself in the mirror, says, "Hi, Sammie."

I think her lip gloss looks like she smeared shiny bubble gum across her mouth, but before I can say anything, Raven weighs in, agreeing that it definitely does not make her look washed out, and is, in fact, *perfect*.

Just then, the door pushes open and I'm almost knocked down by Carli Martin.

"I just said 'hey' to Luke Sullivan," Carli announces. "He is *so* cute."

All the girls look at me. Even Sarah turns away from the mirror and raises one eyebrow, a trick she perfected when we were in third grade. She used to practice in front of my bedroom mirror when she slept over.

They're waiting, expecting me to say something. I stare at them. They stare at me. I stare at them.

"Well?" Sarah says. "What's he like?"

"Luke?"

"Duh!"

I flash to the Fort, the way he pulled me off-balance. What I mostly think about Luke is that I don't like him. I don't like how he stuck himself between me and David, and I *really* don't like the way he makes me feel uncomfortable and unsure all the time. I don't like how every day at lunch I get stuck sitting next to him. But I can't put any of that into words. And even if I could, I wouldn't want to tell this group, so instead I say, "He's okay."

"Okaayyy?" Carli screeches, the "kay" part of the

word drawn out and three octaves higher than the "oh." "That's all you can say? He's 'okay'? The hottest guy in seventh grade is *okay*? What's he *like*? What do you guys talk about?"

"He's *okay*," I say, remembering exactly what it is I hate about girls. "I mean, he's just a guy. He talks about the same stuff we all talk about—"

"Does he talk about girls?" Marissa interrupts. "Does he like anyone yet?"

"We don't talk about girls," I say impatiently. But then I wonder: Do my friends—David's friends—talk about girls when I'm not there? Are they sitting around our table in the cafeteria before I get there talking about girls?

"You," Sarah says, pointing at me. "He likes you. I see you two in math class."

"He sits next to me," I protest. "He was assigned that seat."

"Oh puhleeze," Sarah says, rolling her eyes and tossing her blond hair. "He so flirts with you. All the time."

"No," I say. "He's not flirting."

"He's got a thing for you," Sarah says, like she really knows.

I flash on his hand holding mine in the tunnel yesterday, the way he pulled me on top of him. My face grows hot. "It's not like that."

"The real question," Sarah says slowly, looking right into my eyes, "is whether *you* like *him*."

"No," I say, loudly. "I'm not . . . I don't . . ."

I want to get out of here, even though I still really have to pee. But before I can make my escape, the door opens and I'm shoved from behind. I stumble forward, right into Sarah, who steps back but is caught by the crush of girls around her.

"I need the mirror," says a voice that I recognize as Amanda Archer's. "Hair emergency."

Amanda doesn't even notice that she's pushed me, or that the mirror is already in full use. But apparently an Amanda Archer hair emergency is pretty serious because the other girls back out of her way. Even Sarah and Carli. I stand there, amazed, as they all grab their backpacks and disappear, silently, out of the bathroom.

"What is with my hair?" Amanda says to herself, looking in the mirror. "I hate frizz." She turns to me. "Got any Bed Head?"

I have no idea what she's talking about. I shake my head no. "Sorry," I say. Then, before she can ask me anything else, I slip into a stall.

After school, when I get on the bus, Luke's in my seat, and David's across the aisle in the seat they usually share. I walk back slowly, trying to figure out what to do.

"Hey," I say to Luke. He smiles a wide, white smile, like he's going to eat me. I turn to David. "Can I sit next to you?" He starts to move over, so I quickly add, "By the window." I want a whole person between me and Luke's grabby hands.

"Sure," he says.

I crawl over him and plop my backpack down at my feet. "I love Fridays."

David laughs. "Me too. They're the best. I don't have to think about homework or school for forty-eight hours."

"You're nuts," I say. "The weekend is the best time to get ahead on work. I can't wait to start reading *Tangerine*. And do the first vocabulary assignment too, and maybe the first set of reading comprehension questions."

"*Tangerine*? When did you guys start reading that? We're still working on our essays for *The Giver*." He turns to Luke. "We didn't get *Tangerine* yet, did we?"

Luke shakes his head no, and leans forward, trying to be part of the conversation, but I ignore him.

DAVID

When Sammie asks to sit next to me instead of Luke, I know it's a sign, because if she really liked Luke she would sit next to him, but she doesn't. She *asks* to sit next to me. I look up at the bus ceiling and say, silently, "Thank you, God." She crawls over me to sit on the inside, by the window, and shoves her backpack down between her feet. Then she launches into a typical Sammie story about how she has homework due in a month that she's going to do this weekend.

"You're nuts," I say.

Luke's leaning into the aisle, trying to be part of our conversation. I want to keep him away from her, and out of whatever's happening in our seat, so I turn to him and say, "You watching the Knicks game tonight?"

"Maybe," Luke says. "If there's someone to watch it with. It's no fun watching alone. I used to go over to my friend Ty's house."

"I would *love* to watch a game alone," I say. "But Pop is the hugest Knicks fan in the entire world. Every game, we have to put on our Knicks jerseys, and we have special Knicks cups that we drink out of. On school nights, I have to have my homework done before game time. Sometimes, he practically does it for me so I can finish before the tip-off."

While I'm talking to Luke, I put my hand down on the seat, next to Sammie, curl my fingers into a loose fist, to make it smaller, and really casually, slide it over until I'm just touching her leg. She pulls her leg away.

I wait a beat, then turn toward her. "How about you? You watching the Knicks game?" I slide my hand over and make contact again.

"You know I don't watch until the playoffs," she says. "Besides, they stink right now." She looks down at my hand, but doesn't say anything, and doesn't tell me to move it. I leave the hand there, knuckles brushing her thigh, and turn back to Luke, who's leaning forward to try and be part of the conversation.

The hand that's touching her leg feels tingly and hot, like it's charged with electricity, like it's sending off sparks, or maybe smoke, and I'm afraid to look at it or to look at her, so I ask Luke what he thinks will happen in the game, who will score the most points, who will maybe get into a fight.

We're almost to Sammie's stop when Luke says, "The three of us should watch the game together tonight."

The three of us together? I shake my head. "Sorry. It's a father-son thing. Pop gets all mopey if I invite friends."

"Okay," Luke says to Sammie. "You and me, then." He holds his arms out wide, like he wants to hug her.

My hand is still hot against her leg. She shakes her head no, turning down Luke's offer, and I'm sure she's giving me a sign, a green light.

So when the bus starts slowing for her stop, I know I have to do something, now. I stand up and turn so my back's toward Luke. Sammie grabs her backpack and steps out into the aisle, but then, weirdly, Luke stands up too, behind her.

"How about a good-bye hug?" he asks her teasingly. She looks over her shoulder at him. I take a couple of steps backward, toward the front of the bus, to put some distance between the two of us and Luke. Then I stop. I'm shaking and I kind of feel like I might puke.

"I need to get off now," Sammie says, looking past me. "What are you doing?"

Right then, I pucker up and lean in, like I hope she wants me to, like Luke would, aiming my lips for her cheek, and that's when it goes all wrong. Because Luke moves in super close from behind, so he's pressed against her. And she turns toward me, her eyes wide and her mouth slightly open like she's about to say something. Then the bus jerks, and I lose my balance and kind of fall into her. With one hand I grab the back of the nearest seat, but I'm off-balance and my mouth ends up half on hers and somehow my other hand lands right where it shouldn't, right where it's not supposed to be, on her chest.

The bus monitor hollers from the front of the bus,

"What's going on back there?" and Sammie pushes me, with both hands, hard, her eyes wide and scared.

I stumble back and she takes off past me. I watch her run off the bus, and down her walk, then stand on her doorstep, shoulders hunched, and even though I'm just looking at the back of her, I know she's upset.

"Man, she's so adorable," Luke says. "That was so funny. Hey, you make a good wingman."

I turn and look right into his big, stupid blue eyes. Luke grins and holds up his hand to high-five me.

I push past him and his raised hand, and sit back down in my seat, feeling sick and dizzy.

SAMMIE

"Please, God," I say, "just let me get inside."

I imagine David and Luke laughing and high-fiving each other as they watch me, stuck outside on my front steps, my hands shaking too much to get the key in.

Finally, as the bus pulls away, the key slides in, I push the door open, shrug off my winter coat, and head straight upstairs, through my bedroom and into my bathroom. I can hear my mother in the kitchen, talking on her cell, but I don't call hello or say anything. Dump my backpack in my bedroom and just make it to the toilet to heave up everything in my stomach. I'm shaking and can't seem to catch my breath.

I flush, strip off my clothes, turn the shower on, hot, and get in. I soap up my washcloth and scrub and scrub. I scrub where they touched me, as hard as I can, trying to erase the feel of their hands on me. "Shake it off," I tell myself, just like when I'm at bat and I swing and miss. "Shake it off. Get back in the game."

I make the water a little hotter, stand still under the shower, trying to concentrate on the heat, but I can still feel Luke behind me, pressed against me. I shut my eyes and see David's face, my best friend's face, coming toward me, too close. I'm trapped between them. I open my eyes. The shower is filled with steam and the water's plenty hot, but I'm shivering.

"It's all right," I say out loud in the shower. "It's over. It was nothing."

I'm still in my bathroom, wrapped in a towel, when my mother knocks on my bedroom door.

"Just a minute," I say. The clothes I wore to school are lying in a heap on the floor. I grab a wad of toilet paper, pick them up, and dump them into the hamper. In my bedroom, I pull on clean underpants and my pj's.

"Come in," I say.

She pushes the door open, sees me in pj's with my hair wet, and frowns. "Is everything okay?"

Before I can answer, her cell phone dings with a text

message. She looks down at her phone.

"Fine," I say.

She types a response, then presses send and looks up at me.

"What's with the shower in the middle of the day?"

"David—" I blurt out. "And Luke—"

Her phone dings again. "Luke," she says, looking down at the screen and frowning. "The new boy?"

"Yes," I say, but it's obvious that she doesn't really care why I'm in pj's at two thirty in the afternoon. I can't talk to her about any of this.

She looks up from her phone. "What happened with Luke and David?"

"They . . . they were fooling around on the bus, and spilled a bottle of Snapple all over me. I was all sticky."

"That stinks, but I'm glad everything's all right. I've got to scooch. Showing a house at four."

"Great," I say. "Hope it goes well."

She pulls the door shut and is gone. I sit down on my bed and listen to the sounds of her leaving—car starting, garage door opening, then closing. She gives a little toot of her horn as she drives off.

Time to start homework, I tell myself. I usually like working in the kitchen because I can lay out all my binders and see everything I have to do. Plus, I'll know as soon as anyone else comes home, which won't be for hours now.

I pick up my phone, hoping for a text from David. An apology, maybe, or an explanation. But the screen is blank. I slide under the covers, trying to get warm, and scroll through my contacts, looking for someone I can talk to. They're all boys—David, Jefferson, Andrew, Kai, Max, Spencer. No one who would understand. Of course, I do have Carli's number, and Sarah's, from before, when we were friends, but what would I say? And what would they say? I flash on Sarah, in the girls' bathroom. *He's got a thing for you. Do you like him?* She wouldn't get it either.

I grab my purple squishy pillow and my stuffed bunny, and curl up under the covers.

"It was nothing," I say out loud. "It didn't mean anything."

Then I do the stupidest thing ever: I bury my face in Bunny and start crying.

DAVID

I drop my backpack by the kitchen table and go right to the refrigerator. Sometimes, Inez makes Brazilian desserts, like *brigadeiros*, which are these yummy chocolate fudge balls rolled in chocolate sprinkles, or *quindim*, which are little coconut-topped custards. They're my favorite. I open the fridge and there's nothing sweet and delicious, but I keep standing there like I'm looking for something, and what I see is me, leaning in toward Sammie and—

I slam the fridge door shut. "Inez?" I call. "Inezzz!"

In the basement, the dryer clangs shut, which means she's doing laundry. I know she can hear me but she doesn't respond because she doesn't like it when I holler for her. It's disrespectful, she says. I don't want to be disrespectful, but I also don't want to be alone. I want her to stay with me, to talk to me, to take care of me.

I wait, listening as the dryer hums to life and Inez clomps back upstairs.

"You're waiting on me to get you a snack?" she asks.

"Please?" I say. "I know I can get it myself, but I want something you make."

"What?"

I want something special, something that will taste really good, something I can't even name. I think and think about all the great things Inez cooks, and I finally decide. "A broiled banana. Please." Inez makes the most awesome broiled bananas, with butter and brown sugar.

"All right," she says, and then in a singsong voice,

adds, "since you asked so nice."

While the banana cooks, I turn on the little TV that my parents installed in the kitchen for Inez, so she can watch her favorite Brazilian shows on Netflix. She clomps over and turns it off. "No TV on school days. You know that."

The "no TV on school days" rule is one of my parents' stupidest rules.

"It's Friday," I plead. "The weekend. I've spent the entire week doing schoolwork. I need a break."

"Then go outside and run around, get some fresh air."

First, I am a person who likes stale, indoor air, preferably breathed in while watching TV. Second, yesterday's warm spell was followed by a cold front so everything that melted has refrozen, including my entire backyard, and playing outside could lead to a broken arm or even frostbite. But when Inez decides something, even reason and fact won't sway her.

I sigh, and yank my binder out of my backpack, slamming it down on the kitchen table maybe a little too hard because Inez, who's been preparing my broiled banana, stops and turns slowly and looks at me with her special warning look. I take a breath and very gently, I open my binder.

But I can't concentrate. I think about telling Inez

what happened on the bus, asking for her advice, but I can't imagine saying the words I would need to say out loud, to Inez. Instead, I pull out a stack of drawing paper. I don't plan on it, but my pencil just goes, and I'm drawing a little boy, his father's hand gripped tightly onto to his shoulder, and a ball rolling toward him. I fill the paper with the scene, then take a clean sheet and draw the girl, running, a cloud of hair streaming out behind her. I draw her from the boy's perspective. I draw the boy and a baseball tee, swinging and missing, the ball flying right past his bat. I draw and draw and draw, turning the memories in my head into scenes on paper. The drawings feel stronger and truer than what happened on the bus. They're the real story, the story I want to remember. I'm so caught up in them that I don't even notice when Inez sets my snack down next to me. When I finally look up, I've got half a dozen sheets of paper strewn over the table, and the melted brown sugar on my banana has hardened into a shiny coating.

MONDAY, FEBRUARY 9

DAVID

On Friday night, right before I got into bed, I texted Sammie, *I'm sorry*. But I hit delete instead of send because the whole thing was an accident, and I knew Sammie would know that, and it would be weird to apologize for something that was just an accident. I texted her about hanging out on Saturday, but she never answered. She didn't answer last night either when I texted her about the math homework.

So just in case, if she *is* mad, I'm going to tell her the truth. About how I didn't mean it like maybe it happened, and about how Luke ruined everything. Because the real truth is that it was all Luke's fault.

At the bus stop, I joke around with Kyle and Kevin Jenkins, who're twins and in eighth grade, and even though I can't exactly hear what they're saying because there's a funny pounding sound in my ears, I crack silly jokes and laugh at whatever they say back to me.

When the bus pulls up, I'm planning how I'll sit in my regular seat, next to Luke, and Sammie will get on two stops later and sit in her regular seat, across the aisle, and I'll tell the elephant fart joke, and Sammie and Luke will laugh.

Except when I step into the bus, Luke's in Sammie's seat, and I know they arranged it this way. They texted each other last night when Sammie was ignoring me, and she likes him and not me. So I walk right to that seat and sit down next to Luke so Sammie can't.

"How come you're sitting here?" I ask.

"I just felt like it," Luke says. "Hey, great game last night, huh?"

I don't even answer him because he's such a liar. Instead, I pull out my phone and start playing Candy Crush, and I ignore him the entire rest of the bus ride. Even when Sammie gets on and sits in the front row, next to the bus monitor, which is a really weird thing to do, I don't say anything.

★ ★ ★

120

SAMMIE

It will be like it never happened, I tell myself. And besides, it was just a joke. One of David's stupid jokes. But when I step up into the bus and they're both in my seat, I feel like I've been punched in the face. The two of them. A team. Ganged up against me. Again.

Without thinking, I sit down in the very first seat, next to the bus monitor.

No one sits in the front seat. Ever. The empty space next to the bus monitor is like the no-man's-land between two opposing armies.

I turn and look right at her, ready to give her a big smile to show that I'm completely normal and there's some kind of logical reason that I'm sitting next to her. But she won't even look in my direction. Every time she stands up to survey the rest of the bus and holler at the kids who are messing around, she completely ignores me.

At school, I shut myself into the girls' bathroom by the main office, where no one ever goes, until the bell rings for first period.

I make it through the morning, spend lunch in the girls' bathroom, and am on my way to math when I remember where I sit: right between the two of them.

My stomach clenches into a small, hard knot of fear, and it's not even a lie when I go to the nurse's office and tell Mrs. Sirkin that I feel really sick.

She has me lie down on one of the cots, and pulls the curtain around me.

As long as I'm lying down and not thinking about math class, I feel okay. But when Mrs. Sirkin pokes her head in and asks, "On a scale of one to ten, how bad is the pain?" the knot returns.

"Seven," I say. That's not totally true, but I triangulate between the real-pain score, which is a four, and the fear-of-math-class score, which is a ten.

So she calls Dad. "No fever," she tells him. "The pain seems to come and go. But Sammie's not a frequent flyer here. This is only the third time she's been in my office in a year and a half. I'd give her the benefit of the doubt."

She hangs up and comes to tell me that Dad has a break in patients and can pick me up in twenty minutes, and I don't protest.

In the car, Dad waits until I've got my seat belt on, then hands me a plastic bin, in case I'm going to puke. "I'm seeing a lot of stomach bugs in the office," he says. "Usually it's a twenty-four-hour thing."

I think about trying to explain what's going on, but I don't know how to. I glance over at him. He's loosened his tie and unbuttoned the top button of his shirt. A few white chest hairs poke out.

"David and Luke," I say.

"Are they sick too? No surprise you've got it, then."

"On the bus," I try.

A picture pops into my head, of Dad and me at the beach, maybe four or five years ago. My mother and the Peas are lying on towels, all reading their summer beach books and working on their perfect tans. Dad and me? We're in the water, with our boogie boards. It's up to my chest, and there's a giant wave heading straight toward us. I'm scared but I don't want to show it. Dad shouts, "Paddle, Buddy!" I climb up onto my board, turn to face the shore, and start paddling as hard as I can. But the wave catches me and crashes right on top of me and I'm tumbling underwater, over and over. I'm lost and choking, and I don't know which way is up or where the ocean floor is. When I finally surface, salt water in my nose and the back of my throat, hair plastered all over my face, Dad is right there, grinning, ready to drag me back out to the deep water and the big waves. And I go.

"What about the bus?" Dad asks.

"Nothing," I say. "I just—I started to feel sick this morning on the bus."

He reaches over and pats my knee. "It'll pass."

TUESDAY, FEBRUARY 10

DAVID

Sammie's not at lunch or in math on Monday, and not on the bus home. Then this morning she does that weird thing of sitting in the front row, next to the bus monitor. I want to ask Luke if he knows what's going on with her, but I don't want him to know that I care. Or that she's not talking to me.

I walk into school with Luke, past the Corey-Markus crew ("'sup," "word," "dude"), trying to figure out some way to get Sammie alone, and thinking about faking stomach cramps so Luke will go to first period without me. But then he says, "I have to go to the guidance counselor's office. I'll catch up with you in social studies."

The office is in the west wing, down the hall from

Sammie's first-period science class, so I say, "I'll walk with you."

"It's okay," Luke says. "I'll just meet you in class."

"No biggie," I say. "I have to pick up something in the science room anyway."

We're on our way there when we pass Spencer and Kai, standing by their lockers.

"Hey," I say.

"What are you guys doing over here?" Spencer asks.

Luke mumbles something about picking up a form and keeps walking.

I stop, wondering why Luke is being so weird about going to the guidance office. "I'm looking for someone," I tell Spencer and Kai.

"Sammie?" Spencer asks. "Are you looking for Sammie? I heard about you guys on the bus on Friday."

"What do you mean?" I say, my voice sounding odd. Guilty.

Spencer blushes. "You and Luke and Sammie. On the bus."

"We heard—" Kai interrupts. Then he stops, and starts to blush too. "You guys were teasing her."

"Touching her," Spencer says. "Like—"

"No," I interrupt. "*Nothing* happened."

Andrew appears, with Jefferson and Max trailing behind.

"What happened?" Andrew asks.

"Nothing," I say. "Nothing happened."

"On the bus," Spencer says. "David says nothing happened on the bus on Friday, but *we* heard—"

"Oh yeah," Jefferson says. "I heard about the bus on Friday. You and Luke with Sammie."

Andrew chimes in. "We heard you had Sammie trapped between the two of you, and—"

"No," I say. "I didn't do anything. I was just . . . trying to give her something. And then the bus stopped short, and I kind of bumped into her."

"The girls on my bus," Kai insists, "said you kissed her, and you and Luke were, like, grabbing—"

"No," I say. "I mean, Luke was flirting with her, but I—"

"Who was I flirting with?" Luke asks, appearing out of nowhere.

"Sammie," Kai says. "Did you kiss her on the bus? On Friday?"

Luke makes a *psht* noise. "On the bus? Why would I try to kiss her on the bus? I was just flirting. Fooling around a little. Girls like that stuff. They like the attention."

I was on the bus, and I know Sammie didn't like it. But if I say that, I'm back in the story. So I keep my mouth shut. The rest of it doesn't matter. The person I need to explain things to is Sammie.

SAMMIE

It's the only way I'm going to be able to get through math class. So before school, I go straight to Mrs. Knell's room and knock on her door.

She looks up from her computer and smiles. "Come on in, Sammie. What can I do you for?"

"I was wondering if I could move my seat."

"Is everything okay?"

"Fine," I say. "I just . . . want to be closer to the board."

Mrs. Knell loves me. I'm not the best math student in the class—Sean Cibelli is—but I *always* do my homework, and I always raise my hand.

"What's going on?"

I can't tell Mrs. Knell about the bus or the boys, so instead I lie. "I think I might not be seeing the board clearly. I think it would help to be closer."

"Have you had your eyes checked?"

"My dad made an appointment for me," I lie some more, "but it's not for a couple of weeks."

"Let's see, then," Mrs. Knell says, pulling out her

seating chart. She looks at the paper, then at the desks in the room. "How about here?" she asks, pointing to Amanda Archer's desk in the second row, between Haley and Sean.

Amanda Archer gets whatever she wants, including choosing her seat in every class. If she's sitting in the second row between Haley and Sean, that's where she wants to be. But I figure Mrs. Knell knows what she's doing.

"I think it'll be a nice change for you," Mrs. Knell says as she erases Amanda's name and pencils me into that spot. "Nice for Haley too."

"Sounds great," I say. I wonder why Mrs. Knell thinks it'll be nice for Haley, and if she'd still think it was nice if she knew about our "stuck-up" conversation.

After lunch, I'm in my new seat when the first bell rings, and still in it when Haley arrives. She sits down and gives me a quick smile.

"Mrs. Knell moved my seat," I say. I try to smile a friendly, not-stuck-up sort of smile.

"Oh," says Haley. "Nice."

She leans over and pulls a binder out of her backpack. The whole front is decorated with stickers and washi tape. There are three silhouette stickers of softball players, a couple of quotes, and a cute kitten photo. My binder is completely plain and boring. And yellow. Which suddenly seems like a dumb color. I'm wondering whether the Peas have washi tape and might help me decorate my binders, when Haley pulls out her planner and opens it. Everything is color coded. I kind of gasp.

"Wow," I say. "That's the most organized planner I've ever seen."

Haley smiles. "I love my planner."

"Me too," I say, then roll my eyes. "I mean, I love *my* planner." I pull it out to show her. "But I think you have me beat with the color usage."

"Hey, Sammie," Sean says from the other side of me. "How come Mrs. Knell moved your seat? Are you failing math?"

I know Sean's not trying to be rude. He's just wired differently. I turn and smile at him, but he doesn't notice because he's drawing some kind of bird in the white space of his math homework paper. There are four colored pencils neatly lined up at the top right corner of his desk.

"No, I'm not failing math," I say. "I asked to sit closer to the board because I was getting headaches. I kind of have one right now, actually."

"You should take some Tylenol," Sean says.

"Thanks," I say.

"I like sitting in the second row," Sean says. "I sit in the second row in all my classes. I have an accommodation for it. I don't like the front row."

"Same," I say. "About the front row, I mean."

Amanda walks into class, and stops when she sees me in her seat.

"What's going on?" she asks no one in particular.

I figure it's not my job to explain the seat change to *everyone*, so I take out my pencil case and dig around to find my favorite pencil, a mechanical one with a really nice, squishy purple grip.

"Where am I supposed to sit?" Amanda says.

Mrs. Knell, who has been writing the Do Now on the board, turns around.

"Oh, Amanda," she says, "I made a few seat changes. You're right there." She points to my old seat.

Amanda stares right at me, stabbing me with her eyeballs. She stomps to her new seat.

"Whoa," I say under my breath, kind of to Haley, "if looks could kill, I think I'd be dead."

Haley grins and whispers, "Off with your head!"

I start to laugh, and turn it into a cough.

At that moment, Luke and David walk in. The two

musketeers. My stomach clenches up and I try to focus all my attention on copying the Do Now into my notebook. I keep my head down and work the problem out. Then I look up and keep my eyes on the board. I don't turn around at all. The entire class. But I can feel them, behind me, together.

WEDNESDAY, FEBRUARY 11

DAVID

On Tuesday, I made a whole plan to talk to Sammie right at the beginning of math, before Luke was there, and I even spent the last fifteen minutes of lunch in the bathroom across the hall from class so I could get there early. I was carrying my binder and racing from the bathroom to math, a man with a plan, when I got knocked from behind and the binder flew out of my arm and exploded all over the hallway. It was Luke, of course, who knocked into me, so instead of being early to class I was late.

If I could just get Sammie alone for five minutes, I could explain everything, but wherever I go to try to catch up with her, Luke's right there, ready to butt in and ruin everything. He's not a sidekick, he's a side-stick.

I finally catch a break when Mrs. Dougherty asks Luke to stay after in English. Sammie's in Spanish, only two doors down, so I'm packed up before the bell starts ringing, and out the door before it stops. I spot her right away, practically running down the hall, but I manage to catch up with her in front of the doors to the stairwell.

"Hey," I say, grabbing her arm. I'm panting and a little sweaty, and my heart's racing. "Can we talk?"

"About what?" Sammie says, pulling her arm away from me.

"About what's going on. About why you're not answering my texts and avoiding me at school. Are you . . . mad at me?"

Sammie stops walking and looks at me. "I'm not mad," she says, and I feel a whoosh of relief. But then she goes on. "What happened . . ." She looks down at the floor, then back up, but her eyes don't meet mine. "What happened on the bus on Friday—"

What happened on the bus on Friday was awkward and embarrassing and weird. But I don't want to say that. I want to pretend that what happened on the bus didn't happen. And I want Sammie to pretend that too. I open my mouth to try to say something, but just then,

Jefferson and Spencer come walking up.

"Hey, Sammie," Spencer says. "David told us about you and Luke."

"What?" Sammie says, glancing at me.

"About how you were fooling around on the bus," Spencer says. "With Luke. Are you guys going out?"

"David told you I was *what*?" Sammie asks, her voice high and sharp.

"He told us what happened on the bus on Friday—"

"I did not," I interrupt. "It wasn't—"

"You said you were *giving* something to Sammie," Jefferson tells me, "not kissing her, even though all the girls on my bus said it was kissing. You said *Luke* and Sammie were fooling around, and that Sammie liked it." He turns to Sammie. "Are you guys going out?"

Sammie looks right at me, and there's something in her eyes that I can't read. I wait for her to tell the guys that nothing happened with Luke, that she wasn't flirting with him, that it was all a big mistake. But she doesn't. She doesn't say anything.

Just then, Luke joins our little circle. "Hey," he says, putting his arm around Sammie. "You and David making up?"

"Shut up," I say. "We're *friends*. We don't have to make up. Sammie said she's not mad. Right, Sammie?"

She keeps staring right at me, saying nothing. She

doesn't seem to even notice Luke's arm around her shoulder. *Or maybe she's used to it*, I think. Maybe Luke puts his arm around her all the time because she really does like him, not me, and she wants his arm around her like that.

"Cool," Luke says. "Then maybe you want to kiss and make up with me?" He starts to leans in toward her, like he's really going to kiss her right here in the hall, but before his lips make contact, Sammie pushes him away. She still doesn't say anything.

Luke laughs, then lightly punches my arm. "C'mon," he says. "We're going to be late for drama class." He pulls me away from Sammie and down the hall.

I can't believe the way he moved in, so smooth, and practically kissed her right in the hallway, in front of everybody. Or the way she almost let him.

I push through the door into drama class, but before I can sit down, Carli Martin grabs my arm and whispers, "Follow me."

She pulls me to the back corner of the room, where I'm surrounded by her friends.

"What's going on with Luke?" Carli asks in a hoarse whisper.

"That he's secretly a pod person?" I ask. "I'm pretty sure it's not true—"

"No," Sarah interrupts. "What's going on with Luke

and Sammie? We heard that something happened on the bus. Between them. And we heard that they are . . . that they might be . . ." She stops talking and looks me right in the eye, raising one eyebrow.."*You* know."

"Going out?" I say, feeling a sudden, hot rush of frustration. It's unfair, the way Luke's so smooth, the way everything that's hard for me is so easy for him. "Why don't you ask him. They were practically kissing in the hall just now."

Carli starts crying, big, fat tears rolling down her cheek. I'm kind of amazed that anyone can make tears appear that fast, but I ignore her and push right past Carli's wet face and Sarah's open mouth, and sit back down next to the person who's ruining everything.

"What was that about?" Luke asks.

"Nothing," I say.

Sammie doesn't come to lunch, again.

SAMMIE

David Fischer is telling lies about me. My *best friend* is saying stuff he *knows* isn't true. I don't know what to do.

So I decide to ask two girls who are a lot more experienced with flirting and drama and boy problems than me: the Peas.

They've been picking me up from school every day this week, and even being nice about it.

Today, Rachel's in the driver's seat and Becca's riding shotgun. I open the back door and slide in, but neither one says a word. I don't take it personally. They can't talk because they're both looking in the little mirrors on the backs of their sunshades to reapply their lipsticks.

Becca flips her sunshade up and caps her lipstick. "How was your day?"

"Okay," I say.

"That doesn't sound very Sammie-like," Rachel says. "There must have been at least one A-plus on a paper, or a quiz you killed."

"Classes are fine," I say. "I mean, they're the same."

"Hmm," Becca says. "Is it personal? What's going on? C'mon, dish."

I take a deep breath and try. "There was this thing on the bus Friday—" I stop, not sure how to say what happened.

"Like someone threw up?" Rachel asks. "Remember when we had to ride the bus, Bec? It always smelled like barf."

"Oh my gawd," Becca says, making a gagging face. "That stink, I can still smell it."

"No. No one threw up," I say. "Friday, well, I always

sit in the same seat. I sit in one seat and David and Luke sit across from me. But Friday, Luke was sitting in my seat, and David was in the other seat, so I sat with David because Luke—"

"Middle school," Rachel says to Becca like it means something.

Becca shakes her head. "Gawd."

"It was weird. He started touching my leg."

"Luke was touching your leg?"

"No, *David* was."

"Did you tell him to cut it out?" Rachel asks.

"No. I moved my leg away but then he moved his hand so he was touching me again. I didn't know what to say. I wasn't even sure he was doing it on purpose."

"Seventh-grade boys," Becca says like she's talking about something gross. "They have no sense of personal space. They're like puppies, all wiggly and awkward but not nearly as cute."

"Seventh-grade boys are the worst," Rachel says. "They're so handsy. Half of them haven't figured out deodorant and they stink." She pinches her nose with one hand and waves the other like she's waving away a really bad smell.

"Nobody smelled," I say, "but Luke—"

"Luke?" Becca interrupts. "That cute boy from the fro-yo place? I bet he's figured out deodorant."

"I don't know about the deodorant," I say, "but a lot of girls are flirting with him, and David told everyone that I was too, and that Luke likes me—"

"You go, girl!" Rachel says, taking a hand off the wheel to air high-five me. "Flirting with the cute new boy!"

"Look," Becca says, turning around to look at me. "Seventh grade is the worst, but you'll get through it. Don't let those other girls push you around about Luke. If the two of you have something going on, that's your business, not theirs."

"We don't—" I protest, but the Peas aren't listening.

"First it's boy trouble," Becca says to Rachel. "Next thing you know, she'll want us to take her shopping for thongs."

"Urban," Rachel says. "They have the best."

"Our little angel," Becca says.

"She's growing up," Rachel says, pretending to wipe away a tear.

I turn and stare out the window, wondering if maybe there's something wrong with me. I *have* boy trouble, but not the kind the Peas think I have. And no one seems to understand that.

THURSDAY, FEBRUARY 12

DAVID

Sammie's not at lunch again, and someone else doesn't show: Luke. I'm not even sure when my sidestick suddenly unstuck. We were in science together, and the bell rang, and I packed up my bag and walked out of class with him right there beside me. But when I got to the cafeteria, he was gone.

He shows up in math class, his nose kind of red like he has a cold.

"Where were you?" I whisper while Mrs. Knell explains the Do Now.

Amanda leans forward so I can't see Luke at all. I lean back and whisper again, "Where were you? At lunch. You weren't in the cafeteria."

He shrugs, staring at his desk.

"I had to meet with someone," he whispers, opening his math binder. "A teacher."

Amanda leans back, blocking Luke again. I lean forward so I can see him. "Who? Why?"

"It was nothing. Mrs. Dougherty wanted to talk about the *Giver* essay we turned in last week. She wanted to go over it with me, I guess because I'm new."

Mrs. Dougherty is the kind of teacher who gives you back your essay a month after you hand it in. She for sure *never* reads essays in a week.

At the front of the room, Mrs. Knell says, "I'll be collecting and grading these Do Nows. You have five minutes to complete them."

I haven't even written the problem down, and didn't hear Mrs. Knell's instructions. I sigh and open my math binder, wondering why Luke would lie about where he really was at lunch. I take out my pencil and have a horrible thought: maybe he's not telling the truth because he was with Sammie, and he doesn't want me to know. I picture them, together, in the back stairwell, Luke's blue eyes wide open, staring into her dark brown ones, as he moves in to kiss her right on the lips. My pencil snaps, and the vision disappears just as Mrs. Knell says, "David, what answer did you get for the problem?"

★ ★ ★

SAMMIE

When the dismissal bell rings at the end of the day, I grab my stuff and head straight for the girls' bathroom by the front office. It's the safest place to wait for the halls to clear. Then I can head to the library, where I wait until five for the Peas to pick me up.

Except today, someone else is in my bathroom, in one of the stalls, and I know by the sneakers who it is: Haley.

I'm standing there, trying to decide if I can squeeze out a bit of pee or if I should turn around and leave so she doesn't think I'm a stalker, when the door pushes open and Carli, Sarah, Marissa, and Mackenzie flood into the bathroom. Carli's eyes are red-rimmed and puffy, and there's shiny clear snot below one of her nostrils. She hiccups.

Sarah walks right up to me, her green eyes narrowed and angry, and hisses, "Liar."

The only lies I've told anyone are the little ones to Mrs. Knell about needing glasses. She can't possibly mean those, can she? I look past her angry face, at Marissa and Mackenzie, who are in math with me.

"You *said* you didn't like him," Sarah says, her hands on her hips and her chin jutted out.

"What?"

She pokes her index finger at my chest. Her painted fingernail is dark red, the exact color of blood. "You lied to us about Luke. You *said* you didn't like him."

Luke. His name stabs me right in my gut. I wince. And somehow, what I feel as pain must look like something else, because her scowl turns to a look of triumph.

"I knew it!" she says. "Liar! Carli has had a crush on him since his first day here. But you've ruined everything. David told us you guys were *making out* in the hall."

I open my mouth and close it. Open it again. Why would David tell them *that*? I can't make any words come out. I want to say that I didn't lie, and that I'm not going out with Luke, and that I've *never* made out with anyone, in the hall or anywhere else.

Unless . . . what if? On the bus? What if I did something to cause that? To cause all of it?

I'm standing there with my mouth hanging open, when there's a groan from behind the stall door. Haley. I'd forgotten about her. The groan is followed by an awful retching noise and then the sound of something splashing into the toilet. Another retching sound, and more splashing. Haley's full-on barfing. I look from Sarah to Marissa to Mackenzie, and they're all standing,

143

frozen, eyes wide. Even Carli has forgotten her tragic situation and is staring open-mouthed at the stall door.

"Haley?" I say, unsure.

Another moan, then more splashing sounds. In unison, Carli, Sarah, Marissa, and Mackenzie put their hands to their mouths. Sarah makes a small gagging noise and runs for the door, with Carli and Marissa right behind her. Mackenzie, with one hand over her mouth, touches my shoulder. I'm not sure whether she's trying to comfort me or steady herself, but I try to give her a reassuring smile. From behind the stall door comes a wave of retching. Mackenzie makes a little sobbing sound, turns, and runs out of the bathroom.

I wait for a pause in the puking sounds. "Haley?" I say. "Are you okay? Do you want me to see if the nurse is around?"

"I'm okay," Haley says weakly. "Can one of the other girls go get her?"

"Umm," I say, "the other girls bailed. Sorry. It's just me."

The stall door swings open. "Cool," Haley says. "It worked." She's holding her water bottle, smiling.

"What worked?"

"The fake puking."

"You mean you weren't just barfing up your insides?"

Haley laughs. "Nope. I learned that trick at softball camp. We used to use it to get out of dining hall duty."

"Wow. It sounded really real," I say. "But why?"

"I thought you could use a distraction. I don't know what's up with you and Luke, but those girls were freaking out."

"Nothing's up with me and Luke," I say.

Haley shrugs, then pulls her phone out of her back pocket. "Whatever," she says, looking down at the phone screen. "Do Carli and Sarah and crew take a bus?"

"I think so. Why?"

"They'll start pulling out in a couple minutes."

I sigh with relief. "Thanks."

Haley grabs her backpack.

"Aren't you going to miss yours?" I ask.

"I don't take a bus," she says, pushing the bathroom door open. "My mom picks me up on her way home. I'm going to hang out in the library until then."

"Me too," I say, following right behind. "Get some homework done."

"We could work together," Haley says. "At least on math and English." She turns and grins. "Give you a chance to prove you're not stuck-up after all."

I laugh, half at the joke Haley's made, and half with

pleasure at the idea of doing homework with someone.

The last time I did homework with a friend was at the very beginning of sixth grade, when Sarah and I did a book report together. We had to make a "quilt," and Sarah was focused on gluing pink ribbons in between the quilt blocks and writing the headings in purple puffy glue, like that was the part of the assignment that really mattered.

"Cool," I say, and we head into the library.

DAVID

In PE, we're playing badminton golf, which is super boring and mostly involves standing around, so I start thinking about Saturday because it's Valentine's Day. Pop always grumbles that it's a holiday made up by greeting card companies, but I think what really gets him is that it's a holiday when no one buys sporting goods. Jock straps, mouth guards, and baseball bats are not Valentine's Day gifts.

In middle school, everyone acts like they don't care about Valentine's Day, but they do. Last year, when it fell on a Friday, the halls were crazy all day because kids kept leaving classes to slip valentines into other kids' lockers. Girls were coming into classes crying.

One eighth-grade boy got slapped in the face during lunch. The rumor was he gave valentines to three girls. None of my crew gave cards to anyone. I wanted to give one to Sammie but I didn't. We both pretended like it was just a regular day.

I wonder if Luke's going to give Sammie a valentine. Maybe he's bought a card already, and maybe he'll give her candy too. I wonder if he knows that Sammie's favorite candy is Sour Patch Kids. I wonder if I should buy some Sour Patch Kids and take them to her house on Saturday. It's not fair that I know Sammie so well, and Luke barely knows her at all, and he's maybe going out with her. It's not fair that what happened on the bus made everything weird and awkward between us. I wish I could remind her of our history, of our friendship, before the bus. Before Luke.

Then I have a flash of inspiration. I *can* remind Sammie about us, through my drawings. I can draw our friendship, the story of us. Sammie loves my drawing, and always asks me what I'm working on. She's the only friend who knows how I feel about *The Northern Province*. She's the only friend who's seen my real drawings. I decide right then: I'm going to draw my way back into Sammie's life.

At the end of PE, I'm so deep into thinking about

what I can draw, running through different story ideas and thinking about what scenes I could draw, that I don't bother changing out of my stinky gym shirt. I just grab my backpack and coat and head for the bus.

I'm still lost in my own head, thinking about what story to tell and how to tell it, when Luke sits down next to me. "What happened to you at the end of PE? You disappeared."

"Sorry," I say. "I have a lot on my mind."

Luke pulls out his phone and starts playing Candy Crush, and I go back to staring out the window and thinking about what I can draw.

When the bus is coming to my stop, Luke says, "Want to come over later?"

"Can't," I say, standing up and grabbing my backpack. "I've got a ton of homework."

Luke looks at me funny, and I remember that he has all the same classes as me, and knows exactly how much homework we have, which is practically zip.

"For Hebrew school," I say, even though no one *ever* has homework for Hebrew school.

In the kitchen, Allie's sitting at the table, eating a Rice Krispies treat.

I cut myself a couple of squares, pour myself a glass of orange juice, and carry my snack to the table.

When I take out the drawing stuff, Allie says, "I'll

write the story, if you want."

"No thanks," I say.

Her chin gets all quivery, which means that any second she's going to start crying, so I say, "I have to do the whole thing myself. It's an English assignment. If you do the story, that would be cheating." I personally believe getting a little help with homework never hurt anyone, especially when it comes to English assignments, but Allie thinks it's practically the same as murdering your parents with an ax.

"Oh," she says. "Never mind."

The story I want to tell happened at a baseball game two years ago, when Sammie scored a run because of me. On her at-bat, she whacked the ball way into the outfield, over the heads of everyone out there, and made it all the way to third base. Then the next kid up, Jason Diaz, struck out. A kid named Trey went next and hit the ball into the infield, right between the second baseman and the shortstop. There was a little bit of bumbling with the ball, so Trey got on first base, but Sammie was still stuck at third. Then another kid got up to bat, and struck out. So it was two outs, with Sammie on third, and I was up.

Basically, I hate being at bat. I hate standing there, waiting for the ball to come flying toward me because most of the time, I'm 100 percent convinced that it's going to hit me. I'm thinking, *What kind of idiot would stand here and wait to get hit by a small, round rock?* Which makes it hard to focus on trying to hit the ball. I mean, it would be *nice* to hit the ball, but it feels more urgent to avoid being hit *by* the ball.

Anyway, Sammie was on third, and she needed a hit by *me* to score a run, so I managed to almost stay in the box. The pitch was thrown and I stayed in and stayed in and stayed in and . . . backed out. But as I started to back out, swinging the bat, I came down hard on my front foot, which propelled the bat right into the ball, and I got an awesome hit! It went over the head of the second baseman, plunked down on the grass, and rolled out into the outfield, far away from anyone out there. I made it to first, and Sammie got home, and when the opposing second baseman bobbled the catch, Trey ran to third and I got onto second.

I didn't honestly care about making it to second, and when the next batter up hit a high pop that was caught by one of the outfielders, the inning was over without me scoring, but I didn't care about that. What mattered was Sammie. I got her the run.

I don't want anyone except Sammie to know what this story is about. I want it to be like a secret message that only Sammie will be able to decode. My hero,

Melvin Marbury, has animals who act like people in his comic strip, so I decide I'll make the people in my story into animals. I draw Sammie as a cat, and I make myself a dog. The other guys, I make all dogs too. It takes me six pages to tell the story, and I have a little trouble making enough different-looking dogs for all the other players, but in the end it's a great story. A great Valentine's Day gift for Sammie, to remind her of our friendship, of who we were, together, before. I staple the pages together like a book, but I don't write anything. I fold the whole thing in thirds, get an envelope from Mom's desk, and slide it in, then write *Sammie* on the front.

FRIDAY, FEBRUARY 13

DAVID

I spend another lunch period in the bathroom, eating peanut butter crackers instead of spaghetti and meatballs, so I can get to math class early, right after Sammie. I mostly don't mind the bathroom or the crackers because I'm pretty sure those meatballs are made from horse meat.

When the first bell rings, I'm out in the hall, holding my math binder with the valentine envelope slipped underneath so no one can see it. I watch Mrs. Knell's door, and Sammie doesn't even notice me as she walks into the class—first, as usual, with her apparently new best friend, Haley. Two beats later, Sean Cibelli appears. I count slowly to five, and then follow. In the room, Sammie's backpack is on the floor between her and Sean's desks. She's bent over it, getting her math binder, so I stand awkwardly at the front.

"Are we going to have homework tonight?" I ask Mrs. Knell, watching Sammie out of the corner of my eye.

We always have homework in math, unless we're having a test the next day, and then we still have homework, but it's not checked because our homework is to redo the test review problems that we got wrong. Which Sammie always does, and I never do.

But Mrs. Knell smiles and says, "Of course."

Sammie's still bent over her backpack, so I follow up with, "Is it a lot or a little? I mean, how many problems?"

Mrs. Knell stops writing the Do Now and tips her head a bit. "Exactly the right number of problems, David."

Sammie finally straightens up, sets her binder on her desk, and turns to talk to Haley, facing away from her backpack.

"Thanks," I say, starting down between the rows of desks, then stopping between Sean's and Sammie's.

Sean is bent over his desk, drawing something.

"Did you do the homework?"

Sean looks up at me, puzzled. "Are you asking me?"

"Yeah," I say, keeping my back to Sammie, with her backpack at my feet.

Sean motions with his chin to the paper on his desk. It's the math homework, but in the margins are some tiny drawings. I lean over to get a better look. They're all birds, done in pencil. One is sitting like it's perched on a branch. Another is drawn in flight, its wings wide.

"Super cool," I say. "That's so good."

"My math homework?" Sean asks, puzzled.

"The drawings," I say. Then I remember why I'm standing here and ask him, "What'd you get for the first problem?"

Sean looks down at his paper, and I drop my envelope straight into Sammie's backpack.

"Two seventy-three," Sean says.

"Me too," I say. Then I make my way to my seat while Sean stares at his math paper. As I sit down, Haley turns and looks right at me. I ignore her.

SAMMIE

David is standing next to my desk, with his back to me, talking to Sean Cibelli. I keep myself turned toward

Haley, leaning a little bit to the side, away from David. I tell her about the latest episode of *The Great British Baking Show*, which the Peas watch religiously. When David finally moves away, I exhale and sit back in my seat. And see the envelope, faceup, resting on top of the binders in my backpack like it floated there on some gentle breeze. I recognize the handwriting: David's. Which is smaller and neater than you'd expect from a guy. I bend over and push the envelope down in between two binders.

Haley catches my eye. "A valentine?" she mouths. I pretend I don't understand, then turn my focus to the board and the Do Now.

At the end of math, when I put my binder away, I shove the envelope down to the bottom of my bag so no one can see it. I leave it where it is, buried in my backpack. I don't even take it out in the library after school.

DAVID

As we're walking to the bus after school, Luke says, "Want to hang out?"

I'm sleeping over at Kai's tonight. Luke isn't invited, because Kai's mom will only let him have three friends over and he picked me, Andrew, and Spencer. But I fudge a little. "Can't. I'm working at the store."

"Tonight? How late is it open?"

"Uhh, tomorrow morning I mean," I fumble. "Early. Pop said something about taking inventory."

"What about Sunday?" Luke asks. "Or Monday, since we have off. I could ask my dad to take us to the diner."

He doesn't ask about hanging out tomorrow afternoon, or having a sleepover tomorrow night, probably because he already has romantic Valentine's Day plans with Sammie. There's no way I can go to the diner on Sunday, or Monday, and listen to Luke brag about his date with Sammie, so I say, "Big Presidents' Day sale weekend. It's going to be crazy. Everybody loves a sale." I sound almost like Pop, which kind of freaks me out.

"Okay," Luke says, sounding super dejected. "What about the other guys? Maybe they want to hang out?"

"Maybe," I say. And then, to test him, I add, "Or maybe Sammie."

Luke nods slowly like he's thinking hard about it. "Good idea," he says, like he hadn't thought of it. "I will. I'll ask Sammie to hang out."

"Great," I say, kicking myself.

★ ★ ★

SAMMIE

At home, in my room, alone, I take David's envelope out of my backpack and open it up. Inside there are several pieces of paper, neatly folded. I unfold them. They're stapled together like a book. Like one of the kitten books that David and Allie make, except this one is just David's drawings. No words.

And the characters aren't kittens. They're all animals, though. Mostly dogs and one cat. They look a lot like the animals in one of Melvin Marbury's *Northern Province* comic books, which no one our age except David, and me, has ever heard of. I flip through the pages. It's a story about a baseball game. The cat gets a hit and gets on base, but then two dog teammates strike out, and it looks like the cat's never going to get past first base. Then this kind of basset-houndy-looking dog gets up to bat.

Which is when I realize that this story is not about cats and dogs. It's about David and me. I flip to the last page, which shows the cat sliding into home.

I flip back through the pages, but there's no note. No explanation. No apology.

I remember that game. We won. In the car afterward, David kept congratulating me on the run. Mr.

Fischer was proud and happy and laughing, retelling David's hit, and how it turned the game around. The whole team met for fro-yo at Milly's Vanilli Yogurt Bar and everyone was replaying the play and high-fiving David and me.

The thing is, David should have been proud of that hit. It was a good hit, and he doesn't get many hits at all, to be honest. But reading his book, I realize that his hit meant something else to him: it was a gift. For me. A gift I never knew had been given.

I never thought about what David might be feeling or dreaming or hoping. He was my friend. My best friend, when I needed one. But maybe David wanted something else.

MONDAY, FEBRUARY 16

SAMMIE

Luke texted me on Saturday, asking if I wanted to catch a movie. A dark theater with him? I texted back *No*.

Then he texted me again on Sunday morning. Same question. I texted back *No*, then turned my phone off.

Ten minutes after I turned my phone back on this morning, it buzzed. This time it was David: *The fort?*

I turn my phone back off.

DAVID

I spend the whole weekend waiting for a text from Sammie, some sign that she got my valentine book. I know I dropped the envelope right into her backpack, and I think I saw her lean over and look at it. I keep replaying that moment in my head, and sometimes I'm sure she saw it, and sometimes I'm sure she didn't. On Sunday afternoon, I pull my phone out and start to text her, but then I remember Luke and I don't send the text because maybe she's with him. So instead of hanging out with Sammie, I spend Sunday afternoon drawing another Sammie story.

On Monday morning, I text her *The fort?* But she never responds.

An hour later, Luke texts me, *Heading to the diner. Want to come?* I do, because I want to find out whether he hung out with Sammie and if he kissed her on the lips, but I'm too bummed about everything, so I pretend like I don't even see the text. I figure I'll see him on the bus in the morning.

TUESDAY, FEBRUARY 17

SAMMIE

After all the texts from Luke and David, I wake up with a stomachache and raging headache. Dad takes my temperature, which is normal, gives me Tylenol, kisses me on the forehead, and says, "You're fine."

As I walk out the door, he high-fives me. "Have a super day!" I try not to puke on the sidewalk.

Shake it off, I tell myself as I stand at the bus stop. But when I hear the sound of the bus engine, a block away, I know I can't do it. I turn and run down the Anands' driveway and crouch behind their garage until the bus pulls away from my stop. Then I head for the Greenway. It runs between my house and David's, of course, but if I keep going past David's, I can take it all the way to Quaker Ridge Road. And from there, I figure it's only a half hour walk to school. I'll probably be late, but at least I won't be on the bus with David and Luke.

There's still snow on the ground, but I follow the path I made through my backyard the last time I went to the fort. And the Greenway is plowed, so it only takes me about thirty minutes to make it to Quaker Ridge Road. Where there are no sidewalks. I have to walk on the side of the road. Car after car passes, splashing me with slushy brown yuck until my jeans are soaked and I actually think about turning around and going home.

I'm starting to feel very sorry for myself when a white Honda Civic pulls over in front of me. The passenger side window opens, and Haley leans out.

"Want a ride?"

"Yes, please," I say.

I climb into the back seat.

The woman driving must be Haley's mom, but she's nothing like Haley. She turns her head and smiles at me. She reminds me of my mother, not in looks but in style: full makeup, big movie-star sunglasses, gold bangles on both arms, and long, dark red nails.

"Lousy day to have to walk," she says. "Good thing Haley and I were running so late. I'm Dana." She puts her blinker on and slowly pulls out into traffic, bangles clinking as she turns the steering wheel.

"Thanks for picking me up, Mrs. Wilcox."

"Please, call me Dana. Or Ms. Wilcox. I never married."

"Do you live near here?" Haley asks.

"Not exactly," I say. "I missed my bus, and my parents had already left for work, so I had to walk. I came along the Greenway."

"Oh, man," Haley says. "Missing the bus must stink."

I think to myself that it was better than making the bus, but I say, "It wasn't so bad, until I got to Quaker Ridge. Every car that drove by splashed me. My jeans are soaked."

"Do you have anything you can change into in your locker?" Ms. Wilcox asks.

Some girls have a whole wardrobe in their lockers: extra pairs of pants, just in case a blot of ink or splash of tomato sauce should render the ones they're wearing unfit to be seen in public; cute shorts in case the temperature should suddenly zoom up by forty degrees; spare T-shirts and sweaters for when the super-low-cut tops they're wearing don't meet dress code. I'm *not* one of those girls.

"I think I have a pair of sweats," I say. "I usually wear shorts in gym, but I think I brought sweats in at some point. They're probably a little stinky, though."

"I have a clean pair in my backpack," Haley says. "I was going to wear them after school, for softball practice, but you could borrow them. I'll wear the stinky pair I have in my locker. Only Coach Wright will have to smell me."

"Really?" I say, because I don't know Haley that well, and I'm not sure I'd do the same if the situation were reversed.

"Sure. You can give them back to me tomorrow."

"Thanks," I say. "Okay."

"How do you girls know each other?" Ms. Wilcox asks.

"We're in a couple classes together," Haley says. "And Sammie's a jock too. She plays baseball."

"On the boys' team?" Ms. Wilcox asks.

"Yep," I say. "Since I was five. Little League."

"Haley did Little League first too," Ms. Wilcox says. "Until girls' softball opened up in second grade. You didn't want to switch over?"

"I never thought about it," I say.

"This year, playing for the school team—it's a whole new world," Ms. Wilcox says. "That's why we moved up here from the Bronx. Coach Wright has a great reputation."

"You moved just for softball?"

"Yep," Haley says.

"I teach down in the Bronx, so living up here makes my commute a bit longer," Ms. Wilcox says. "But I wanted Haley to play for the best team possible. To give her a shot at a college scholarship." She glances over at Haley, sitting next to her. "Right, sweetie?"

Haley smiles back at her mother. "Right."

I'm surprised at how seriously Haley and her mom talk about softball. And surprised, also, that the New Roque softball team is "the best." Until the batting cages, I didn't even know there was a softball team. But I don't say anything. I don't want to be called stuck-up again.

DAVID

Luke's not on the bus Tuesday morning, and neither is Sammie.

Then Luke's not in Spanish class. He finally shows up, halfway through the period, with a late-to-school pass.

I lean over toward him and whisper, "Everything okay?"

"I missed the bus," he says, looking down at his desk. "I overslept, and then we had to wait like an hour until Lily woke up before my mom could drive me. I just got here. How was the sleepover?"

"What?"

"The sleepover at Kai's house. I texted Spencer about hanging out Friday night, and he said he couldn't because you guys were having a sleepover at Kai's."

"It was pretty lame," I say, feeling my face flush. "I mean, Kai's parents are almost as strict as mine, so we could only play sports games on his Xbox, and only for an hour."

"Better than my Friday night," Luke says. "I watched about six episodes of *My Little Pony* with Lily and had to eat my mom's homemade pizza for dinner."

"Why do moms try to make homemade pizza?" I ask.

"I stopped by the store on Sunday, and again on Monday," Luke says, "because you said you'd be working all day, but you weren't there."

"Oh," I say, remembering the lie I told him. "Last minute, one of the sixteen-year-olds wanted both shifts. Pop let me off the hook." Before he can ask me any more questions, I say, "What did you end up doing?"

"I went to the diner with my dad on Monday," he says. "I texted you to invite you, but you never answered."

"Oh. Sorry," I say. "My phone battery died. I didn't even realize it until last night."

"You missed out," Luke says.

Yeah, I think to myself. *Missed out on hearing Luke brag about Sammie.*

"Sorry," I say. And then I can't help myself. "Did you and Sammie hang out?"

Luke gives me a small, tight smile. "Wouldn't you like to know."

My stomach knots up.

Señora Alicea claps her hands together and says in her high-pitched voice, "*Clase, clase, miren a Señora Alicea.*"

I turn my attention to Señora Alicea and the whiteboard, figuring I can get the details about Luke's super-fun weekend with Sammie at lunch.

But he doesn't come to lunch, again. I check out the Corey Higgins–Markus Johnson table, thinking maybe he finally got a clue, but he's not there.

"Anyone know where Luke is?" I ask the other guys at our table.

"I haven't seen him all day. Is he out sick?" Spencer says.

"No, he's in school. Just not *here*."

"He texted me on Sunday and asked if I wanted to go to the movies," Jefferson says. "But I was already going with Max, so I said I couldn't."

167

"He texted Kai and me on Sunday too," Spencer says. "But we were going to Squiggy's Hangout to play Magic and Luke doesn't play Magic."

"I'm pretty sure he hung out with Sammie," I say.

"He texted me on Monday," Andrew says. "To go to the diner with him and his dad."

"Did you?"

"Couldn't," Andrew says. "Do you think he kissed her? I mean, if he was hanging out with her."

"Maybe they're hanging out together now," Jefferson says helpfully.

"Making out in the stairwell," Kai adds.

"Maybe," I say, wishing I'd never brought up the subject of the missing Luke.

Then he's in math class after lunch, and Sammie is too, and they don't look at each other or pass notes or anything, but there's something funny about Luke. His eyes look bloodshot. I wonder whether making out with someone can make your eyes bloodshot. I think it makes your lips all red, so I try to look at his lips, to see if they're redder than usual, but every time I lean forward, to see around Amanda, she leans forward too.

After math, as we're walking to PE, I ask him right out, "Where were you at lunch?"

"What do you mean?"

"Why weren't you in the cafeteria today? Where were you?"

"I . . . I had to go to the nurse. To have my eyes checked."

"I thought maybe you were hanging out with Sammie. She wasn't in the cafeteria either."

"Oh," Luke says. He's quiet for a minute, then says, "Yeah. I saw her."

THURSDAY, FEBRUARY 19

DAVID

On Thursday, at lunchtime, Luke vanishes again. He was right next to me in science, then the dismissal bell rang and we were both packing up our stuff, but when I turn to say something to Luke, he's not there.

I can't spend another lunch period imagining Luke and Sammie sucking face, so I head upstairs, away from the cafeteria. I'm wandering the halls, half hoping I'll spot Luke and Sammie and half hoping I won't, when I walk by Mrs. Olivar's art room. It's full of kids, and there's music playing. Curious, I stop and take a step through the open door.

Everyone is drawing or painting, except for two girls

who are working at the pottery wheels in the back of the room. Mrs. Olivar looks up and sees me.

"David," she says cheerfully, "I was hoping you'd make your way to us."

I start to say something about meeting with a teacher when Arnold O'Neill, who's in my English and science classes, and isn't a complete nerd even though his name is Arnold, waves at me. "You can sit here," he says, pointing to an empty stool between him and Sean Cibelli. Then I smell pizza. I look around, and everyone has a slice. I spot a giant box of doughnuts on Mrs. Olivar's desk. Pizza and doughnuts and drawing cartoons for an hour. I'm still not sure I'm staying, until I remember that it's taco day in the cafeteria, and everyone says the taco meat comes from pigs' butts, which I don't really believe, but still, they never taste right. So I walk over to the empty stool, set my backpack down, and grab a piece of white paper.

"Is this a club or something?" I ask Arnold.

"Duh," Sean says. "The art club."

I look over at what Arnold's drawing. He's working on a piece of paper with six large squares inked out on it. It's a comic strip, and he's filling in the squares with one of those Japanese manga stories—there's a girl with huge eyes and a boy with spiky hair wearing a turtleneck.

"Nice," I say. Then I look at Sean's drawing. He's got a sheet of plain paper, and is doing a pencil sketch of a bird. Even though it's just pencil, the bird is so detailed and realistic that I half expect it to lift right off the paper and fly away.

"That's amazing," I say.

"Thanks," he says. "Do you draw? Or paint? Or make comics?"

"I draw, but not as good as you, and not comics. I *read* comic strips, but I've never tried to draw one myself. I don't know how you can tell a whole story in those little blocks."

"Comic strips are the best," Arnold says, shading in the boy's spiky hair in the second box.

"*Birds* are the best," Sean says. "I'm going to be the next David Sibley. He's my hero. What do you draw?"

I shrug and feel my face start to get hot, thinking about all the cute kittens and puppies I've drawn for Allie's stories. Luckily, Arnold and Sean are both looking down at their papers and don't see my tomato face. "All kinds of stuff."

"Animals or people or fruit or exploding spaceships?" Arnold asks, beginning to sketch in the third block of his comic strip.

"Animals mostly, I guess," I say, my face slowly cooling down and returning to its usual white-with-freckles state. "I make picture books sometimes, with a lot of goofy animals, but I also do realistic stuff. I'd like to learn how to draw a comic strip."

"They're easy," Arnold says. He points to his drawing. "You use a template, like this. Mrs. Olivar has tons of them. You plan out what you're going to draw on one template, and then you draw it on another."

"How do you fit a whole picture in such a small space?"

Arnold laughs. "You just have to scale things down. Decide what's really important. It's like a puzzle. What kind of comics do you read?"

"Not manga. More like old school stuff."

"Like the *Peanuts* and *Family Circle*?"

"Not that old school. *Calvin and Hobbes*. *Garfield*. *Bloom County*. And *The Northern Province*. That's my favorite."

"*The Northern Province*. Melvin Marbury, right?"

"How'd you know? Nobody our age has even heard of him."

Arnold tips his head to one side and studies his half-done comic strip. Then he nods and looks up at me. "I didn't know him either, until about two weeks ago. But he's going to be at the New Roque public library in a couple of weeks—"

"No way!"

"Way," Sean says, nodding. "He's in town because of the Big Apple Comic Con."

"I wanted to go to that," I say. "But my parents say I'm too young to go by myself. And they won't take me, even though my dad was a huge Melvin Marbury fan when he was a teenager and gave me all his Melvin Marbury comic books. Why's Mr. Marbury coming to our library?"

"Mrs. Olivar said one of the librarians went to college with him or something, and she arranged it," Arnold says. "There's a comic strip contest too. He's picking the best ones. And giving a talk."

"Comic strips," Sean says disgustedly.

"Wait a minute," I say, because I completely can't believe it. "How come I didn't know about any of this? The library or the contest?"

"It's only open to kids in the art club. Have you ever come to the art club before?"

"No, but I come to art *class*."

"A *class* is not the same thing as a *club*," Sean says, carefully shading in the beak on the bird he's drawing. "And besides, Mrs. Olivar did put up the poster about the contest."

He points his pencil at the front wall of the art room, where Mrs. Olivar hangs all her inspirational posters and notices. There's a Dr. Seuss poster that says, "You'll never be bored when you try something new. There's really no limit to what you can do!" and that "Be the change" poster that all the teachers seem to love, plus one of North American birds, a creepy one of a human skeleton, and one that's a Picasso painting. I scan the wall and finally pick out a small nine-by-twelve sheet of yellow paper with a bunch of writing and what looks like a comic strip. I can't read any of it except for the word "contest," which is larger and darker than the rest of the paper.

"I guess I never noticed it," I say. "Am I still eligible? Can I still meet Melvin Marbury? And have him look at a comic strip I draw?"

"I don't know about the meeting part," Arnold says, "but you can *listen* to him. And it's not a guarantee that he'll choose your strip. There'll be like a hundred kids submitting strips, and you've never even drawn one before—"

"Yeah but I can *draw*."

"I can draw too," Sean says, setting his pencil down and holding up his bird drawing. "But who would want to draw a comic strip when you could make a beautiful white-breasted nuthatch like this?"

"Nice," Arnold says, nodding appreciatively at Sean's drawing. "I could never do that kind of detail. That bird looks like it's about to fly right out of the paper."

"It's all in the shading," Sean says. "You need to think about where your light source is, and really think through the shadows."

Arnold nods, then he turns back to me. "You have to submit the comic strip to Mrs. Olivar by the end of next week, and it has to illustrate that quote from *Calvin and Hobbes*," Arnold says, pointing to the whiteboard, where Mrs. Olivar has written, *Things are never quite as scary when you've got a best friend. —Bill Watterson*

I grab a blank piece of paper and copy the quote down.

"And you have to come to a meeting after school on Tuesday," Arnold adds.

"Anyone can submit?"

"Anyone who wants to draw a comic strip," Sean says. "And is an official member of the art club."

"How do I become an official member?"

Arnold laughs. "Tell Mrs. Olivar. She has a copy of the contest submission rules on her desk, and the permission slip for the field trip. It's during school, so you'll have to miss all your morning classes."

Miss classes *and* meet Melvin Marbury? I don't even wait for Arnold to finish talking before I head to Mrs. Olivar's desk.

★ ★ ★

SAMMIE

In math, Haley passes me a note: *Are you staying after school?*

Yes, I write back.

Want to do something fun?

Sure. In the library?

In the gym. It's a just-for-fun softball practice

I look at the piece of paper. I pick up my pencil to write *no thanks*, but then I think: Why not? Haley's nice. And wants to be friends. And doesn't care about Luke or David. And *isn't* Luke or David. *Shake it off*, Dad said. Maybe hanging out with Haley will help me shake it off. The preliminary baseball meeting isn't for two weeks, and real practices won't start for another week after that, so fooling around with a couple of girls playing softball can't hurt anything.

Okay, I write, and hand the note back to her. She reads it, grins, and holds up her hand for a high five.

When the last bell rings, she's waiting outside my social studies class, and we walk to the gym together.

I push through the locker room doors and am hit by a wall of chatter. I stop, frozen. I thought there would be a couple of girls showing up, but instead, the locker room is packed with them, all talking and fixing their hair and laughing.

I almost turn around and leave because there are so many girls. I don't need to spend my after-school time comparing hair products or being yelled at for poaching someone's boyfriend. But Haley puts her hand on my shoulder and says, "Take the locker next to mine."

"Okay."

"We gotta move," she says, pulling her sweater over her head and kicking off her Converse. "Coach Wright doesn't like stragglers."

"Got it," I say, opening my backpack to pull out my gym clothes. Haley sits down on the bench and takes off her no-show socks, revealing hot-pink-painted toenails.

"You paint your nails?" I ask.

"Just my toes. I don't like how polish feels on my fingernails, but I love the colors." She holds one foot out and admires the pink. "It's fun, don't you think?"

"Sure," I say, pulling my gym T-shirt on. I look down and realize it's my fall ball team shirt. I waver for a moment, thinking that maybe I should put my regular T-shirt back on. But that one's from summer baseball camp. Not any better. I pull the fall ball tee off, turn it inside out, and pull it on.

Out in the gym, the girls are standing in a circle, with

Coach Wright in the middle. I jog up and join them, making sure I'm next to Haley. Looking around, there are white girls and black girls and Hispanic girls, and one eighth grader—Jelly Lee—who's Asian, I think. I realize that I know most of the seventh graders. Adriana and Izzy are in PE with me, although I never talk to them. I recognize Malia Martinez and DeeDee Kalama too. Olivia's in Spanish and social studies with me. We were in the same class in first, second, and third grade, and she played Little League with me one season.

"Let's start with a warm-up," Coach Wright says. She turns to an eighth grader, a tall black girl I recognize but don't know. "Savanna, you and Valerie take it from here."

Savanna nods and steps into the middle of the circle along with a white girl, also an eighth grader, who I figure must be Valerie. She's got long red hair braided in two French-braid pigtails and a ton of freckles.

"Okay," Savanna says. "Right arm across your chest." I pull my right arm across my chest, along with all the other girls in the circle, and Savanna and Valerie.

"One," Savanna calls.

"Two," all the other girls respond, holding the stretch.

"Three," Valerie says.

"Four," the rest of us call.

We count that way up to ten, then switch arms, repeating each ten-second hold three times. I've never warmed up like this before. Usually, in baseball, the coach just tells us what to do and we do it on our own. But before I can decide if I like it or not, Valerie says, "Thirty toe touches. One!"

We count the toe touches the same call-and-response way, then do thirty lunges, and I'm just getting used to this all-inclusive kind of warm-up when Savanna says, "Now, we're gonna pair up—"

I turn to Haley, because if I have to pair up with someone, I want it to be her. But Savanna's still talking.

"Each new girl with a veteran. New girls, raise your hands."

Haley's arm shoots up, like she's proud to be new. Reluctantly, I hold mine up too.

"Newbies, hold those hands up high!" Valerie shouts.

It's been a long time since I worried about being picked for the team. Even back in elementary school when we played jail tag or capture the flag at recess, I was always one of the first to be chosen. But today, holding my hand up as one of the seventh-grade new girls, wearing my inside-out baseball team T-shirt, I'm praying that I won't get left out.

An eighth-grade girl with tan skin bounces over to me. Her hair is as wild and curly as mine, even though it's pulled into a ponytail. "Hey," she says. "My name's Zari."

"I'm Sammie."

Zari smiles and holds out her fist for me to bump.

"Okay, with your partner, two laps around the gym," Savanna tells us. "Then find a spot and alternate sit-ups and push-ups."

"C'mon," Zari says, touching my arm. Together, we jog around the gym, Zari talking the whole time about how Coach Wright is really great with skills drills, and how she has a ton of homework in English class, but thank God they just finished a unit in science, so she doesn't have any homework in that.

After that, we take turns doing sit-ups and push-ups. Zari counts for me and I count for her.

"Awesome," Zari says, high-fiving me when I get twenty-five push-ups in a minute.

After the general warm-up, we do some more running drills and then move on to softball drills. Savanna and Valerie demonstrate each one before we start. Coach Wright walks around while we do the drills, but she doesn't yell at us like Coach D does during PE. It feels weird. Like everyone is too nice.

At the end of practice, we huddle together around Coach Wright. "Great job, girls," she says. "Official practices don't start for almost a month, but I want to get ahead of the curve. These 'fun' practices are a great way to get to know each other and build the team from the inside out."

Back in the locker room, I change into my dry T-shirt, and listen to the girls all around me talking.

Olivia and DeeDee are discussing the science test we all have on Friday. Savanna's telling Zari some story about her sister, who plays on the high school softball team. The chatter doesn't seem so overwhelming.

"What'd you think?" Haley asks me, grabbing her backpack out of the locker.

"It was fun," I say. "I know most of the seventh graders."

"You sound surprised by that."

"Not surprised," I say, but I don't know how to explain it to Haley. It's like I forgot about girls besides Sarah and Carli and their crowd. The others were there, all along, but I stopped seeing them.

"Want to come again tomorrow?" Haley says as I grab my backpack.

I shrug. "If my sisters can pick me up after, I guess so."

The Peas pick me up at five on the dot, and say

they're happy to get me at five all week.

At home, Dad is already in the kitchen, getting dinner ready, when I walk through the door.

"Hey, Buddy," he says. "The letter came today!"

He nods toward the fridge: the baseball team first meeting letter. The letter Dad and I have been waiting for all year.

"Want to read it?"

Actually, right now, I don't feel like reading it. I know everything the letter says. Coach D's completely pointless mandatory first baseball team meeting is famous at E. C. Adams Middle School. "Sure," I say.

"How about you set the table and I'll read it to you?"

I shrug, grabbing the napkins and silverware and distributing them around the table.

Dad takes the paper off the refrigerator and shakes it with a flourish, then clears his throat. "'Dear parents, You are receiving this letter because your child has expressed an interest in joining the E. C. Adams Middle School baseball team'—blah blah blah—'A mandatory meeting will be held on Tuesday, March third, during the lunch and recess period. At that time, all completed paperwork must be handed in, including medical forms, transportation permission forms and proof of academic eligibility'—blah blah blah. We've got those forms all done, right, Buddy? The letter goes on to say that boys who show up without the proper paperwork will be immediately cut. 'There are always more interested players than the team can accommodate, so participation is not guaranteed.' Coach is trying to separate the boys from the men, I guess." Dad laughs. "He doesn't scare us, right, Buddy?"

Boys from the men, I think to myself.

"Why'd you stay late today?" Dad asks.

I planned to tell him. The truth is, I didn't think about exactly how or when I would tell him, but I always thought I would. Until right now. When I say, "Group project for English."

MONDAY, FEBRUARY 23

SAMMIE

I go to softball practice again on Friday. We do more partner drills, plus a side-to-side drill to work on lateral movement. We also practice walking while pumping our arms because Coach Wright says it improves your running speed.

We even run laps in the halls. I've never run inside before, and it's fun. We thunder down the hallways, past open classroom doors. Mrs. Knell, still working in her room, waves at us as we run by. By the time practice is over, my face is flushed, my hair's damp with sweat, and I feel loose and warm and good.

"You coming to the cages this weekend?" Zari asks

me as I'm packing my stuff in the locker room.

I shake my head no. "Can't," I say, trying to think of a good reason why.

Luckily, she doesn't ask. "See you Monday, then," she says.

On Monday, I'm changed and standing next to Haley in the gym when Amanda Archer walks out of the locker room and strolls over to Savanna.

I watch her, wondering what the queen of the seventh grade could possibly be doing at a softball team practice. But apparently she's doing the same thing I am, because when Valerie and Savanna start the warm-up, Amanda pairs up with Jelly Lee, and when we have to get into groups of four for catching drills, Amanda and Jelly join Zari and me.

"I thought I heard you were playing boys' baseball," Amanda says to me.

"I did," I say. "I mean, I am. But I'm trying this out too."

"Me too," Amanda says. "I'm trying it out. I play field hockey in the fall, but I wanted a spring sport too."

I never thought I had anything in common with Amanda Archer, but maybe I do.

TUESDAY, FEBRUARY 24

DAVID

I spent the entire weekend trying, and failing, to come up with an idea for a comic strip about friendship and scary things. When I should have been working on my science lab homework, I was trying to tell the story of how Sammie and I went trick-or-treating together and some kids were throwing eggs, and we were afraid we'd get in trouble, so we skipped a whole street of houses. But I couldn't make the story work. When I was supposed to be reading *Tangerine* for English, I instead spent two hours outlining a story about Sammie and me finding the fort, but there wasn't anything scary about that. And of course, Mr. Phillips collected the science lab on Monday, and Mrs. Dougherty gave us a reading quiz.

When the dismissal bell rings, I pack my backpack and head upstairs to the art room for the after-school meeting. Stepping out into the hall, I'm surprised to see Sammie at the other end with that new girl Haley. They're walking away from me, toward the back stair-case, so they don't see me at all. I watch them, Haley talking and waving her hands around, and Sammie nodding and watching Haley and even laughing a little.

That used to be me, I think. I'm the person who used to make Sammie laugh.

All of a sudden, I remember our trip to Splish Splash Water Park last summer. Pop had taken the day off and Sammie's dad drove, and it was just the four of us because Allie was too short for most of the rides—and too much of a scaredy-cat anyway—and Sammie's sis-ters would never do that kind of thing. They're more the lying-in-a-lounge-chair type.

We started with the rides we could all do together—a couple of circuits on Mammoth River, and then down the Bootlegger's Run water roller coaster. The dads wanted to go on a couple of the double raft slides with us. Sammie and me, we wanted to go by ourselves, but we compromised and did Dinosaur Falls three times.

Then the dads told us we could go by ourselves for a while. I think they were kind of tired by that time, and needed a break. But we didn't.

I was psyched to do Dinosaur Falls on a raft with Sammie instead of Pop, but she wanted to go down Dr. Von Dark's Tunnel of Terror.

The truth is, I didn't really want to, but I couldn't tell Sammie, so I went. My teeth were chattering while we waited in line, and not because I was cold. When we got into the raft, I was shaking all over. Then we were off, into the tunnel. I've never been as scared as I was inside the tunnel. It was pitch-black, and just when I was getting used to the total darkness—whoosh! The slide dropped away, and we fell straight down. It felt like a hundred feet, that drop, through pure blackness. I didn't scream because, honestly, there wasn't time. My brain *thought* of screaming, and then we hit the bottom of the drop and we were sliding again.

When we came out through the waterfall and into the sunlight, Sammie said, "That was totally cool. Let's do it again!"

Of course I went, even though I kind of felt like I might poop my pants. So we did (and I didn't). We rode the Tunnel of Terror three more times, and then, after lunch, we did the Abyss on a double raft and raced down the Giant Twister body slides.

It's the perfect story for this contest.

At the far end of the hall, Sammie and Haley push through the doors and disappear into the stairwell. I turn and walk to the art room, feeling like there's something heavy and painful inside my chest, right behind my ribs. I wonder if it's indigestion, like Pop gets, and whether Mrs. Olivar has any Tums.

I sit down between Sean and Arnold, who leans over and whispers, "Want to sit with us on the bus?"

"Sure," I say.

Mrs. Olivar goes over all the details about the field trip—that we'll be leaving in the middle of second period and arriving back at school during lunch, so just in case, we should pack a lunch.

The whole field trip review takes all of ten minutes, so Mrs. Olivar tells us we can work on our comics until four thirty, when the late buses come.

"I want to tell the story of two friends at a water park," I say to Arnold.

So, with Arnold giving me pointers and suggestions, I start drawing the first frames of my first comic strip ever, the story of me being terrified at Splish Splash. I draw Sammie as a cat, again, and me as a dog, but I draw Pop as a polar bear, wearing a bathing suit and a

Mets baseball cap that are both too small, and I draw Dr. Goldstein as a cheetah, kind of lean and hungry-looking, but with a goofy smile so you know he's not a *scary* cheetah.

"I'm doing a story about a princess who's a secret ninja," Arnold says. "Her bodyguard is the only one who knows she's a ninja, because he's one too."

"Cool."

Arnold slides his paper over toward me so I can see. "In this episode they're battling a giant glostosphere that wants to poison the Earth's atmosphere."

Arnold's comic has the same large-eyed girl and spiky-haired boy as the strip he was working on last time, so I figure that's the princess and her bodyguard. The two kids are battling a giant round thing that looks kind of like Jabba the Hutt.

"Is that the glostosphere?"

"Yeah. It eats the enemies it vanquishes. That's why it's so big."

"Cool," I say. "Eating your enemies seems like a really good way to get rid of them."

"Thanks," Arnold says.

"If I were an evil villain, I'd want to be one who ate my enemies, with whipped cream and hot fudge, and a hot chocolate after to wash them down."

"My glostosphere doesn't bother with whipped cream," Arnold says, sounding a little defensive. "He's not *tasting* his enemies."

"Do you have any snacks?" I ask Arnold. "I'm kind of hungry."

"Sorry," he says. "I've got nothing."

I turn to Sean, who's drawing some kind of bird with a long, curved beak. "You got anything to eat?"

He reaches into his backpack, pulls out a plastic container, and twists the lid off. "I have an apple cut up, with the skin off. Two of the pieces have brown on them, so I can't eat them. You could have those. If Mrs. Olivar has a clean plastic fork you can use." He sets the Tupperware down in front of me. The slices of apple all look white to me, and I'm afraid I'll take the wrong slices and ruin Sean's snack. Also, apples are too healthy.

"Never mind."

Sean slides the apple container so that it's in front of him, leans over it, looks at the apple slices inside, then screws the lid back on.

I point to the bird drawing in front of him. "What's that?"

"What's what?"

"That bird you're drawing."

"A long-billed curlew," Sean says. "It's a North American shore bird found primarily in the western

United States. Curlews mostly eat insects, although they sometimes also eat small amphibians, like frogs. I saw one this summer when I went bird-watching in New Jersey with my dad. A curlew, not a frog."

"Would you rather eat a frog or a bug?" I ask Sean.

He tips his head to one side, thinking. "I personally would rather not eat either of those things, but if I were a curlew, I think I'd rather eat a frog. It's bigger."

"I agree on both counts," I say. Then I turn back to Arnold, who's focused on his comic strip. In one panel, the princess shoots out some kind of rays from her eyes, but they seem to be bouncing off the glostosphere. Then she does a spinning kick and kicks the glostosphere right between the eyes.

"I like how you drew the spinning," I say. "That's really cool."

"Thanks."

I slide my partly done comic over toward Arnold. He looks at it, and laughs. "That's hilarious," he says. "That dad polar bear in his tiny bathing suit, that's really funny."

"Thanks," I say. "I need to show the two friends going into Dr. Von Dark's Tunnel of Terror, but I can't figure out how to draw it when they're inside because it's pitch-black."

"Draw the characters first, wherever you want them

in the frame," Arnold tells me. He grabs a blank comic template and sketches two stick figures in the middle of the first frame. "Then make the rest of the frame really dark, right up to like a millimeter away from the characters. You have to leave that little bit of white space, to make the characters pop out from the background." He shows me, shading in around the two stick figures.

"Thanks."

I grab my pencil and get to work. I draw and draw and draw until Mrs. Olivar claps her hands and says, "Start cleaning up. It's almost four thirty."

I look down at my first ever comic strip, and feel proud. I grin, then glance at Sean and Arnold, hoping they haven't noticed. They're both busy packing up. I put my comic strip in my backpack, carefully so the paper doesn't get wrinkled.

"This was fun," I say.

"What?" Sean asks.

"Drawing. Hanging out in the art room. With you guys."

Arnold snorts. "You're weird."

"Thanks," I say, wondering who they sit with at lunch.

WEDNESDAY, FEBRUARY 25

SAMMIE

I didn't plan on going to the cafeteria. I was going to spend my lunch period in the nurse's office, or maybe with Mrs. Knell, but when the bell rings at the end of English, Haley turns and says, "Do you have plans for the weekend?"

So I tell her about how Dad and I were psyched to get in one more weekend of skiing, but my mother has a big Realtor event on Sunday night, and Dad has to go too.

"I've never been skiing," Haley says.

"It's totally fun. Dad's taking me up to the Berkshires for the day on Saturday, just the two of us. I can't wait."

"How long have you been skiing?"

I launch into the story about how Dad took me on the bunny slope when I was three, and by the end of that first day, we were doing green trails on the big mountain. I only remember it from Dad's telling, but I'm so caught up in the story that I don't realize where we're going until we're pushing through the glass doors and I'm hit with the smell of grease and frying meat.

And then it's too late. I follow Haley through the lunch line, accept the plate with a burger, fries, and overcooked green beans that the lunch ladies pass to me, and walk with Haley to her table like it's nothing.

Savanna and Jelly are watching something on one of their phones. They look up and nod hello. Haley takes a chair at the end of the table, and there's not an empty one next to her, so I end up between DeeDee and Izzy, with Adriana across from me.

"Are you coming to softball practice again today?" Adriana asks.

"I think so," I say. "Probably." Then I take a bite of my burger and chew slowly, hoping she'll change the topic of conversation.

"What's not to be sure about?"

"The first baseball team meeting is in one week. Softball's fun and all, but I'm playing baseball."

"Boys' baseball?"

"Yeah," I say. Then, before she can ask me anything more, I turn to Kennedy, who's in my Spanish and science classes, and ask, "Are you doing softball?"

"Can't," Kennedy says. "I run track in the spring."

"Me too," a girl named Faith chimes in. "We do hurdles together. Except I'm better." She grins at Kennedy. "Right?"

"No way!" Kennedy says. "I rock the hurdles. I leave you in the dust."

Haley leans over and stage-whispers to me, "They have this fight all the time."

I turn to Olivia. "Weren't you on my Little League team?"

"Yep. In first or second grade, I think. I switched to softball after that. My mom played in high school and college, so she really wanted me to. I'm psyched to finally be able to be on a school team."

Two other seventh-grade girls sit down at the end of our table.

"Does anyone really eat green beans?" asks one, whose name, I remember, is Simone. "I mean, they have to know that we all just throw them right in the trash. It's such a waste of food."

"I eat mine," Haley says, popping a forkful into her mouth. "They're not so bad."

"How about you, Sammie?" Faith asks.

"No way," I say. "I hate all beans. Especially over-cooked green ones." I poke at the pile of them on my plate for emphasis.

"Do you still hate clowns too?" DeeDee asks.

"Not anymore. I used to. How'd you know?"

"We were in kindergarten together. In Mrs. Battapaglia's class."

"Oh, right," I say. "I remember. Room 101."

DeeDee dips her burger in a blob of ketchup. "I invited the whole class to my birthday party. You came, but no one knew where you were for most of the party."

A memory from that party flashes in my brain: a horde of kids running around in the backyard on a warm, sunny spring day. "I completely blocked it out. It was a lady clown, right?"

DeeDee takes a bite of burger and nods. "She made balloon animals for everyone."

"I remember being nervous about her, and then when she started doing the balloons I freaked. I thought they'd pop. Carli Martin was there, and I grabbed her arm and made her come hide with me."

"Your mom couldn't find you guys," DeeDee says.

"She was pissed," I say regretfully. "I think that was the last birthday party I went to for three years. I don't hate clowns anymore." I stab a green bean on my fork.

"They're better than cafeteria green beans."

Olivia and DeeDee laugh.

"Hey, since you're around on Sunday," Haley says, "maybe you want to come to the cages with us? We're having a practice there in the morning."

"Maybe," I say, wondering if I can ask the Peas to drive me so Dad won't know.

When the bell rings, I pick up my tray and head out of the cafeteria, but instead of being all alone, I'm with a group. Of girls. And I realize something: it was fun. And then I realize something else: not one of them mentioned what anyone was wearing.

DAVID

Completely randomly, when I get home from school, Mom says, "How about you have a little sleepover party this weekend?"

The last time I had a sleepover party was my ninth birthday, because the morning after the sleepover, as we were watching the last kid walk down the sidewalk with his pillow, duffel, and goodie bag, my mom said, "I am *never* doing that again! That was the worst night of my entire life." Something about my friend Benjie being awake until one in the morning, and then Kai and Andrew getting up at five. Mom can be kind of dramatic sometimes, but in the three years since then, she's stuck to her guns on the sleepover party thing. I'm allowed to have *two* friends, max. Not three and definitely not four. *Two*. And never Benjie with Kai or Andrew, which isn't a problem because I'm not such good friends with Benjie anymore.

I think about feeling her forehead, the way she always does to me when she wants to let me know I'm saying something crazy, but instead I say, "Sure. How many guys can I invite?"

"How about three?"

"Okay. Jefferson, Kai, and Andrew."

"Three plus Luke. You've been such a good friend to him, but, you know, it's not easy being new. He's still having a hard time finding his way."

"He seems to be adjusting pretty well," I say, thinking about how he got two slices of pizza from the lunch ladies today without even asking. "I think he's fine."

"Sometimes a person can look fine on the outside but not really be fine."

"I see him every day. He's really fine."

"I'm not so sure."

"Trust me, Mom," I say, remembering how Carli was practically drooling on him in the hallway. "Luke's doing great. He doesn't need to come to my sleepover."

Mom sighs. "Was he invited to the sleepover at Kai's house?"

"No, but not all the guys were. Only three of us."

She crosses her arms in front of her. "How about the sleepover at Spencer's house last weekend?"

"No. But *I* wasn't invited to that one either. Not everyone gets invited to every sleepover."

She sighs again and looks at me like she's going to say something else serious. Then she glances up at the ceiling and back down at me.

"Four friends, and one of them is Luke," she says. "We'll order in pizza, and I'll get out the fondue pot, and you guys can have chocolate fondue."

Curses, I think. *Foiled again.*

Mom bought the fondue pot two years ago, as the family present on the first night of Chanukah. On the second night of Chanukah, instead of the traditional jelly doughnuts for dessert, we had chocolate fondue. Mom put out a giant platter with pieces of banana and pound cake and strawberries and marshmallows to dip. It might have been the best night of my entire life, and *not* because Pop's idea of a great second night of Chanukah present was a pair of regulation baseball pants.

Since then, we've only used the fondue pot three

times: the night before I left for sleepaway camp, when Mom said she'd make any meal I wanted; on my birthday, when ditto; and on the second night of Chanukah *this* year, when I made the very compelling argument that chocolate fondue on the second night of Chanukah was a *family tradition*.

Then Mom says, "You can skip Hebrew school on Sunday. Being as it's a special occasion."

"Deal," I say.

SATURDAY, FEBRUARY 28

SAMMIE

I'm on the chairlift with Dad when my phone buzzes. A text message. I pull my ski gloves off and take out my phone. Dad laughs. "Your generation," he says. "Can't even sit on a chairlift without checking your phone." He pats his chest. "Mine is safely tucked in here, and on 'Do Not Disturb.'"

It's a text from Haley. *Batting cages tomorrow?*

"Anything urgent?" Dad asks.

"No," I say, putting my phone back in my jacket pocket. "Just a friend. She wants to hang out tomorrow."

"Nice," Dad says. "Now, do you want to do another boring blue trail, or can we go for one of the blacks?"

"I'm ready for a black," I say.

We do three black diamond runs, different ones each time, and then break for lunch. While Dad stands in the food line, I head to the bathroom, where I pull out my phone and answer Haley: *OK*.

DAVID

At six o'clock, with snow falling steadily, Jefferson, Andrew, Kai—and Luke—arrive at my house, sleeping bags in tow.

The forecast says we'll get six inches tonight, and everyone's excited about fresh snow.

"How about a snowball fight?" Andrew says.

"I'm in," Kai says. "I brought snow pants, and a hat and gloves, just in case." Kai is that kid who's always prepared for everything. He probably has a bathing suit in his overnight bag too, just in case.

"I didn't bring gloves," Luke says. "Or snow pants."

"I didn't bring snow pants either," Jefferson says to Luke. "Just wear your jeans."

"I don't have another pair," Luke says. "If I get these wet, I won't have anything to wear. And my mom will freak."

"Well, I'm in," Jefferson says. "I brought a spare pair of jeans. We can split into two teams. Me and Kai against you and Andrew, and Luke can be the ref since he doesn't have the gear."

"I don't have snow boots," Luke says, sounding kind of pathetic. "But it's okay. I can hang out in the kitchen and ref from the window."

"Cool," Andrew says. "Let's do it!"

There is no way Mom is going to be okay with me leaving left-out Luke in the kitchen while the rest of us are having fun in the yard. "No worries about the gear," I say, slapping Luke on the back. "I have gloves and boots and probably even an extra pair of snow pants you can borrow, thanks to L. H. Fischer Sporting Goods. Come shopping in my garage."

"Oh, right," Jefferson says. "The Fischer family garage. I forgot about that."

"What are you talking about?" Luke asks.

"Follow me," I say.

I lead the guys out into our garage, where Mom and Pop have turned one end into a giant sports gear closet. Sleds, skis, and ice skates are all neatly stacked in one area of shelves. Another section contains a selection of jackets and snow pants hanging up, organized by size, and, below that, large covered plastic bins, each labeled with what's inside: socks and long underwear; gloves, mittens, and hats; yada yada.

We find a pair of snow pants that will fit Luke, and

then Andrew and Jefferson want snow pants too, so we find some for them. I locate gloves and boots for Luke, and even dig out a pair of ski socks, so his feet will be super warm.

And then we head out into the yard, with me reffing the other guys as they compete to see who can get the most hits on the other team. We draw lines in the snow that each team has to stay behind. It's my job as ref to make sure no one strays over their line. We agree that the first team to score six hits wins the round. And then they're at it, heaving snowballs at each other as fast as they can.

Luke gets a point with his third throw, and then another two throws later. Within minutes, his team has won, with every point scored by him.

They play a second game, and Luke and Andrew win again.

"Okay, my turn," I say after they've won their third game. "Andrew, you ref now, and give me a chance."

"But I won," Andrew complains. "One of the losers should be ref."

"Okay," Kai says. "I'll be ref, and Andrew, you be on Jefferson's team."

Andrew doesn't like that any better, but he has to agree. Which puts me on Luke's team.

Andrew gets me twice and Jefferson hits me once, but by the time they've got three hits, Luke's gotten five and I've made one.

After Luke and I win a second game, Andrew says, "I want to be on Luke's team."

"Your turn to be ref," I remind him. "Jefferson, how about you and me against Kai and Luke?"

We play three more games—because Jefferson and I pull off one win—but after Kai and Luke win their second, Kai says, "Let's go inside. I'm cold. And hungry."

Everyone except Andrew is ready to give up. "I want to play *one* game on Luke's team," he insists.

After Luke and Andrew win their one game, we head inside and strip off our snow gear in the back hall while Mom orders us two pizzas, plus garlic knots and a couple of big bottles of Sprite. When the food arrives, we take it down to the basement and eat while we play *Madden NFL 17* on the Xbox. When we get tired of that, we switch to *Guitar Hero*, and then *FIFA 17*.

When Mom brings down the fondue pot and the tray of stuff to dip into it, everyone crowds around. Mom hands out the fondue forks.

"I love fondue," Andrew says, pushing a strawberry onto his fork. "Remember when we went to the Melting Pot last year for my birthday?"

"That was the best," Kai says, dipping a piece of pound cake into the chocolate.

"I had diarrhea for two days after that," Jefferson says. "All the cheese, I think."

"Cheese blocks me up," I say, putting two pieces of pound cake on my fork. "It forms like a cork in my butt."

"TMI," Kai says.

"I've been to the Melting Pot," Luke says. "When I lived in Villemont. I took my girlfriend there, for our three-month anniversary."

"Your girlfriend?" Andrew asks, then pops his chocolate-covered strawberry into his mouth.

"Yeah, my girlfriend. Courtney."

"Ooh," Jefferson says. "Luke has a girlfriend."

"Had," Luke says. "We broke up. But she wasn't my first girlfriend." He pushes a marshmallow onto his fork and dips it into the melted chocolate. "I dated a girl in sixth grade too. Vera."

"I have a girlfriend," Jefferson says, sounding very cool and casual about it. "I only see her in the summer, though, at sleepaway camp. She lives in Massachusetts." Jefferson's so-called girlfriend is the girl he went to the camp social with, and I know for a fact that all they did was take a picture together and dance a couple of slow dances.

"Me too," Andrew says, putting two pieces of strawberry on his fork. "I have a girlfriend. But she doesn't go to our school either."

"Does she live in Massachusetts with Jefferson's girlfriend?" Luke asks, like he doesn't believe either story.

"No," Andrew says defensively. "She lives in White Plains. I see her every weekend."

What Andrew doesn't say is that he sees her at church and at Greek school, which is like Hebrew school but for Andrew's church, so it's not like they ever have the chance to *do* anything.

"Have you guys kissed?" I ask Andrew.

He glances at me, then turns back to the tray of dipping goodies, which I'm pretty sure means no.

"Luke definitely kissed his girlfriend," I say. "Maybe he can give you some pointers."

"I don't need pointers from Luke," Andrew says.

"I could definitely give all of you some girl pointers, that's true," Luke says.

"I don't need *any* pointers," Jefferson says.

"You guys," Luke says, leaning back in his chair, "could *all* learn from me."

"But you don't have a girlfriend now, right?" Kai says. "I mean, you said you *had* a girlfriend. Past tense."

"I'm working on it," Luke says confidently. "Sammie's definitely interested."

I hate that he's so sure of himself. And I hate that he's probably right. I wish I could go back to that stupid day on the bus and do things right. So maybe I'd still have a shot.

"Sammie's so . . . Sammie-like," Jefferson says, studying the tray of dipping goodies. "I mean, she's Snergir. Not girlfriend material. I heard Carli Martin has a major crush on you. She's hot."

Luke laughs. "Carli Martin is an idiot."

"She's popular," Jefferson says, sliding a piece of banana and a piece of pound cake onto his fork.

"And pretty," Kai adds, copying Jefferson's banana–pound cake combo.

Luke shrugs. "Who cares. She's an airhead. Sammie's much better girlfriend material."

"I'd go out with Carli," Jefferson says. "I mean, if I didn't already have a girlfriend. Which I do."

"When are you going to ask Sammie out?" Kai says.

"I'm working on it," Luke says.

"At lunchtime?" I ask.

Luke glances at me, puzzled. "What are you talking about?"

"When you don't come to lunch some days, you're with Sammie, right?"

"Oh. Yeah. Right. Yeah. Sometimes." He looks

around the room like he's looking for something. "And anyway, we're going to be spending a lot of time together during baseball season."

Jefferson laughs. "Yeah, right. Coach D is going to love you guys making out on the bench."

"I don't plan to spend much time on the bench," Luke says. "I'm thinking about all those bus rides to away games. Coach D isn't going to be in the back of the bus. But I will, with Sammie." He grins. "The back of the bus is great for making out."

"It doesn't seem so great to me," Kai says. "All that shaking around."

"The back of the bus makes me nauseous," Jefferson says. "And anyway, don't you guys already have some-place better to make out?"

"What?" Luke asks.

"Where you go at lunch."

"Oh," Luke says. He picks up his fondue fork and studies it, then puts it down and announces, "I gotta whiz."

When he's out of the room, Jefferson rolls his eyes and says, "He talks like he's such a player."

"I bet he's lying about being with her at lunch," Kai says. "I bet she doesn't even like him."

"You're her best friend," Andrew says to me. "She

talks to you. Tell her that Luke's bragging about making a move on her, and ask her if she likes him back."

Currently, Sammie's *not* talking to me, but I can't tell these guys that because then they'll ask why and we'll be back to what happened on the bus, and I don't want to go there. "Mmm," I say.

"I bet if she fell right into his arms he wouldn't even know what to do," Andrew says.

I bet Luke Sullivan would know *exactly* what to do with a girl in his arms, unlike me. But I don't say that. I don't say anything.

"Hey!" Jefferson says. "I've got an idea. Let's *put* Sammie in Luke's arms. See if he'll put the moves on her then. We get them together in the back stairwell after lunch one day."

"I bet Sammie will tell him off," Kai says gleefully.

"Let's see if he's really the smooth player he says is," Jefferson says, making a fist. "Deal?"

The toilet flushes.

"Deal," I whisper, my throat dry.

"Deal," Andrew and Kai say in unison.

We all bump fists.

SUNDAY, MARCH 1

DAVID

As Mom is putting boxes of Frosted Flakes and Honey Nut Cheerios on the table, she says, "One of the high schoolers called in sick this morning. Your father's going to need you at the store later."

"*Today?*" I say, motioning toward my four sleepy friends, who are silently passing and pouring the cereals. "What's the point skipping Hebrew school if I have to work at the store instead? Where are all the actual employees?"

"David," Mom says in her disappointed voice. "It's important. That store supports our family."

Which is completely not true because Mom works

full-time, so the store only *half* supports our family.

"Your father needs you," Mom says.

"Can't he need someone else?"

"I'll go," Luke says, looking suddenly wide awake. "I'll help out. I could go instead of David, even."

Mom laughs. "That's so sweet of you to offer, but David knows the ropes. Mr. Fischer needs someone with experience."

How much experience does it take to open a big box, take out whatever smaller boxes are in the big box, slap each one with a price label, and put it on a shelf? A trained monkey could do it, honestly. That's what I am at L. H. Fischer Sporting Goods: a trained, *unpaid* monkey.

"I can go with David," Luke says, looking at me for support. "He can teach me how to do stuff."

None of my other friends has ever offered to come with me to the store. Sometimes, Jefferson and Andrew drop by when I'm working and hang out for a little while, but they've never offered to *do* anything, and it's honestly kind of awkward. I look at them, to see what they think of Luke's sudden goofball offer, but they're hunched over their bowls, shoveling spoonfuls of sugary cereal into their mouths.

"If it's okay with your parents," Mom says.

Which is how Luke ends up coming with me to the store after the other guys get picked up.

"Dave-O!" Pop says when we walk through the front door of L. H. Fischer Sporting Goods. He holds out his arms like I'm the messiah, then wraps them around me and hugs me. I keep *my* arms at my side because I don't want to give him any encouragement. "And Luke! The Dynamic Duo to the rescue! I'm so glad you boys are here because we just got a huge shipment of baseball cleats. Four giant boxes. How about you boys unpack them in the stockroom and price them, and then after lunch we'll get them out on display?"

"Okay," I say to Pop, because at least the unpacking part of the plan happens in the stockroom.

Pop pats Luke on the shoulder. "So nice of you to offer to help David out. You stick with him. He'll show you what he's doing, and you can jump in when you're ready. It's learning on the job around here."

"C'mon," I say to Luke. "Let me show you the stockroom."

"I always wanted to see what a stockroom looks like," Luke says, sounding super excited.

There is *nothing* exciting about the L. H. Fischer Sporting Goods stockroom, which is basically a dusty back room full of metal shelves and boxes. Usually, at least two light bulbs need to be replaced, so you can't see all that well. And apparently sixteen-year-old paid employees can't see trash cans at all because the one in the stockroom is always overflowing. Throw in a rolling stepstool, a couple of metal folding chairs, and a lot of dust bunnies, and that's the stockroom.

The pile of shipping boxes that we need to unpack is pretty obvious because it's right in the middle of the main aisle. I take a box and show Luke how to open it, which you do by flipping it over and peeling off the packing tape. "You could get scissors and cut through the tape," I explain. "But then you have to worry about damaging the merch inside. So it's better to peel off the tape."

"Peel the tape so you don't damage the merch," Luke says. "Got it."

I take the packing slip out of the box, grab a pencil, and hand it to Luke, then show him how to check off the merch as I unpack it.

"Baseball cleats in February," I say, as I pull out the first shoebox. "Bathing suits in March, ski gear in August. It's always the wrong season inside L. H. Fischer Sporting Goods."

Luke laughs and makes a check mark on the invoice. I pull out another box of cleats.

When we finish unpacking the first box, Luke says, "That was fun."

"Five more to go," I say, opening the second shipping box. "But unpacking's not the *worst* job in the store. It's better than working in the shoe department."

"What's wrong with the shoe department?"

"Stinky feet," I say, waving the box of cleats I'm holding in front of my nose. "Even nice people's feet stink, people you'd think would have great-smelling feet. Even people who come in with *wet hair*, like they showered on purpose to be completely clean. Their feet still stink."

"I never thought of that," Luke admits. "Stinky feet are gross."

"Yep, they are."

After we've checked the second box of merch against the packing slip, I show Luke how to work the price gun, and we get a little assembly-line thing going where I hand him the shoebox, he puts the price on, and I put it on the appropriate stockroom shelf.

When we've emptied four shipping boxes, I show Luke how to break one down, and where the flattened boxes go, by the back delivery door. Luke takes the whole thing weirdly seriously, insisting that he break down the second and third packing boxes by himself, which is fine by me. I don't mind sitting on the step-stool while he works.

We've just started unpacking the last big box when Pop calls over the intercom, "David, I need you at the register."

"Do you think you can finish this up without me?" I ask Luke.

"Sure," he says. "Is it okay if I put the boxes on the shelves after I price them? I see how you've been doing it, by style and then size."

"Okay," I say. "If you're not sure about something, just don't shelve it."

There's a line of five customers at the register, so I step in to help speed things up. I take the items from each customer, hand them to Pop one at a time, and then slip them into the bag after he's rung up each one. Then I hand the bag to the customer with a smile and a "thank you." We've rung up four customers and are down to only one waiting when Luke comes out of the stockroom.

"I've finished all the cleats," he says. "Is there anything else I can do?"

Someone is waiting in the shoe section to try on running shoes, so Pop turns the cash register over to me, and Luke becomes my bagging wingman. "Thank you for shopping at L. H. Fischer," he says to our first customer. "Have a great day, and come back to see us soon!"

Finally, at a little past twelve, the store begins to empty out. People don't shop at lunchtime on a Sunday because they go home and have lunch, or they go out to the diner. This is both a good thing, because it gives us a breather at the store, and a bad thing, because it reminds me that I'm not home or at the diner.

Mom and Allie come by and drop off bagels with cream cheese and lox, which Dad and Luke and I take turns eating in the stockroom. Afterward, Dad gives us money to go down to Dunkin' Donuts for a treat.

We each get a Boston cream and a large hot chocolate, and a plain cruller and a coffee for Pop, then head back to L. H. Fischer Sporting Goods.

"I like working at the store," Luke says as we walk slowly up the street. "Maybe your dad could hire me for real."

I laugh. "You're twelve. It's not legal."

"I'll be thirteen in a month."

"It's still not legal. You have to be sixteen. Unless you're family, like me."

When we walk in, Pop is waiting right by the front, like something exciting has happened.

"I've got a really great surprise!" Pop says. In my experience, what Pop thinks is "really great" would probably not be rated "really great" by anyone else, and would *definitely* not be rated "really great" by me.

"You boys have been such a help this morning that the store's in excellent shape. Jeanine's here, and I know I can leave the place in her capable hands, plus Fletcher's coming in from two until close. So we're taking a break for a couple of hours this afternoon. "

Pop rubs his hands together like he can't wait to spring this really great surprise on us, and I'm honestly starting to get excited because a couple of hours is just the right amount of time to take in a movie, which is my favorite thing to do on a Sunday afternoon, but then Pop says, "I just called and reserved us two hours at the batting cages."

My tiny flame of excitement flickers out.

"Luke, check with your dad and see if he can join us. And I'll call Mike Goldstein. Maybe he and Sammie can make it. Be nice for you three to practice together, right?"

"Umm," I say. But Pop is already dialing, and before I can say "Guantánamo Bay torture chamber," he's got Dr. Goldstein on the line.

"Mike," he says. "I reserved a couple of cages at

Frozen Ropes. You and Sammie up for joining us?"

He listens, then says, "Why don't you come without her, then? Hang out with the guys. You're a better coach than I am. Maybe you could offer David some pointers on his form. He's rusty, you know."

He listens again, says, "Great!" and hangs up. "Sammie can't make it—"

I start to offer a silent thank-you to God for this small favor, but then Pop says, "Mike's going to join us anyway." He winks at me. "He wants to keep his eye on the competition."

I look up at the ceiling. *Really, God?*

Luke calls his dad and gets an okay. "He's still in the city, but he says he'll meet us there in an hour."

Why? I think. *Why this particular torture now? What would be so wrong with a nice movie, a big tub of popcorn, maybe some Raisinets?*

I pick up Pop's cruller and take a bite.

"The preliminary baseball meeting's coming up this week," Pop says. "This may be your last chance to warm up, get into fighting form."

My mouth is full of cruller so I don't say anything, but what I want to say is that Tuesday is the day *after* the field trip to meet Melvin Marbury. I wish I could tell Pop how excited I am to meet my artist hero, and have him be even one-tenth as happy as he is when he talks about baseball.

SAMMIE

Haley texted me early this morning to say I could catch a ride to the batting cages with her. I said yes, figuring that if Dad dropped me off at Haley's, I wouldn't have to tell him about the practice. I'd go to the cages this one time, and hang out and have fun. Then baseball will start on Tuesday and I won't have time for softball. Dad won't ever need to know.

As we're eating breakfast at the diner, I casually say to Dad, "My friend Haley invited me over. Can you drop me off there later?"

"Sure," he says. "Is that the friend who was texting you yesterday? Haley? I haven't heard that name."

"Yeah, she's in my math class. And English. She's nice."

"Is this for a school project?"

"Umm, no," I say. "Just hanging out."

Dad drops me off right at one thirty. "Are you sure this is right?" he asks as I open the car door. The address Haley gave me is for an apartment building. Even though there are a lot of them in New Roque, no one else I know lives in one. My grandma lives in an apartment in Riverdale, but she used to have a house, before Grandpa died.

"I'm sure," I say. I walk into the building's lobby, and turn and wave at Dad. Then I text Haley, *Here. In the lobby.*

Down in a sec, Haley texts back.

I walk over to the elevators and pretend to press the up button, then turn and wave again to Dad, who finally drives away.

A minute later, the elevator doors open and Haley and her mom are inside.

"Hop in," Haley says. "Car's in the parking garage, one level down."

In the car, I ask, "How was your Saturday?"

"We went to visit my grandparents in Yonkers," Haley says. "And then we went to the movies."

Ms. Wilcox chimes in. "We saw two movies in a row. That's my favorite way to spend a Saturday afternoon."

"How about you?" Haley asks. "How was skiing?"

"Great. It was just me and my dad, so we could do all the black diamonds."

"Black diamonds?" Ms. Wilcox asks.

"The hardest trails."

"It's a shame he couldn't come with you to practice today," Ms. Wilcox says. "I'm sure he'd enjoy seeing you in the cage, and meeting the coach."

I don't say anything.

"Next time," Haley says, glancing back at me.

"Right," I say. "Next time."

When we get to Frozen Ropes, the whole team is there. Valerie's in one cage, batting, and Zari's in another. It's the first time I've seen most of the girls bat, and Valerie's killing it.

"Glad you could make it," Coach Wright says as we join the others. She puts one arm around my shoulder and gives me a squeeze. Jelly comes over and gives me a big hug. I smile, feeling warm and light and happy.

Coach Wright hands me a bat. "It's going to be lighter than what you're used to," she tells me, which I already know from practicing our stance during the after-school sessions. I take the bat and lift it up over my shoulder. Then I take a few practice swings, my shoulders loosening as I work the bat.

"I want you to let some of the other girls go first," Coach says. "You've had a lot of experience with baseball, and as you already know, the stance and swing are basically the same in fast-pitch softball. But I think it helps to watch other players. See how they move."

"Sure," I say, even though I'm dying to get into the cage.

After Valerie goes, I watch Jelly and then Haley and

Savanna. Finally, Coach calls to me, "You're up next."
I grin and bounce up and down on the balls of my feet,
loosening my legs and hips.

When Savanna finishes, I pick up my bat and step
into the cage.

"Keep your front shoulder down," Coach reminds
me. "Keep the flex in that front elbow."

I nod, because I want her to know I've heard, but my
body already feels what it needs to do. Until the first
ball comes out of the machine. I swing and miss.

"It's a slower pitch," Coach says. "And the ball's
coming at you a little differently."

I miss the first five pitches, then connect, then miss
another couple, and then I finally get it. And I'm in
the zone: plant my back foot, begin the swing, dip my
front shoulder, and connect.

I'm there, pitch after pitch, and my bat's connecting,
and it feels great.

I'm in mid-swing when a deep voice behind me says,
"Samantha?"

Dad. I miss the ball, and turn around, getting hit
with the next pitch. He's standing right behind the
cage.

"What are you doing?" he asks, his voice sharp and
angry. "What's going on?"

Another ball hits me squarely on the back.

"Softball," I say. "Some of my friends play. I wanted to give it a try."

"What friends?"

I look around at the other girls, who are standing back, pretending to be focused on Jelly in the other cage. "Haley?" I say, and even I can hear the question mark in my voice. Behind Dad, I see Luke and David, watching me, not even pretending to look away.

"Why are you here?" I ask. "With them?"

"Don't try to change the subject, Samantha. You lied to me."

"I didn't mean to."

"And worse, you're ruining yourself for baseball. What were you thinking?" His voice gets louder, harder to ignore.

"I wanted to try it," I say. Haley steps into the other batting cage and starts swinging at pitches.

"Why?"

I step out of the batting cage. "Can we go somewhere to talk?" I ask.

But Dad doesn't budge. "What's gotten into you? We've been waiting all year for baseball season. Now you're risking it all to try some . . . some *girls'* game."

Coach Wright walks over to us. "Can I help you?" she says to Dad.

Without even looking at her, Dad jerks his head in her direction. "Did she talk you into this?"

My stupid eyes fill with tears. "No one talked me into it. I wanted to try it. It's actually fun, and I'm good at it. And in case you haven't noticed, I am a girl. I'm a *girl*, playing a *girls'* sport."

I push past him and run into the ladies' room, but he calls after me, "I won't give you permission to play softball. It would ruin you for baseball. Trust me, I'm doing what's best—"

The bathroom door slams shut behind me, and I'm breathing hard, like I've been running. I feel trapped. Stuck. I lean my forehead against the cold, white tile walls, and wish I could disappear.

DAVID

We all stand there, no one talking, and watch as Sammie runs down the hall and into the bathroom, with Dr. Goldstein following behind.

She pushes through the bathroom door and it shuts behind her. Dr. G stops short, takes a step back, and stands right outside the ladies' room. His back is to us. He doesn't turn around.

"All right," Pop says, handing me a bat and acting

like nothing happened. "We're in cage three. Which of you boys wants the first crack?"

"Luke," I say, because I don't want to go at all.

Luke grabs the bat and heads into the cage. I'm half watching him hit pitch after pitch, replaying the embarrassing Sammie-and-her-dad scene in my head, when I notice that the guys in the batting cage next to us have stopped swinging and are watching Luke. Two eighth graders whose names are Shane and Nick, plus, of course, Corey Higgins and Markus Johnson.

The pitching machine runs through its fifty balls, and Luke gives a final swing, like he's wishing for just one more pitch, like he can't get enough, then ambles out of the cage.

"Your turn," he says to me, handing me his bat.

The last thing I want to do is swing at—and miss— fifty pitches while Markus and Corey and those guys are watching.

"Gotta pee," I say, dropping the bat and heading for the bathroom.

When I come back, Pop's in the batting cage, swinging away, and Luke's talking to the cool crew. They're standing in a circle, and no one moves to make room for me, so I end up kind of behind Luke, trying to get one foot into the circle.

"—the Diamondbacks," Luke is saying.

All the other guys nod their heads silently, looking like four really cool bobblehead dolls.

Then Corey says, "Good team."

"Yeah," Luke says. "But I'm psyched to play on the school team."

"What position?" Nick asks.

"Catcher," Luke says.

"That's my position," Shane says, running his hands through his shaggy brown hair. "And there's another eighth grader who plays catcher. Joe Garcia. I heard there's a girl in seventh grade too."

"Sammie," Luke says.

"Is she playing baseball or softball?" Markus says. "I thought I saw her hanging out with the softball girls."

"Baseball," Luke says, and I nod in agreement and mumble, "Baseball."

Which is when Shane notices me. "Hey, little man," he says.

"Hey," I say.

Nick, who is standing next to Luke, and therefore next to my foot, turns, looks at me, and shifts a few inches to the right so I can get a shoulder and an arm into the circle.

"Sammie's really good," I say.

"At what?" Corey asks, grinning.

Shane and Nick snicker, but I ignore them. "At baseball. She was the best player on our Little League team last year. And she played in a summer league and did fall ball too."

"She's cute," Nick says.

"You think so?" Shane says. "She's kind of . . . I mean, she's got that crazy hair, and she's skinny and flat as a board. And her clothes? I mean, come on. She's a nerd."

"I think she's cute," Nick says. "Does she have a boyfriend? Some seventh-grade guy's gotta have his eye on her."

"How about you, little man?" Shane asks me. "You're carrying a torch for Sammie, right?" He smiles widely at me, like we're sharing a secret, and for a moment I think he's actually reading my mind. Then I realize it's just talk. He's guessing.

"Not me," I say. "Luke."

Luke shoots me a look like I just made a big, loud, juicy fart, then laughs. "I like nerdy girls," he says, like he's sharing a big secret. "They're so . . . easy."

The guys all laugh. Corey slaps him on the back.

I hate Luke, and I hate what he's saying. I hate the way he's talking about Sammie. I hate the way he changes his story to fit in, to be like them, but then I realize I'm nodding, like I agree, and my mouth opens and I mumble, "Easy."

SAMMIE

Dad waits for me to come out of the ladies' room. Together, we walk, silently, to the car. I don't look back at the softball girls. I don't want to see their faces.

We drive home in silence, and walk into the house in silence. The only sound is the whir of the treadmill in the basement, which means my mother or one of the Peas is running.

I start to head upstairs.

"Buddy," Dad calls after me, his voice soft and forgiving. "I'm sorry I got so upset there at the batting cages. It's just that I was so surprised, and hurt, that you'd lied to me. I thought we told each other everything."

"I'm sorry," I say. "I wanted to tell you, but I didn't know how."

"If you'd come to me, we could have hashed it out. I could have helped you work through whatever was going on."

"I just . . . Haley invited me, and at first I only went

because she asked. But then the other girls were so nice and the practices were—"

"Buddy," Dad interrupts me. "you'd be wasting your time and your talent playing on a girls' team."

"I only was going to do it until baseball practices started. But, Dad, it was fun, and the girls—"

At the word "girls," Dad makes a kind of huffing sound, then puts one hand on my shoulder. "We've invested too much in you to have you throw yourself away on girls' softball. You love baseball, and you're so good at it. You're a real athlete, Buddy. Don't you want to make something of yourself? Be unique?" His voice starts to get louder.

I want to say something to Dad about how the girls help each other during practice. About how they make everything fun, even the warm-ups and drills. But being nice and having fun isn't what it's about. Is it?

My mother walks into the kitchen. Her hair is pulled back into a ponytail, and her forehead is shiny with sweat. The sports bra she's wearing is wet with sweat too, and she's still breathing hard. "What's going on? What are you guys talking about?"

"Nothing," Dad says. "Sammie got pulled into trying out for the girls' softball team. I don't think she realized how much it could harm her baseball playing."

"I didn't get pulled in," I say. "I wanted to try it. I like the other girls who play." But Dad doesn't even hear me.

"And she lied to me about it," he says.

"What's wrong with girls' softball?" asks my mother. "Why would she lie about playing a sport?"

Dad barks a fake laugh. "*Girls'* softball? It's not a serious sport. I told her I wouldn't give her permission to play. They use these giant neon-yellow balls—"

"I don't think the color of the ball has any bearing on whether it's a serious sport," my mother says. "There are college-level women's softball teams Sammie could play on."

"There are college *baseball* teams Sammie can play on," Dad says.

"How many women make it onto college baseball teams?" my mother asks.

"Some," Dad says, crossing his arms in front of his chest. "A few. There's a precedent. But if Sammie starts softball now, her baseball career is over. Everything about how you play softball is different from baseball. So just 'trying' softball could ruin Sammie for baseball. It's like . . . like practicing ballet if you want to play football."

"I think I've heard of football players who do ballet,"

my mother says. "It improves their coordination or something."

"Stop trying to help," Dad says. "You just don't understand. You don't play baseball. You haven't spent hours and hours coaching our daughter, taking her to the batting cages, rooting for her, like I have. This conversation is between Sammie and me." He reaches out and squeezes my shoulder so hard it hurts.

I move to stand next to him, closer, like we're a team. The way it's always been.

My mother opens her mouth, then closes it. She looks right at me, tipping her head to one side like she's puzzled. I stare right into her eyes and what I see is sadness. I don't say anything.

"Okay, then," she says, turning and walking out of the kitchen.

MONDAY, MARCH 2

DAVID

Last Monday, while she was frying onions and watch-ing *Judge Judy*, I handed Inez my field trip permission slip and asked her to sign it. Mom and Pop usually aren't around for those kinds of things, so Inez has been signing school forms for years, and she never asks what they're for. I turned the papers in the next day, and got up early this morning, before Pop came downstairs, to pack myself a lunch. So basically no one, except Arnold, Sean, and Mrs. Olivar, even knows I'm going on this field trip.

Ten minutes into Spanish class, Mrs. Merola comes on the PA system and announces that art club students should report to the main office. I close my binder and shove it into my backpack, then stand to leave. I glance at Luke, and he's smirking at me like I'm doing something funny. I ignore him and head toward the door, which is when I notice that Andrew and Max are also grinning like I'm making a joke. They all think I'm pulling a prank, that I'm pretending. I give a little wave and walk out of the room, wondering how long it will take before they realize that it's not a joke, and I really am going on the art club field trip. As I walk toward the main office, I realize that the only person who wouldn't be surprised is Sammie.

On the bus, Arnold and I get a seat in the very back row. The seat across from us is empty, but Sean sits in front of us. "I don't like the last row," he explains.

When we get to the library, there are already four other school buses there, and I have to admit that I'm surprised because I didn't think there were so many kids who were interested in comics, or at least in the kind of comic strips that Melvin Marbury draws. I sort of thought I was one of the only ones.

We get off the bus and file into the library.

A black man with a shaved head is standing just inside the doorway. He's wearing gray pants and a black cardigan sweater over a T-shirt that has a picture of a black cat holding a white bone and saying, "I found this humerus."

I laugh at his shirt. "That's funny."

"Thank you," he says, smiling. "Librarian humor." Then, speaking to the group, he says, "Up the stairs and to the right."

Upstairs, in the conference room, there are probably fifty kids already sitting in folding chairs. The E. C. Adams crew gets the second to last row back, which I feel pretty bad about until the Ardsley kids show up and get the last row.

A moment later, the humerus guy steps to the front of the room and claps his hands together. "Boys and girls," he says. "I'm Tobey Simmons, one of the librarians in the children's room. We have a very special treat today." He pulls a piece of paper out of the pocket of his cardigan, exactly the way my grandma Gert pulls crumpled-up tissues out of her sweater sleeve to mop up the drop of clear liquid snot that's always hanging from the end of her nose. "Our guest today is the creator of the Pulitzer Prize–winning comic strip, *The Northern Province*. He is also the author of two wonderful children's picture books. Please welcome Mr. Melvin Marbury."

Everyone starts clapping as a white guy wearing

jeans and a rumpled pullover ambles to the front of the room. He's not very tall, his hair is gray, and he looks more average than I expected. But when he starts talking, I know it's Melvin Marbury.

"How many of you follow anime?" he asks. About half of the kids in the room raise their hands.

"I don't know anything about anime. I can't talk about that. I'm here to talk about dreamy moose and ice-hockey-loving dogs and pugilistic beavers. Hope that sounds good to you."

Then he talks for half an hour about how he started doing a comic strip when he was in college. He tells us he can't draw, which is ridiculous because he's a great artist. He tells us that the comic strip is dead, but that shouldn't stop us from drawing ours anyway.

Then he announces the first-place winner, who gets a Percy the Penguin doll, and it isn't me; it's some girl from Ardsley. The librarian puts an image of the winning comic strip up on a giant screen, and it isn't even funny because it's about Malala Yousafzai, but Mr. Marbury talks about how great the storytelling is. I honestly don't pay much attention because I'm bummed about not winning Percy the Penguin. I bet the Ardsley girl doesn't even care about Percy. I wonder whether I can find her afterward and offer to buy it from her.

The girl goes up and gets to shake hands with Mr. Marbury, and everyone claps. I'm trying to figure out how much money I have and whether Pop would drive me to Ardsley, if the girl is interested in selling Percy, when Melvin Marbury says my name.

"What?" I say, feeling my face get hot.

"Come on up," Mr. Marbury says. "You're the second-place winner."

I walk up to the front of the room, shake Melvin Marbury's hand, and take the prize he holds out, which is a framed, autographed copy of one of his comic strips, and I recognize it.

"That's from *Oliver Shoots a Biscuit in the Basket*," I say.

Melvin Marbury looks surprised. "Yes, it is. I'm impressed." Then he hands me back my second-place-winning comic strip. "I like your cat. And your dog looks a little like my dog, Carleton, don't you think? You know—the one who refs for the hockey team."

I feel my face getting hot.

"Don't be embarrassed," Mr. Marbury says. "I did my fair share of cribbing from the pros when I started. I'm flattered by your dog, actually." He leans closer and says, almost in a whisper, "I think that dog might be someone very close to your heart. You're telling something real and true with him." He leans back and says in a regular voice, "You draw some great characters, David. Keep it up." Then he winks and holds out his hand for me to shake.

"Thanks," I say, shaking his hand.

Everyone starts clapping, and I turn to walk back to my seat. I look down at my Splish Splash comic strip, and along the bottom, outside the frames, I see handwriting that isn't mine. It says, *Buddha taught, "Three things cannot long be hidden: the sun, the moon, and the truth." Keep drawing the truth. —M. Marbury.*

In my seat, I read and reread Melvin Marbury's message. My Splish Splash story does tell the truth. But in the rest of my life? Nope. I haven't told Sammie the truth about my feelings, and I haven't told anyone the truth of what happened on the bus. I've never told Pop my honest feelings about baseball. The guys don't know about my artwork or my membership in the art club. I didn't even tell Melvin Marbury the whole truth about how much his comic strip means to me.

For now, I decide I can at least be honest with Mr. Marbury, so after the third-prize winner is announced, and Mr. Simmons tells us to give Mr. Marbury one more round of applause, and he stands and thanks us, and everyone starts shuffling toward the door, I say to

Albert, "Save me a seat on the bus. There's something I've got to do."

"You should hold it until we get back to school," Sean says. "You don't know who's using these bathrooms. They're public."

"That's not the thing I have to do," I say, "but thanks."

Melvin Marbury is standing with Mr. Simmons, and they're talking. I step up next to him, take a deep breath, and say, "Excuse me."

"David," he says, smiling. "The Splish Splash man."

I don't know how to respond to that, so I say what I planned to. "I have all of your books. The older ones— *Lester and the Lip Lettuce, Goose Tales, The Night of the Skating Zombie Moose*—those were my pop's from when he was a teenager, and he gave them to me." Melvin Marbury is nodding, so I keep talking. "My pop gives me a lot of stuff that I don't really want, mostly sports stuff, but those books . . . your books . . . I started reading them, and it was like finding a new planet. It was like learning a new language that most people didn't know."

Mr. Marbury smiles and his eyes get kind of shiny. I take a breath. "Then I found out there were other books, ones my pop never got. I saved up my allowance money to buy *Oliver Shoots a Biscuit in the Basket*. It took me like a month. I started asking for the others for my birthday and Chanukah. I usually ask for candy or Wii games, but I wanted your books that much. I even have your picture books, but I don't think they're nearly as good as the comics, to be honest."

I sound like an idiot. I sound like Allie that time she ran into some *America's Got Talent* girl at the fro-yo place. Starstruck. But Mr. Marbury chuckles. "Clearly you're not trying to BS me. Or you're doing a lousy job of it. But I appreciate your honesty, David. It's a good quality in a cartoonist."

But I'm not done. I have to say it all to him. "I'm glad I got to hear you speak today, and it was cool that I won second place, but if I'd never met you, it wouldn't have mattered. Because of what you drew. Thank you."

He smiles, puts his hands together in front of his chest like he's praying, gives a quick nod with his head, and says, "Thank *you*, David."

I don't know how to respond. Should I do the praying thing back to him? Try a high five? Hold out my hand to shake his? I shift from one foot to another, then clear my throat, and say, "Okay. Bye now." I give a little wave, which is the stupidest thing I could do. But I don't care. I turn and race for the bus, feeling for the first time ever like I could run a hundred miles.

★ ★ ★

SAMMIE

When the bell rings at the end of math on Monday, Haley leans over and says, "Will I see you at softball practice? My mom can give you a ride home."

"Not today," I say.

"Tomorrow?"

I shake my head, not looking at her. "Nah. I'm done with softball. The baseball meeting is tomorrow."

"I heard your dad say he won't let you do softball."

I hate the way she says that, like she feels sorry for me. "No," I say, focusing on getting my math binder into my backpack. "It's not like that. My dad was just surprised. I lied to him about where I was. He was upset about that."

"Why would anyone lie about a softball practice?" Haley asks, sounding almost exactly like my mother. I look over at her, startled, but she's focused on zipping up her backpack, not even looking at me.

"I'm good at baseball," I say, folding my arms in front of me. "It's what I've always played. I mean, softball was fun and all, but . . ." I think of the way Jelly hugged me at the batting cages, the way all the girls seemed happy to see me and psyched that I was there. And then I hear Dad's voice. *You'd be wasting your time and your talent.* "Honestly, softball is just a waste of my time."

Haley snorts. "How can softball possibly be a waste of anyone's time? You sound like you think softball is less important than baseball. That's just stupid." She picks up her backpack and slings it over one shoulder, then turns and walks toward the door.

"I'm not stupid," I say to her back. "I have straight A-pluses, if you really want to know."

Haley turns and looks at me. "You sound pretty stupid."

"I'm a good baseball player," I say. "I don't want to screw that up for something that's not real."

"Softball is as real as it gets," Haley says. "You're making a mistake. You would have been a great addition to the team, even with your giant ego. But if that's the way you want it to be . . ."

"It's not the way I want it to be," I say to her back. "It's the way it is."

The rest of the day, I feel weird and lonely. When the dismissal bell finally rings, I text the Peas and tell them I don't need to be picked up, then head to my locker to get my stuff. Everyone else is clustered in groups, talking and laughing. On the bus, I sit down next to Mrs. Caputo, and she *tsk*s and shakes her head. "What the heck happened to you?" she says. "You look like a balloon with half your air gone."

I try to smile, but it won't stick. "I'm just tired," I say.

"No twelve-year-old should be that tired."

At home, the kitchen is dark and cold. There's a note from my mother on the counter: *Showing two properties to a client. Home by four. Baby carrots and grapes in the fridge.*

Carrots and grapes. Yuck. I crumple the note up and toss it in the trash, then turn on all the lights, pour a mug of milk, and stick it in the microwave to heat up for hot chocolate.

I stand in front of the microwave, waiting, and suddenly remember Haley's bright pink toenails, that first day in the locker room. "Silly," I say out loud. "Silly and girly." But it's like somebody else's words are coming out of my mouth. I can't make myself believe them.

"We barely knew each other," I say. "We weren't friends." But saying it doesn't make the lonely feeling go away.

DAVID

On the bus, I tell Sean and Arnold about my conversation with Melvin Marbury. Arnold whistles at the part where I say I saved my allowance for a month to buy a comic book, and when I get to what I said about the picture books, Sean says, "Wait. You *told* Melvin Marbury they weren't good? That's not polite."

We make it back to school for the last fifteen minutes of lunch, but I don't want to go to the cafeteria and talk about baseball. I want to keep talking about Melvin Marbury and drawing the truth and winning second place, so I go to the art room with Arnold and Sean.

"Your folks are going to be super proud when they hear about your second-place win," Arnold says.

I shake my head. "They don't even know I entered the contest."

"But you had to have the permission slip signed by a parent," Sean says.

"My babysitter signed it."

"I'm pretty sure that's not legal," Sean says.

"I do it all the time. It's easier asking Inez."

"Well, you still have to tell your parents about the prize," Arnold says.

"Yeah," Sean agrees. "You can't be *drawing* the truth, like Mr. Marbury said, if you don't *tell* the truth."

I sigh. "It would be easier to tell my pop the truth if it was a baseball truth instead of a comic strip truth."

Sean looks confused. "What's a baseball truth?"

"I mean it would be easier to tell my pop something exciting that happened if it involved baseball."

"Is baseball exciting?" Sean asks.

"To Pop, it's the most exciting thing in the world."

"What about for you? Do you think baseball's exciting?"

"Umm. Sometimes," I say, remembering the time Sammie scored off my hit, and the time Kai's mom brought homemade lemonade for the team instead of Powerade.

"You don't sound excited," Sean says.

"My dad thinks NPR news is exciting," Arnold says. "Every night at dinner we have to hear all about it."

"My dad's an engineer," Sean says. "He thinks buildings are exciting. When we went to Chicago last spring, the whole family had to take a boat tour just to look at buildings. But the next day my dad and me went to Montrose Point Bird Sanctuary, and I added seven birds to my life list. We even saw a Leconte's sparrow."

The bell rings, and we grab our backpacks. Arnold heads to English class and Sean and I start toward math together.

"Did your pop always like birds?" I ask him. "I mean, is he the reason you started birding?"

Sean laughs. "Nope. It was the other way around, actually. He tried to get me interested in buildings. And then he wanted us to bake stuff together. He's an amazing baker. He makes the best cakes and pies you've ever had."

"I like cakes," I say. "And pies. Can he make a sour cream apple pie? That's my favorite."

"My dad can bake anything," Sean says proudly. "But I hated baking. Way too messy. I don't like messy. You have to be okay with gunk on your hands to be a good baker."

"So how'd you end up doing the birding thing?"

"I'd sit in the kitchen while my dad baked and watch the birds landing on our bird feeder. One day, my dad was making a pecan pie, and I was watching these two yellow-and-black birds fluttering around the feeder. My dad put the pie in the oven, and took a book down from the cookbook shelf, and handed it to me. It was the *Sibley Guide to Birds*. He challenged me to find a picture that looked like the birds at the feeder. It only took me about five minutes. Then he asked me if I'd want to go somewhere and look for birds with him. I was so excited, I fell off my chair. My dad said that if I didn't want to build stuff or make cakes with him, that was okay. But he wanted us to share something more than just our genetics. He said if what I loved was birds, then he wanted to love birds too."

"Wow," I say. "My pop would never say something like that."

"How do you know?" Sean asks. "You haven't even tried. Maybe you should tell him your comic strip truth, and see what happens."

All afternoon, I think about Sean and his dad, and Pop, and baseball, and truth. I make it through my classes without any of my friends asking awkward questions about the art club, and then, when the dismissal bell rings, I grab my backpack and head outside, not to my regular bus, but to the one that will take me downtown, to the store.

When I walk through the doors of L. H. Fischer Sporting Goods, Pop's at the register, his reading glasses perched on the very tip of his nose. He looks over the top of them at me and smiles.

"David," he says cheerfully. "What a surprise!"

I nod, but can't say anything.

He tips his head to one side, looking concerned. "Everything okay?"

I nod again, take a big breath, then sigh it out.

"Did something happen?" Pop asks worriedly. "Bad day?"

I take another breath and say, "Yes, and no. I mean, yes, something did happen, but it wasn't bad, it was good. But it made me feel bad—well, it made me think, and *that* made me feel bad . . ." I stop because I don't know how to say the rest.

Pop comes out from behind the register and puts his hands on my shoulders, then bends over and looks right into my eyes. "Whatever it is, good or bad, champ, you can always tell me."

So I try again. "I'm in the art club," I say. "And I won second place in a contest."

"Second place? Nice," Pop says, sounding exactly like he did when Allie came in third in her class's geography bee.

"It wasn't just a school-wide contest," I explain. "Kids from all over Westchester entered."

Pop nods.

"Melvin Marbury judged the contest."

Pop furrows his brow, and then his eyes go big. "Isn't that the guy who drew the *Northern Province* comics? I loved those comics when I was your age."

"I know," I say. "You gave me all your old books. I loved them too. I still do. They're what turned me on to drawing, and then I drew a comic strip myself, and it won second place. From Melvin Marbury."

Pop nods his head some more and smiles at me. "I

knew you liked to draw. I've seen those kitten sto-ries you and Allie do. But I didn't realize how much it meant to you. I'm so glad you told me, David." He turns to go back behind the register.

"There's something else," I say.

He turns around.

"Baseball."

He nods, smiling so widely that all his teeth show. "Tryouts tomorrow! I bought the eggs already!"

"The thing is," I say. "I'm not sure . . ." I stop and look down at my feet and then up at Pop. He looks at me, puzzled, and then he understands, and his mouth makes an O, and he nods, and sighs.

"You're not sure you want to play?"

I nod. "I'm not sure I *don't* want to play. But I'm not sure I do."

"Well," he says. He clears his throat, then says "well" again. I can't look at his face because I know I'll see dis-appointment there.

"I—just have to check on something in the stock-room. I'll be right back," he says.

It takes him almost five minutes to fake-check on the fake-something in the stockroom. He comes back carrying two metal folding chairs, opens them, and sets them out, facing each other.

"Sit down," he says.

I sit in one and he takes the other.

"Son," he says. I look up, startled, because Pop never calls me "son." That's what my bubbie and zaydie called *him*. His eyes are bloodshot and his nose is running a little, but he doesn't look sad, or disappointed. He looks determined. "Did I ever tell you how your mom and I met?"

"In college, I think."

"We met in law school," he says.

I look at him, surprised. "I never knew you went to law school. I thought only Mom was a lawyer."

"I didn't finish. I quit at the end of my first year. You see, law school wasn't *my* dream, it was my parents' dream for me. It took me a long time to see that, and to see my own passion. I'd started working in this store when I was sixteen—it wasn't called L. H. Fischer then, of course; old Mr. Blumenthal owned the place. I kept working here every vacation during college and even the summer before law school, and I loved it. But making a career in retail? Not what a nice Jewish boy was supposed to want to do. I figured I'd stay connected to the sports world by going into entertainment and sports law, maybe representing professional athletes. Then I met your mom during orientation and fell pretty hard for her. She loved the law, and she loved law school, and she could see almost right away that I didn't. You know where I brought her on our third date?"

I shake my head no, afraid if I say anything Pop will stop talking, stop telling this surprising story that I've never heard.

"Right here." Pop says, pointing at the store's check-out counter. He laughs. "I wanted to show her New Roque, where I'd grown up. We were both living in the city, so we took the train out here and I took her to dinner down the street, at a little Italian restaurant. We walked to the high school and got ice cream at the Häagen Dazs place. Then I brought her here, introduced her to old Mr. B."

He stops talking and looks around at the store, seeing something I can't. Then he pats my knee and says, "We were only a couple of months into our first year. Mom saw how much this place meant to me. She convinced me I should come back to work over the Christmas break. Told me Mr. B needed me. Then she kept prodding me, asking me questions, making me see what was already in my heart. What I really wanted to do. Making me see that I already had a passion, and a path, and it was right here." Pop pats the counter like it's a living thing and smiles a small, crooked smile. "I didn't know how to tell my parents. But your mom, she gave me the courage to do that too."

He puts his hands on his knees and leans forward a little, chuckling. "It took Bubbie and Zaydie a long time to forgive me, and to forgive your mom. But following my own passion instead of the dream someone else fashioned for me? I have never once regretted it. I love what I do." He puts his hands on either side of my face so I'm looking right at him. "I love what I do, son. And you should too. Whatever you decide about baseball will be fine with me."

TUESDAY, MARCH 3

SAMMIE

I wake up with a headache. In the bathroom I wet a washcloth and press it to my forehead, closing my eyes. When I open them, I know that the face staring back at me in the mirror is mine. But it doesn't feel like mine. "You got this, Sammie," I say out loud to the face. I watch the mouth move, but the words don't help.

I'm in my room, packing my backpack, when my mother comes in. "Sammie," she says quietly.

"What?" I say, making my voice cold and angry so she won't see my sadness.

She shifts from one foot to the other, not saying anything, and I realize she's holding some papers.

"That baseball meeting is today?" she asks.

"Yup. Are those the forms?"

She holds them out to me and starts to say something.

"Thanks," I say, cutting her off. I take the papers, shove them into my backpack, and push past her.

In the kitchen, Dad's waiting, pacing back and forth. When he sees me, he smiles and holds up a hand to high-five me. Like we're victorious. Like we've won something. I don't feel victorious, but I hold up my hand anyway and let him slap it.

I pour myself a bowl of cereal and eat it in silence. When I'm done, I put the bowl in the dishwasher, grab my stuff, and head for the door.

"Hey, Buddy," Dad says. "Aren't you forgetting something?"

I turn around, puzzled. He's holding the paperwork that I already put in my backpack.

"Thanks," I say. "Mom already—"

"Don't worry about your mother," he says, cutting me off. He holds out the papers. "I'm proud of you."

I take the papers and unzip my backpack to show him the other set, the ones my mother gave me. But he pushes past me and opens the front door. "Better hurry," he says. "Don't want to miss the bus on your big day!"

I shove the second set of papers into my bag and head out to catch the bus.

"You show those boys who's boss, Buddy!" he shouts after me.

DAVID

I stumble into the kitchen, still mostly asleep in my usual morning fog, and am surprised to see Pop, cooking his world-famous first-day-of-baseball scrambled eggs with cheese and salsa. For a moment I think maybe yesterday, in the store, never happened. Maybe I only imagined that I told Pop about my comic strip and that I wasn't sure I was trying out for baseball.

But Pop heaps some eggs onto my plate, sets it down in front of me, and says, "I'd already bought the eggs. I figured, what the hay, it's never a bad morning for a healthy, stick-to-your-ribs breakfast, right?"

"Thanks," I say, mixing some salsa into the scrambled eggs.

"Don't forget the toast," he sings, nodding toward the toaster, where two slices are waiting for me.

Allie's neatly cutting her eggs into tiny, rabbit-poop-sized bites.

"Good morning," she says cheerfully, placing a poop

pellet of egg on her piece of toast and taking a tiny bite.

I grunt at her because it's just too early to speak words.

She picks up her phone, looks at it, and announces, "It's going to snow today. A lot."

"Really?" Pop says. He walks over to the kitchen window. "It's not snowing at all right now." He leans over and looks up at the sky. "Looks a little gray, though."

"According to the weather app, six inches by this afternoon," Allie says gleefully. "My snow day calculator says an eighty percent chance of early dismissal!"

SAMMIE

The snow starts falling during first period. During Spanish, third period, I go to the window, and the parking lot is completely white. By fourth period, when English class starts, it's all everyone can talk about. Mr. Pachelo keeps clapping his hands and trying to get our attention, but no one even notices. Carli and Sarah are twittering and giggling, and Haley's telling Marissa about how they never had snow days in the Bronx. Raven and Max and Andrew aren't even in their seats. They're clustered at the window talking and high-fiving each other. I'm the only one even half paying attention to Mr. P, and that's only because I don't have anyone to talk to.

Apparently, the stress of trying to get our attention is not good for Mr. Pachelo's bowels, because five minutes into class, when Raven and Andrew are still at the window, Mr. P coughs, and the entire room is suddenly filled with a stink bomb of rotten eggs. I cover my nose with my hand.

"Uugghhh," Carli groans. She whips out a mini bottle of perfume and a tissue and douses the tissue in perfume.

"Everyone, take out *Tangerine*," Mr. P says. "Let's talk about Paul, and his relationship with Erik. According to Paul, what's the biggest difference between football—Erik's sport—and soccer, which Paul plays?"

Normally, I would raise my hand right away, but today I just don't feel like it. I want this day to hurry up and be over. So I watch the clock and count down the minutes until the period's over. Then I can go to the baseball meeting, and turn my paperwork in, and everything will be all set. Everything will be done and final.

I won't play softball. Everything will go back to the way it was.

The bell finally rings, and I pack up as fast as I can and head to the gym. I don't bother stopping in the cafeteria to pick up lunch. I'm not hungry.

DAVID

When the bell rings for lunch, I grab my backpack and head for the cafeteria. I have all the baseball paperwork—Pop zipped it into the front pocket of my backpack weeks ago, so we wouldn't forget—and I could still go to the crap mandatory meeting, and maybe make the team. But when I get into the cafeteria, I see Arnold and Sean sitting with a couple of girls from the art club, and the girls are talking while Arnold nods. Sean sees me and waves. Luke and Jefferson are walking toward the door with trays of food.

"See you in the gym," Luke says as he passes me. "Save you a seat?"

I glance toward Arnold and Sean, and I know what I really feel. I shake my head. "Nah. I'm not going to do baseball."

Luke's eyes go wide. "Wow. Okay. You sure?"

"You're kidding, right?" Jefferson says, looking way more disappointed than I feel. "We've been talking about tryouts the entire year."

"I am sure," I say. "And I'm not kidding. It'll be better odds for you guys."

Luke laughs. "I wasn't so worried about my odds. But thanks."

Jefferson rolls his eyes at Luke.

"Have fun," I say.

"Ha," Luke says. "Somehow I don't think the mandatory meeting will be fun."

"About as fun as getting a flu shot," I say, "continuously, for an hour." Then I turn and walk to Sean and Arnold's table and set my tray down. "Whatcha talking about?" I ask as I take a seat.

SAMMIE

When I get to the gym, Coach D is already talking, even though there are only six guys in the room. Luke and Jefferson are there, sitting on one of the benches in the back row. I choose an empty bench, as far away from them as I can. I sit down and open my backpack. Corey Higgins and Markus Johnson stroll in and sit down next to me. I glance at Corey. He smiles at me. I remember seeing him at the batting cages on Sunday, and wonder if he's smiling because of my fight with Dad.

When I reach down to get the paperwork out, Corey slides over so his leg's touching mine. "Hey, Sammie," he whispers.

I nod, and slide away from him.

He grins at me. I sigh and roll my eyes right at him. Then, ignoring him completely, I pull out the papers Dad gave me.

". . . practice after school every day, Monday through Friday, no excuses," Coach D is saying, staring down at his clipboard. "And if I feel the need for it, we may have additional weekend practices, TBD. Those are mandatory too. No excuses. What I hate more than anything is parents calling with excuses. You're big boys now. Don't go crying to Mommy when you have a schedule conflict. Be a man about it." He looks up from the clipboard, right at me, then coughs into one hand. "What I mean is, be a grown-up. No crybabies on this team."

While I'm trying to straighten out all the papers, Corey picks up my bag and hands it to Markus, who sets it down on the floor on the other side of him. Coach D doesn't notice or doesn't care.

Just then, Max and Spencer walk in. I slide over and wave at them, so they'll sit between Corey and me. But Corey slides toward me, and Max and Spencer take the bench behind us. I lean over Corey and Markus and grab my bag, setting it down on the seat beside me to block Corey. He grabs it and passes it over to Markus again, who sets it down on the floor next to him. Then Corey slides over until his leg is pressed against mine.

"Why aren't you sitting with your boyfriend?" he whispers.

"I don't have a boyfriend," I say back, not whispering.

"Sammie," Coach D says, "when I talk, you listen. What's going on back there?" Without waiting for an answer, he starts up his lecture again. "Practices will start next Wednesday. We'll run outdoors no matter what, even if it's snowing like today. None of this girly—err, harrumph," Coach coughs into his hand. "None of this wimpy running in the halls. A little cold weather never hurt anybody."

"I heard you and Luke Sullivan were making out on the bus," Corey whispers.

Behind us, Max shushes Corey, but Coach D doesn't seem to notice.

"You heard wrong," I whisper, keeping my eyes on Coach D.

"Then you're available?" Corey asks quietly. "Playing the field? Looking for the right one?"

"I'm not looking for anything," I say. "I'm not interested."

Corey puts his hand on my leg. I startle, surprised,

and turn to look at him, wondering if this is some kind of cool kid joke. But he's staring straight ahead, at Coach D. I try to pick his hand up and move it off my leg, away from me, but he's strong and holds it there. I glance at Coach D, who is looking right in our direction, but he doesn't say anything to Corey.

"Cut it out," I whisper to Corey. "Move your hand."

"Make me," he whispers back.

"Hey," Max says to Corey. "What are you doing? Sammie told you—"

"Max!" Coach D snaps. "I expect your full attention. Whatever games you're playing back there, they end now."

"But Coach—" Max starts to protest.

"No buts. First two weeks are tryouts. I'm testing you," Coach says. "Figuring out who's truly committed to the team. There will be cuts. Look around at your competition because not everyone will make this team."

Corey squeezes my leg, and leans in to whisper something in my ear. His breath smells like French fries.

"What a jerk," Spencer says loudly.

I push Corey away, stand up, walk past him and Markus, grab my bag, shove the papers inside, and keep on walking.

"Samantha," Coach D says. "Where are you going?

Meeting's not over."

I don't say anything.

I walk out of the gym and am halfway down the hall, on my way to the cafeteria to apologize to Haley, when somebody grabs my arms—two somebodies, actually, one on each side. Corey and Markus.

"Coach D wants you back in the meeting," Corey says.

"Leave me alone."

"Can't," Markus says, grinning. "Coach wants you there."

"Tell him I changed my mind. I don't want to play baseball." I try to speak loudly, to sound tough, but my voice catches in my throat and it comes out wobbly and hoarse.

"I thought you liked playing with the boys," Markus says, backing me up against the lockers.

My heart is racing and I feel out of breath and off-balance. "Get away from me," I say.

Corey shakes his head back and forth slowly. "Can't."

"Cut it out," I say. "Leave me alone."

"Coach D wants you in the gym," Markus says, putting his hands on either side of my head and leaning toward me. "And what Coach wants, Coach gets."

"Stop it," I say. I put my hand on Markus's chest and try to push him away, but I can't.

Suddenly, over his shoulder, I see Valerie, Jelly, and Savanna. Corey sees them too and steps back, but Markus's back is to them, so he's caught off guard. Valerie grabs his arms and pulls him away from me.

"What do you think you're doing?" she says.

Jelly takes one of Markus's arms and Valerie hangs on to the other. Savanna plants herself in front of Corey, so her face is inches from his.

"We weren't doing anything," Markus protests. "Sammie walked out right in the middle of the baseball meeting for no reason. Coach D told us to bring her back."

"Really?" Valerie asks, still holding Markus. "No way Coach D told you to bully her into coming back to the meeting. You guys are idiots. Get out of here."

I'm still leaning against the lockers as Corey and Markus shuffle off down the hall.

"Those two are the biggest jerks in the seventh grade," Valerie says. She puts her arms around me, and I want to say something to thank her, to show her that I'm okay, but what I do instead is start to shake. My whole body is vibrating and I can't stop it. She keeps her arm around me and pulls me into her.

I catch my breath and say, "It happened so fast. They caught me by surprise. I should have fought back harder, but—"

"Shoulda, coulda, woulda," Valerie cuts me off. "There were two of them and one of you. They always work as a team. Luckily, Savanna saw them." She pats my shoulders and lets go of me. "That's what friends are for. Girls got to stick up for each other. Especially around jerks like those two. Right?"

"Right," I whisper.

Jelly flexes her arm. "Of course, it helps that I'm so strong. And tough!"

Savanna does a bodybuilder pose with both arms flexed. "Yeah, and I'm stronger, and tougher!"

I smile, and realize that they're right: they are strong. And tough. They stand up for themselves, and they stand up for each other. They stood up for me, even though I've been ready to give up on them.

I smile a wobbly smile. "You're both strong. You're like superheroes."

Savanna makes a *pffft* sound and waves her hand. "Nah. We're just softball-strong. Athletes. Like you."

DAVID

Sean is explaining to Arnold and Caroline and Ruby and me the difference between a black-capped chickadee and a Carolina chickadee—with pictures—when I look up and see Sammie come into the cafeteria with a bunch of other girls, which is really weird because she's supposed to be in the mandatory baseball meeting. They all grab trays and get into the food line, and they're talking and laughing. One of the girls puts her arm around Sammie and gives her a quick squeeze.

"I've seen black-capped chickadees in New Hampshire, New Jersey, and Virginia. Their range is much bigger than the Carolina chickadees'." When he talks about birds, Sean sounds exactly like Pop talking about some great new aluminum bat he's going to start carrying at the store.

"What does 'range' mean?" I ask Sean, glancing up at the cafeteria doors just in time to see Luke walking by, heading toward the west wing. I *know* the baseball meeting should still be going on, because Coach D has a reputation for keeping everyone until after the dismissal bell rings, so they're all late for their next class. If both Sammie and Luke aren't in there, something big must have happened, bigger even than Coach D having a spontaneous bloody nose, which he sometimes does get.

I can't believe Luke would bail on baseball. He was the starting catcher for the Diamondbacks. So maybe Coach D had a heart attack?

"Hang on, I gotta check on something," I tell Sean. "Medical emergency." Then I grab my backpack and race after Luke.

"Hey," I call after him. "Wait up!"

He turns and sees me, and for a split second I think he might try to take off running and lose me, but he doesn't. I catch up to him, panting a little. "Where are you going? What happened to the mandatory meeting?"

Then Luke does the weirdest thing: he starts blushing. "I . . . have to drop something off in the guidance office."

"Coach D let you leave the mandatory meeting to 'drop something off' in the guidance office?"

Luke's face is still bright red, which doesn't make any sense because there's nothing embarrassing about guidance counselors except maybe for Mr. Lang's seasonally themed ties, but they should make Mr. Lang blush, not Luke, when I suddenly remember who else has an office in the guidance office.

"Dr. Ginzburg!" I say, proud of myself for figuring it out. "You're going to see Dr. Ginzburg."

"You don't have to shout about it," Luke says, frowning a little. He looks down at the floor. "It's no big deal. I've met with her like four or five times, that's all, just because I'm new. But things are better and I don't have to keep meeting with her. She wanted to see me one more time. I suggested today, so I could skip out of at least part of that stupid baseball meeting." He meets my eyes and smiles a small, crooked smile. "Apparently, Dr. Ginzburg has a lot of pull. I was allowed to turn my paperwork in to Coach D, sit politely for fifteen minutes, and then get the nod that I could leave."

"Good one," I say.

"Hey," Luke says. "Don't tell anyone about Dr. Ginzburg, okay? I mean, *you* understand it's only because I'm new, but the other guys . . ." He trails off.

Then the light bulb goes off in my head about where Luke was those times he wasn't at lunch. And I realize that *nothing* has been going on between Sammie and Luke at lunchtime. Luke's been hiding his meetings with Dr. Ginzburg the same way I was hiding my art club membership.

"No problem," I say, feeling suddenly better because maybe Luke hasn't sealed the deal with Sammie. "I won't tell anyone."

"Come with me?" he asks. "It'll only take like ten minutes. Then I can tell you all about the baseball torture and you can tell me why you decided not to try out."

I walk with him to the guidance office and sit and work on my latest comic strip while Luke talks to Dr. Ginzburg. He comes out of her office just as the first bell rings.

We head back to the east wing, round the corner,

and run right into Jefferson, opening his locker.

"What were you guys doing up here?" he asks.

"I had to drop some papers off in the teachers' center," Luke says. "David went with me, to keep me company." He says it so smoothly that even though I *know* he's lying, I believe him.

"What are *you* doing up here?" I ask. "What happened to the mandatory meeting?"

Jefferson smirks. "I think we broke Coach D. So many people were leaving that he gave up and let us all go early." He punches me in the arm, kind of hard. "Sammie was one of the ones who walked out." He looks at Luke. "Right before you left. Did you find her?"

Luke looks puzzled. "What?"

"Sammie. Did you find her? I figured you went after her, to make a move on her, right? Show the rest of us how it's done?"

"Umm," Luke hedges. "On the bus. When the away games start."

We walk toward the back staircase, Jefferson giving a blow-by-blow of the part of the mandatory baseball meeting that Luke missed, and we push through the doors into the back stairwell. I look down and see Sammie coming through the doors below with Andrew and Kai. Jefferson sees them too, glances at me, and calls down, "Guys! Luke's here. With me. Let's do it!"

He steps behind Luke and they start down the stairs. I follow, puzzling over what Jefferson said. Do what? Then I remember: the prank. I stop suddenly, halfway down the stairs, and some girl behind me bumps into me, pushing me forward into Jefferson.

"Watch it!" he says, one hand on Luke's shoulder.

Think! Think! I tell my brain, trying to come up with some way to make this all stop.

Luke and then Jefferson hit the landing. I'm three stairs above them, still trying to figure a way out, when Andrew and Kai take Sammie's arms, one on either side of her. Jefferson pushes Luke so his back's against the wall, and the other guys propel Sammie into Luke.

I stand, frozen, on the bottom step.

Jefferson grins and pulls out his phone.

Sammie's pressed into Luke, and their faces are inches apart. I see her blink, and watch tears fill the inside corners of her eyes, which are wide open.

"This is your chance, Luke," Andrew says. "Show us how it's done. Go for it."

No one moves. We're all frozen there, like some weird stop-action movie that's stopped for too long. Behind us, kids are pushing their way up the stairs, talking and laughing like nothing's going on.

Then Sammie turns, and punches Andrew right in

the stomach. He gasps and doubles over. She kicks Jefferson so hard in his shin that he wails in pain, grabbing his leg and hopping. Then she turns back to Luke, who is still pressed against the wall.

"I'm *not* your girlfriend," she says. "I never was and I never will be. I don't even *like* you. Do me a favor and *disappear*."

She turns and looks at me, and her eyes are hard and angry. "Was this your idea? What happened on the bus wasn't enough? You had to start telling lies about me too? I thought you were my friend. My best friend."

I hold my hands out, trying to look like I don't know what she's talking about, but my face is hot with shame and guilt. And Sammie? She's done with me. She turns and marches up the stairs.

"That hurt," Andrew complains. "What got into her? She knows we were just joking, right?"

I look around to see what Kai thinks, but he's vanished.

"I can't believe she took it so personally," Jefferson says, still sitting on the floor and rubbing his shin. "You did tell her, didn't you, David? About the prank we planned on Luke?"

I look at Luke. He hasn't said a word the whole time. He picks up his backpack and pushes past me, and I think he's going to go after Sammie, but he doesn't.

Instead, he pushes through the exit door, the one that says "Do Not Use," and out into the swirling snow.

I watch the door swing shut, and stand there for a long minute. But I know what I have to do, so I push through the door after him, out into the cold.

He's halfway across the playground, heading toward Quaker Ridge Road.

"Luke," I holler, my voice swallowed up in the snow and wind. "Luke!"

He doesn't even slow down, so I try again, cupping my already freezing hands around my mouth. "Luke! I'm sorry! It's not your fault."

He stops and turns toward me. I gain a little bit of ground, closing the distance between the two of us.

"I thought you'd be different," he hollers. "I thought you were nice. I thought you'd be a real friend."

He turns his back to me and begins running even faster.

I try to follow him, but I know I'll never catch up. He reaches the edge of the school grounds, turns once to look back, then disappears.

I turn and start back to school, and I have the most awful thought: I caused this. I did this to Sammie, and I did it to Luke too. Nobody did anything to me, and this is what I did back to them.

★ ★ ★

SAMMIE

It happened so fast. One second I was walking through a doorway and the next I'm surrounded by boys grabbing at me, touching me, pushing me up against Luke, and it's the bus and the baseball meeting and Corey and Markus all over again. My eyes start to fill with tears, and I feel so stupid, so helpless.

"This is your chance," Andrew says. "Go for it."

Those words go right into my heart, and something changes. I can't run from this. I can't let someone else, or a bunch of someone elses, tell me what I'm feeling. I *know* what these guys, my friends, are doing to me is wrong.

So I go for it. I punch Andrew as hard as I can. I'm ready to hit Kai too, but he backs away, so I turn and kick Jefferson, hard, in the shins.

I should get out of there. Run while I can. But I've *been* running, trying to avoid Luke and David, to pretend none of it ever happened. And what good has that done? I look Luke right in the eye, and I say loudly, so that everyone around us will hear, "I'm *not* your girlfriend. I don't even *like* you." I think of the way Luke ruined everything, and add, "Do me a favor and *disappear.*"

Luke stares at me with his blue eyes wide open. It's

weird, how he's looking at me, so I turn away from him. David's there, blocking my exit. David, who used to be my friend. Who threw me over for Luke. Who grabbed me on the bus, like I was a *thing*. David, who started all the rumors about me.

I almost haul off and punch him. Instead I tell him exactly what I think of him and his lies.

Then I push past him and march up the stairs toward math class. I feel strong and good. But when I get into the upstairs hall, something happens to my legs and they start to shake. My arms are shaking too, and I feel dizzy. I reach out and grab at the wall to hold myself up. Carli and Marissa and Raven are standing in a circle, with the rest of their clique, whispering. They look up at me, leaning on the wall for support, then huddle back into their gossip circle. I know what they're talking about: me.

Haley's standing outside math class with Amanda and DeeDee.

I push myself off the wall and walk on wobbly legs over to where they're standing.

"Hey," I say. "What's up with them?" I nod my head in the direction of Carli's huddle.

Haley rolls her eyes. "Gossip. Who cares?"

The second bell rings, and I turn to go into math class. Behind me, someone says, "I don't even *like* you.

Do me a favor and *disappear.*" I recognize Carli's sweet voice, and I recognize the words because I said them. *Good*, I think. Everyone will know that I am not going out with Luke Sullivan. And maybe my life can go back to normal.

Luke never shows in math class.

David tries to pass me a note. I tear it up without reading it.

DAVID

Five minutes into math class, Mrs. Merola announces early dismissal and that the buses will begin arriving soon. Mine is one of the first called, but when I get on, there's no one for me to sit with. No Luke and no Sammie.

I wonder how long it will take Luke to get home, and how he'll explain being all snowy and wet, and whether he'll tell his parents what happened. What I did. I wonder how deep the snow is on the Greenway, and whether I could walk to Sammie's house and try to apologize. Again.

When I get off the bus, Mom's car is idling in the driveway. She rolls down her window and hollers, "Hop in."

Inez is in the front seat, and Allie's in the back.

"I'm dropping Inez off at the train," Mom explains, "so she can get back home to the Bronx before the trains stop running, and then, David, you need to help your father at the store. None of the high schoolers can make it in this weather."

Does it occur to Pop to close the store early because no normal person would think of going out shopping for sporting goods when it's practically a blizzard? No way. Or, as Pop would say, *No way, José!*

"All of my clients canceled because of the snow," Mom says cheerfully. "I was just organizing myself to go over and help your father at the store when the school called. Thank goodness!"

"You can still go," I say, trying to sound helpful. "I could stay home."

Mom laughs. "Your dad would be so disappointed to see me walking through the door. I'm all thumbs around that place."

When I get to the store, Pop greets me with a hug. "What luck you had early dismissal! Snow like this gets all the skiers thinking about a day on the slopes. And if they can't find their gloves, or need a new pair of goggles . . . Fischer Sporting Goods! Ready to meet their needs!"

I don't know what to say back. There's no way I can even pretend to be excited about spending my early dismissal afternoon selling a lousy pair of ski gloves instead of drinking hot chocolate and watching three uninterrupted hours of TV.

Before I can say anything, Pop pulls out his wallet and hands me a ten-dollar bill. "Why don't you run down to Dunkin' and get us a couple of doughnuts. I'll take a coffee too, with skim milk and two sugars. And you get yourself some hot chocolate, champ. Then we'll get busy restocking the ski gloves and goggles."

"Okay," I say, taking the money.

Mr. Daniels, the owner, is the only person in Dunkin' Donuts, and there are no more Boston creams, with or without sprinkles, but Mr. Daniels says, "You can have four doughnuts for the price of one. I'm getting ready to close up. No one's coming out in this snow."

"Tell that to my pop," I say, wishing he actually would. "He thinks the snow is going to increase business."

Mr. Daniels smiles. "Your father is the eternal optimist. I wish I had his sunny outlook."

I walk slowly enough to eat two of the doughnuts on the way back to the store.

"Mr. Daniels gave me two for the price of one," I tell Pop, "so I brought you back a cruller. And the coffee was free, because he's closing early."

"That's the difference between doughnuts and sporting

goods," Pop says, which doesn't make any sense.

A whopping three people come into the store in the time it takes me to price an entire box of hand warmers, put them out for display at the register, and dust off the entire front counter.

Pop's hunched over the computer, counting up his supply of ski goggles, when the phone rings. I'm closer to it, but I don't make any move to answer it, because if it's some customer wondering whether we're open, I don't want to be the one who has to say yes in a stupid "so happy to serve you" voice, but I can't say no or "we're just closing up" with Pop sitting right there.

On the fourth ring, he picks up and says, "Fischer Sporting Goods." He listens for a few seconds, says, "Oh no," then "Oh dear," then, looking at me, "He's right here. Hang on, let me ask."

He covers the mouthpiece and whispers, "It's Wendy Sullivan."

Right away, I know Luke's said something bad about me, which I probably deserved, but before I can even open my mouth to explain, Pop says, "Luke's not home. Wendy was in the city with Lily, at a get-together with other adoptive parents. Her phone died, so she didn't get the call about early dismissal, and if Luke tried to call her . . . He apparently didn't have a house key. Was he on the afternoon bus today?"

I shake my head no.

Pop tells Mrs. Sullivan that Luke wasn't on the bus, listens for a moment, then turns back to me. "Do you have any idea where he might be? There's no one answering the phones at school, but according to the online attendance, he was marked absent in math, and in the periods after that. You're in those classes with him, right?"

"Yeah," I say, flashing on the image of Luke running through the empty field, the snow falling thick around him. "We didn't have eighth or ninth period, but he wasn't in math."

"Do you have any idea where he might have gone?"

I shake my head no, because the truth is I don't. I thought he'd go home.

"Can you check with your friends? See if anyone knows anything?"

I nod, my mouth dry and my stomach clenching into a hard knot.

Pop says, "Anything we can do, Wendy, just let us know, okay?" He hangs up the phone, then calls Mom and tells her about Mrs. Sullivan's phone call. I take the pricing gun and start slapping price stickers on each packet of hand warmers, but really what I'm doing is listening to Pop because I need to know how bad this is.

"Wendy's hysterical," Pop says into the phone. "He'd been having such a rough transition, feeling lonely and left out, at home and at school. She thought things were getting a little better at school, and so did Dr. Ginzburg. They met again today, and Dr. Ginzburg felt he was more upbeat, finally finding his way, but then he disappeared right after that. He never made it to math."

My hands are shaking and I can feel myself sweating, but at the same time I'm cold. Because it wasn't his visit with Dr. Ginzburg that sent him out into the snow without a coat. It was what happened after. It was what happened because of me, because I wanted to embarrass him, to get him back for being so smooth and cool with Sammie. For being everything I couldn't be with her. I didn't want it to turn out like this. I didn't mean for it to happen like this, but does that really matter? I did it.

Pop and Mom agree that she should go right over to the Sullivans'. Pop says he'll close up early and come home.

He hangs up the phone, then turns to me and says, "We're closing up shop here, champ."

I don't move. I don't say anything. I've finished pricing the hand warmers, but I keep holding on to the pricing gun like I'm drowning and it's the rope that will save me.

Do the right thing, Pop always says, *even if it's the hard thing.* Sometimes I really hate Pop's advice, and he has a lot of it. But right now I know one thing for sure: I've been doing the wrong thing.

Pop flips the "Open" sign on the front door to "Closed," then walks to the back of the store and turns off the lights. I'm still standing at the front counter, in the dark, shaking and sweating and sick to my stomach.

"C'mon," he says, putting a hand on my shoulder. "Where's your coat? We're going home."

"Pop," I say, "there's something I need to tell you. About Luke. And Sammie and me. About what happened today at school. And it's bad."

SAMMIE

When my bus is called, I grab my backpack and head for the front door, but I slip into the girls' bathroom. No way am I getting on a bus with David and Luke.

I start to call Dad, but his first question will be "How was the baseball meeting?" And I don't want to answer that one. So I text Rachel, but she texts back that she and Becca can't pick me up because they have to take a bunch of their friends home. No room in the car.

As a last-ditch effort, I call my mother, hoping maybe this once, just this once, she'll care. I dial her office and get Nancy, her secretary.

"Hi, it's Sammie Goldstein," I say. "Mrs. Goldstein's daughter."

"Hi, sweetie," Nancy says. "You don't have to tell me who you are!"

"Can I speak with my mother?"

Nancy sighs, which I can hear even over the phone. "I'm so sorry," she says, kind of whispering. "Mrs. Goldstein is with a client." That's what they call the people who are buying a house—clients. Not customers, because customer sounds too ordinary.

"Tell her it's important," I say. "Tell her it's me, her daughter, Sammie. And it's important." My eyes fill with tears. I clench my teeth, trying to make them stop, but it doesn't work.

Nancy sighs again. "One sec," she says, and puts me on hold. I listen for about five minutes to some strange woman's voice telling me about all of the great services that Holcrofte and Banner Realtors can offer me, until Nancy comes back on the line.

"Mrs. Goldstein is very busy at the moment, but she'll return your call as soon as possible. She has your number?"

I picture my mother, deep in discussion with her *clients*, waving her perfectly manicured hand at Nancy, too busy to speak to her daughter.

"Yes," I say, and end the call.

I stare down at the toilet, blurry through my tears. Then I take a deep breath and drop my phone in. It makes a plop when it hits the water, then sinks down to the bottom, but the screen stays lit for a long time. Finally, it flickers, then goes black.

"Go ahead," I say out loud to my dead phone. "Call me back when it's *convenient*."

Just then, someone walks into the bathroom. I grab my phone out of the toilet, dry it off with some toilet paper, blow my nose, and use some more toilet paper to wipe my eyes.

"Sammie?" It's Haley.

"Yeah," I say, still inside the stall because I don't want Haley to see me with my eyes and nose all red.

"You okay?"

"I'm great," I say, still inside the stall. "I missed my bus, and no one can come get me."

"You can always walk," Haley says. "Can't you? You have two legs."

Haley's right, of course. I don't have to feel helpless. But the truth is, I do. I feel helpless and scared.

I step out of the stall and face Haley, and tell her the

truth. "I'm scared. I don't feel safe walking home alone. Can I go home with you?"

Haley doesn't say anything for a long minute. "Why would you want to go home with me? You totally dissed me, like . . . yesterday."

"I was being stupid," I say. "I'm really good at baseball, and it's what I've always played. Before I started going to the softball practices with you, I didn't know anything about softball, honestly. I thought it was sissy baseball. Like for girls—"

Haley holds up her hand. "Stop," she says. "You're making it worse."

"What I mean is I thought because it was for girls it wasn't real. Wasn't serious. I know that's wrong—"

"And stupid," Haley adds, crossing her arms, but smiling just a little.

"Yeah," I say, "and stupid. I mean, there's nothing wrong with playing baseball, even if you're a girl. But I was doing it for the wrong reasons. I wasn't seeing what was in front of my eyes. I mean, you and the other girls . . . you're strong. There are some great athletes on the girls' softball team. Girls who are just as talented as me—"

"Maybe more talented," Haley says, grabbing a wad of toilet paper and handing it to me because there's still snot coming out of my nose.

I blow my nose and smile at her. "We'll see about that." I toss the TP into the toilet and say, not looking at her, "I also didn't want you to feel sorry for me. I didn't want to be pitied."

"I never felt sorry for you."

"The way my dad was yelling and making a scene, it was embarrassing. He sounded like a jerk."

Haley makes an *uh-huh* sound, but quietly.

"He's not a jerk. He's always been my biggest fan. And my coach, and my friend. My go-to. He just doesn't know about girls' softball."

"Sometimes even parents can be ignorant," Haley says.

"I think he's stuck in, like, 1980."

Haley laughs. "Maybe even 1950."

I sigh. "I don't want to go home. I know I can walk through a blizzard and make it home, but . . . I don't want to. I made my decision about softball, but I'm not ready to explain it all to my dad. So can I go home with you? Please?"

"What about your mom?"

I sigh. "We're not like you and your mom. I mean, we don't fight or anything, but we just don't get each other. She won't care if I don't come home, and she definitely doesn't have a clue about the whole softball thing."

Haley reaches into her pocket and pulls out a ten-dol-lar bill. "My mom gave me money for a cab just in case. Her snow day app predicted we'd have early dismissal. She's a teacher so she follows the weather like it's her religion."

Haley calls a cab, and we take it to her apartment.

We ride the elevator up to the third floor, and Haley opens the door with her key. "Follow me."

I follow her down a short front hall, past a galley kitchen, and into what seems to be the living room, but with a dining room table at the end near the kitchen.

"We should put our stuff in my room," Haley says. "My mom goes bonkers if I leave it out here."

So I follow Haley down a small hallway off the living room, into her bedroom. "My mom's room is on the other side of the hall," Haley explains.

The walls of Haley's room are covered with post-ers of women athletes, including one of the 2012 USA Softball National Team. I walk over and study it. "I didn't know there was even such a thing as a national women's team."

"Apparently there are a lot of things you don't know," Haley says. "Or think you know but are actu-ally wrong about."

"Yeah," I say quietly. "Apparently."

"Do you want to call your parents and let them know you're here?"

"They're not worried about me," I say. "I'll text them later."

Haley looks at me for a long second without saying anything. Then she shrugs. "They're your parents."

I follow her out to the kitchen.

"How about we make some brownies," she suggests.

"I've never made brownies before," I say. "The Peas—my sisters—are the bakers in my family. They make brownies about once a week. And chocolate chip cookies. But they eat like one brownie and then give away the rest to friends. Or to Dad and me."

"You should know how to make them yourself," Haley says, opening a cabinet door and taking out a box of cocoa, a bag of flour, and a bag of sugar. "Since you're the one eating them."

She pulls out a couple of bowls and sets them on the counter. Then she gets vanilla, a stick of butter, and a couple of eggs, and shows me how to make brownies. It isn't even hard to do. While they're baking in the oven, we rinse all the dishes we used and load them into the dishwasher. Then we make hot chocolate,

"My mom's a stickler about cleaning up," Haley says.

"She says the apartment is too small for messes. I can cook anything I want, as long as I clean up. If I don't, I lose my cooking privileges."

"She sounds tough," I say.

"Not really. She's kind of a softie, except about messes."

When the brownies are baked, and cooled enough to cut, we take them into the living–dining room and flop onto the couch. Haley turns on the TV.

"How about *That '70s Show*?" she asks.

"Love it!" I sit, curling my feet up under me and snuggling down into Haley's couch. She pulls an afghan off the back and drapes it over the two of us.

An hour later, we're still plopped in front of the TV, just starting our third episode and halfway through the pan of brownies when Haley's mom comes through the door like a snowy tornado.

"Oh my GOD," she says, tossing her car keys onto the front hall table. "It's a blizzard out there. I've never been so scared driving in my entire life. I cannot believe those jerks at the board of ed refused to close school early. Every single school up here in Westchester had early dismissal, but New York City? Nope."

Then she sees me, and stops. "Sammie!" She puts one hand on a hip and tips her head. "Sammie Goldstein."

"Mom," Haley says, picking up the remote and

pausing the TV. "Obviously you remember Sammie."

"Yes. Of course. Do your folks know you're here?" Ms. Wilcox asks.

I nod. "I texted them a while ago. They're fine with it."

Haley looks at me with one raised eyebrow, then turns to her mom. "Is everything okay?"

"A while ago," Ms. Wilcox says meditatively, unzipping her coat and hanging it in the hall closet. She bends and slips off her snow boots. She points toward the hall. "I'm going to change into some cozy pj's. I'll be right back!"

We're halfway through an episode when Ms. Wilcox reappears, wearing plaid flannel pj pants, an oversized gray sweatshirt, and fuzzy slippers. She heads to the kitchen and begins making a pot of coffee.

"You'll have to spend the night," Ms. Wilcox says to me, "because the roads are practically impassable. It's all settled."

"Settled?" Haley asks.

"I mean—I think Sammie should spend the night, right?"

A sleepover. Back in fifth grade, I slept over at friends' houses almost every Saturday night. One weekend we'd be at Carli's and another at Sarah's. Sometimes they'd both come to my house, and we would all sleep in the family room, our sleeping bags laid out in a row. But I haven't had a sleepover with a friend since fifth grade. Before the girl drama started. I can't help it—I smile.

"That sounds great," I say.

"Why don't you call your parents?" Ms. Wilcox says. "Let them know the plan. I'm sure they'd like to hear from you."

"They're both still at work," I say, thinking they didn't seem half as concerned about me as Ms. Wilcox is. "I've told them all about you and Haley, but I'll check in with them a little later." I'm amazed at how easily the lie comes out. I glance at Haley. She's watching my face, but doesn't say anything.

"Right," Ms. Wilcox says. She pours herself a cup of coffee, turns and opens the fridge.

"I almost forgot," she says, her voice muffled by the fridge door. "Some boy in your grade is missing. It was on the radio news."

"Did they say his name?" Haley asks.

"Luke something," Ms. Wilcox says.

"Sullivan?" Haley asks.

"That's it! Yes—Luke Sullivan. He disappeared from school and no one's heard from him since. They gave a number for people to call with any information. Do you girls know anything about this Luke? Where he might be?"

Haley looks at me, worried. "Are you okay?" she whispers.

I shake my head no.

"What are you girls whispering about? Do you know something?"

"He's in our math class," Haley says. "We were just trying to remember if he was there today."

"Well, if you know anything, I'll call the hotline for you. Think hard, girls. I'm going to snuggle under the covers and read for an hour."

Ms. Wilcox heads back into her bedroom, shutting the door behind her.

Haley picks up the remote and turns the TV volume up.

"I heard some talk about you and Luke," she says quietly. "That you guys were an item."

I shake my head no again. I can't believe that even Haley heard the rumors about us. And I can't believe she thinks they're true.

"It wasn't like that," I say. "Whatever you heard, it wasn't true."

Haley looks surprised. "Really?"

I look up right into Haley's eyes, because I don't

know how to tell the story of me and Luke. Of me and David and Luke, actually. But I know that I need someone to hear it. I need to try. I take a deep breath and hug my arms against my body.

"We didn't kiss. Ever. Except once on the cheek, on New Year's Eve, and anyway, I didn't kiss him back. But after that, he kept . . . touching me and saying things to me. I didn't want him to. I didn't know how to make him stop. Then David started doing it too. And on the bus, the two of them . . . they ganged up on me. They were grabbing me . . ." I don't even know how to say it. I motion with my hands at my chest.

Haley's eyes are open wide, surprised. "Like they groped you? Right on the bus?"

I nod and hug myself tighter.

"I heard something about the bus," Haley says. "But it was just you and Luke. You were teasing him? I don't know, you guys were making out on the bus? Something like that."

"It didn't happen that way at all. It happened just like I said. I think David's the one who turned it into a story about me and Luke. David tried to act like nothing happened. He actually said it right to my face: 'Nothing happened.' Like I wasn't there. Like it wasn't my . . . Like I wouldn't remember what happened to me."

Haley puts one hand lightly on my arm. It feels warm and reassuring.

I take a deep breath. "Then, today, when I went to the baseball meeting, these boys—you know them: Corey and Markus, the cool crowd—they were all over me, touching me and saying stuff. One of them asked me if I was 'playing the field.' I kept saying I wasn't interested, but I couldn't make them stop. Coach D must've heard them, but he didn't say anything to them. I left the meeting, and Coach D sent those guys to bring me back, and they . . . well, they were even worse in the hall."

Haley opens her arms and pulls me into a hug. "Valerie told me about it," she says quietly. "You must have been scared."

"Yeah, luckily, Valerie and Savanna saw it happen, and they came after the guys." I sit back and look at Haley's face. "The thing is, I might be part of the reason why Luke's missing. Because right after that whole thing with Corey and Markus, in the stairwell, David and Kai and those guys were trying to push Luke and me together. I was so angry after everything that happened that I told Luke I wished he'd disappear. And he did. I mean, he ran out of school, without a coat or anything, and I think that's when he went missing. So it's all my fault."

"Oh, Sammie," Haley says, shaking her head slowly

from side to side. "It's so not your fault. None of it, if you ask me."

"I feel like I should call in to that hotline, but would I have to tell them everything? And how would that help?"

"Do you have any idea where Luke went when he ran out of school?"

I shake my head no. "David went out after him. But he came back because he was in math class."

"So you don't have any helpful information," Haley says, reaching over and taking a brownie from the pan. "David's the one who should call."

I take a deep breath. "I also think I might have blown it for the boys' baseball team. I ran out of the meeting, and I never turned in my paperwork. I don't know what to do. "

"Do you want to play baseball?"

"It's what I've always played. I love baseball. I'm good at it."

"Maybe you could explain to Coach D what happened."

"Maybe," I say doubtfully. "But the truth is, I'm not sure anymore if it's what I want to do. I always loved baseball. I didn't really know what girls' softball was about, so I loved baseball because that was the only option. And it's a good option. I could maybe keep playing it. But I think I really like being part of a girls' team. I like being with a group of girls." I laugh. "I never thought I would say that. The girls on the softball team? They're real athletes. Just like me."

Haley smiles. "Duh."

"Yeah," I say softly. "Duh."

WEDNESDAY, MARCH 4

DAVID

Of course, I wake up right at seven a.m. No reason to be awake, with the massive snowstorm and school closed, so: the sun hits my face and boing! I'm up. I hate myself. I hate mornings, but this morning I hate myself even more than I hate the fact that it's seven o'clock in the morning.

Pop took away everything: cell phone, computer, Xbox, even my old Nintendo DS, which I haven't played in like two years. I felt like saying, "There were no electronics on the bus, Pop. And no electronics in the stairwell either. I didn't need electronics to be a total jerk to Sammie, or to Luke." But I figured it was better to keep my mouth shut. He was a man on a mission.

So I'm lying in my bed at seven o'clock in the morning on what could have been possibly the best snow day of my entire life, feeling sick and guilty and awful, when I hear a kind of soft scratching sound. I think maybe it's a mouse or a squirrel trapped in the walls, and I'm starting to spin a whole fantasy about how I'll tame the mouse/squirrel, and make friends with it, like prisoners do in all those old prisoner movies, and it will be my only companion during my long, lonely years of being grounded for the entire rest of middle school, when I hear the scratching sound again, a little louder, and coming from my door.

"Allie?" I whisper.

"What?" she whispers.

"Why are you scratching on my door?"

"I wanted to see if you were awake."

I sigh. "I'm awake."

"Can I come in?" she whispers.

I sigh again. She's not exactly a tamed mouse/squirrel that I've won over by saving crumbs of my prison bread to feed it with, but she may be my only companion for a very long time, so I decide to be nice.

"Sure," I whisper.

She pushes the door slowly open and crawls in on all fours.

I groan quietly because if she is going to be my only companion for the rest of middle school, I am so screwed.

"What's up?" I whisper.

"Luke," she whispers, and it feels like a punch in my gut.

I catch my breath, then wait, but she doesn't say anything else. I don't know what she knows, and I don't want to say anything that will make her hate me in case she's going to be my only companion. But after three minutes of silence, I can't help myself. "What about Luke?"

"He's missing, right?"

"Yeah."

"Since last night?"

"Since yesterday."

"I think I saw him."

I sit up in my bed. "What? When?"

It would be just like Allie to say that she remembered that she saw him once three days ago, at the supermarket, so that's what I'm expecting, but instead she says, "Last night. In our backyard. Right when you and Dad got home."

"Are you sure?"

"I'm sure I saw someone in the backyard," she says, "and I'm sure it was right when you got home, because I was in my room, and I heard the garage door, so I turned my light off because I was going to come downstairs and I wanted to conserve electricity. That's when I saw something moving in the backyard, and I was afraid it might be the abominable snowman, so I looked, and it was a person." She pauses and takes a breath. "I'm not sure it was Luke. He was wearing a big coat, and he was walking across the backyard, away from our house. So I never really saw his face. But I didn't even know he was missing then, and I thought it was him. I thought to myself, *Why is* Luke *in our backyard?*"

Why would Luke run away in a snowstorm, and end up in my backyard? It doesn't really make sense. But then again, who besides Luke would be running around in people's backyards during a snowstorm? I mean, if it was someone walking their dog, they wouldn't be in my backyard, would they?

Just in case, I ask, "Did this person have a dog with him?"

Allie shakes her head no. "But maybe it was the abominable snowman," she says hopefully, "and he was wearing a coat as a disguise."

"There's no such thing as the abominable snowman.

But why was Luke in our backyard?"

"Maybe he wanted to return something that he borrowed from you."

Allie is not the most logical person, but I don't say this to her. Instead, I ask, "Why would someone who has run away—in a snowstorm—be worrying about returning something he borrowed?"

"Well, then," Allie says, because she's nothing if not full of ideas, "maybe he wanted to borrow something from you."

Which is when the light bulb goes off: the coats and boots in our garage. Luke came to my house to borrow some stuff, all right.

After telling Allie a hundred times that she has to be absolutely quiet, not even a whisper, because we don't want Mom and Pop to wake up, we go down into the garage. Right in front of the coat rack, there's a small partly frozen puddle, made, I'm pretty sure, by someone who was covered with snow and looking for a warm coat. Plus, there's an empty hanger on the coat rack and an empty space in the row of spare boots. I pull out the plastic bin where Mom keeps extra pairs of socks and gloves, and I'm about to lift the lid off when Allie starts jumping up and down. She covers her mouth with one hand and points behind the bin with the other.

"What?" I whisper.

Her eyes are practically bugging out with the effort of not talking, which she's taking extremely seriously, but she shakes her head back and forth, refusing to be tricked into speaking, and points like her life depends upon it. I look, and see: a balled-up pair of cold, wet white socks. Luke's socks, I am 100 percent sure.

And in that moment, as I'm staring at Luke's cold, frozen socks, I know where he is.

SAMMIE

It's six a.m., and still pitch-black outside, but I'm so not used to sleepovers, and the muffled noises of Ms. Wilcox getting ready wakes me up. I yawn and stretch, and look over at Haley, who's sound asleep. I know I'm up for good, so I pad out to the kitchen.

"Good morning," Ms. Wilcox says cheerfully. "Did I wake you? I'm sorry."

"It's okay. I'm an early riser."

"You're going to be on your own for a couple of hours, then. Haley's most definitely not an early riser. She could sleep though a tornado. You guys have a snow day, but good old New York City public schools are open and 'ready for customers.' So I've got to go to work. Thank God for four-wheel drive." As if to demonstrate Haley's sleep-through-anything ability, Ms. Wilcox opens a kitchen cabinet, pulls out a fry pan, and bangs the cabinet shut loudly. She sets the pan on the stove, then grabs eggs and butter from the fridge.

"Scrambled eggs?" she asks me.

"Sure."

It feels nice to be awake with the world still dark. I sit at the kitchen counter and watch while Ms. Wilcox cracks four eggs into a bowl, then pours them into the pan and cooks them up. She sets mine in front of me and eats hers standing in the kitchen.

She takes a bite of eggs, chews, swallows, and says, "I chose this apartment because of the underground parking. Saves me having to shovel off the car. When Haley and I lived in Riverdale, we had street parking. Any time there was any chance of snow, I had to set my alarm for four a.m., just in case I'd need to dig the car out."

"That's doesn't sound safe," I say. "Driving in the snow like that."

"Most city students get to school by public transportation, so as long as the subways and buses are running, schools can stay open. Of course, many of the teachers drive in. But the ones who can't make it safely call in absent. Half the teachers will be out. No learning today. Just babysitting. Trying to keep the chaos a little bit under control."

Before she leaves, she goes to the hall closet and pulls out these things that look kind of like tennis rackets, but with shorter handles and some weird straps across the racket part.

"These are snowshoes," she tells me. "One pair is Haley's and one is mine. But they'll fit you. They're really easy to use. Haley knows how. If you girls want to go out later, maybe to your house or something, you could use the snowshoes." She speaks gently, like she's suggesting something hard and maybe even painful.

"Thanks," I say.

She opens the front door, then hesitates and says, "That alert I told you about yesterday? It was for two missing kids. You were one of them." She looks right at me, into my eyes. "You weren't quite truthful with me, because your parents didn't know where you were. I called them immediately and let them know you were okay. They were very worried about you, Sammie, especially because that Luke boy is missing. There was some thought that the two of you might be together. In any case, I reassured them that you were safe and here, with Haley and me, and we agreed you'd stay the night."

Then she hugs me tightly, wrapping her arms around me and pulling me in close. "Parents make mistakes," she says quietly. "Lots of them." My eyes fill with tears, and I duck my head so she won't see.

After she's gone I think about going back to sleep, crawling into the nice, warm spare bed in Haley's room, but instead I sit at the window and watch the sky turn from black to gray to gray-blue. A small, bright jewel of sun appears, and it changes everything. I watch that tiny drop of brilliance grow bigger and brighter until the whole living room is filled with a beautiful morning light.

I don't know why, but I get up and fish my dead phone from my backpack and shake it, like it's a snow globe, like it will tell me something about my future.

But the screen remains black. I blow on it, as though my warm breath will bring it to life. Nothing happens.

Maybe if I take the phone battery out and blot the insides with a tissue, I can get it to start up. I'm pretty sure I have a pack of tissues somewhere at the bottom of my backpack, so I grab the bag and start emptying it out. Which is when I find the second set of papers, the ones my mother handed me. I set them down on top of my binders, wondering why she didn't tell Dad that she filled them out. And then I see what's printed across the top: "Girls' Softball."

My mother filled out the paperwork for girls' softball.

I pick up the papers and flip through them like they'll tell me something I'm not understanding. But they're just forms. Almost the same as the baseball team ones. But also not.

I wonder if Luke's been found yet. I wonder what I'd be doing right now if Luke had never come to our school. If David and Luke hadn't ganged up on me on the bus. If David hadn't spread rumors about Luke and me. If I'd been able to tell Dad everything, and he'd been able to help me figure it out.

If David were still my best friend.

I close my eyes and try to picture today, but without all the bad stuff. But I can't. Because it did happen. And everything that followed happened too. Including Haley. Who listened to me and was a real friend. And my mother, who filled out the forms for me to play girls' softball.

I realize that I have to go home. That I want to go home.

Haley's still asleep so I get dressed in the living room, pack my backpack, and write her a note. It's two blocks to the Greenway, which, I know, won't be plowed, but that's okay. I'll take Ms. Wilcox's snowshoes. I can walk on top of the snow.

DAVID

The snow in the backyard is up past my knees, so by the time I get to the Greenway, I'm sweating and panting. I think about just turning around and waking Mom and Pop, and letting this be their problem, but I can't. I want to do this one thing right.

Allie begged me to let her come too, but I explained that she needed to stay home, that her job was just as important as mine, and that we each needed to do our own important jobs. Hers is to watch the clock, and if I'm not back in two hours, to tell Mom and Pop where I've gone, and why.

I'm kind of wishing that I'd said three hours, because it's probably been half an hour just getting across the yard. I turn and look back at the house, and Allie's standing at the sliding glass door, waving like mad. I give her a thumbs-up, and she gives me a double thumbs-up back.

I have no idea how long it takes me to get to Fort Maccabee. I just put my head down and walk, or try to, in snow so deep that my legs burn as I push them through it. The sky is clear and blue, and the sun beats down on me and on the silent, white world around me.

When I get to the turnoff for Fort Maccabee, I almost don't recognize it because everything is covered in snow. I kick through the soft snow until I hit the hard-packed stuff that lines either side of the walkway. Then I lean over and see a bit of blackness, which is the tunnel's entrance. I take a deep breath and push away the fresh snow until I'm down to the hard part, climb over it, and stumble and tumble down the hill, glad for the soft new stuff that breaks my falls, which are too many to count.

I'm panting and hot and covered in snow, and I'm sure Luke must hear me, must have heard me come rushing and falling down the hill. But the whole world is quiet, except for the sound of my own ragged breath.

The tunnel is dark. I can't see anything, so I shade my eyes and call out, "Luke?" My voice echoes back at me, and for a second, I feel almost relieved because maybe I'm wrong and Luke isn't here and there's nothing more I can do.

But I step into the blackness, and as my eyes begin to adjust, I make out a dark blob against the dark tunnel wall, and in the center of it, a small patch of lightness.

I step closer, and say again, "Luke?" but the dark blob is silent. I step closer still, and the darkness resolves into a pile of clothing—dark pants and a dark hooded coat, the small patch of lightness becoming Luke's face, pale and still beneath the jacket's hood.

"Luke," I say again, quietly because he is so quiet, and I step closer and stare into his face. His eyes are shut, and his face is so white—ghostly white, I think. Deathly white.

"Luke," I say, louder.

I kneel down in front of him and shout right into his face, "Luke!" My voice comes out funny, like I've been coughing.

He opens his eyes, but the way he looks at me, I know he doesn't see me. He is seeing something else, something terrible and sad.

"Hot," he says. "Is this hell?"

"No," I say, and I put my mittened hands on his shoulders. "It's me, David. You're in the fort—Fort Maccabee."

He shakes his head slightly from side to side. "Hot," he says. "Take my coat off."

"No!" I'm really shouting now because it's freezing cold in this tunnel and Luke is crazy and we are alone together and I don't know what to do. I don't know how to help him, and I was wrong again because I should have told my parents, I should have come out here with someone, but there is only Luke and me. My stupid eyes fill up with tears, and this is the thing Luke sees.

The stupid tears are running down my face, and my nose is dripping, and I don't know what to do.

"Crying," Luke says.

"I'm sorry," I say, not sure whether I'm apologizing for crying, or for everything else.

"I thought we were friends," Luke says sadly. "You were funny. Nice. Not like my old friends. But you pranked me." His face crumples. "And Sammie. I thought you wanted me to—I was a jerk. No one likes me."

"Not true," I say, shaking my head back and forth hard, my jaw clenched tight because the stupid tears keep coming. "I was the jerk. I was jealous of you and Sammie. I thought you guys really were . . . I was the one who messed everything up. You *are* my friend."

Luke is staring right into my eyes, wanting to believe me, and then it's like a curtain comes down and his eyes slowly close and his head sags forward.

I wrap my arms around him, pulling him into me as tightly as I can, and call out, "Help! Someone help!"

but my voice is ragged and hoarse and no one will ever hear me.

SAMMIE

A guy with a mini snow-blower is clearing the sidewalk in front of Haley's apartment building. He's got a narrow path done along the whole block. The sun is shining, and even though there aren't many cars out, most of the stores on North Avenue have opened for business. I walk the two blocks to the Greenway, carrying the snowshoes under my arm and smiling and saying hi to everyone. When I get to the Greenway, which isn't plowed at all, I strap on the snowshoes and step onto the wide, white untouched trail. The snow is almost blinding. It looks like a ski trail, except horizontal. But with snowshoes, horizontal doesn't matter. I feel invincible. Ten feet tall. Almost like I'm floating.

Passing David's house, I see the weirdest thing: footsteps through the deep snow in his backyard. They come right up to the Greenway and head in the direction of the Fort.

I remember the last time we were there, Luke pulling me down on top of him. I want to turn around, to get away from this reminder of David and Luke and from the remembering, but it's my way home. I have to pass the Fort to get home.

So I keep going on the Greenway, trying to focus on the blue sky and snow-covered tree branches. I want to keep my eyes up, but they're drawn to the trail David carved through deep snow. It wasn't an easy walk. I can see in his footprints how hard he had to work. Why? What would bring him out here?

Unless it wasn't David. Unless maybe the footprints are Luke's.

The trail goes right to where the Fort is, then veers off the side. I look over, and see a path of broken snow down the side of the hill, right into Fort Maccabee. Maybe this is where Luke went when he disappeared. But the trail looks fresh, like it was made after the snow stopped.

I stand and listen, but there's only silence. I shiver, and decide I'll tell Dad about it. That maybe someone should check and see if Luke or David is in there. But not me. Not alone.

I'm just about to start walking again when I hear a sound. Something like a sob or yelp, I'm not sure.

I stop and hold my breath and listen.

"Help," a faint, hoarse voice cries. "Somebody help."

It's coming from the tunnel, and it's a voice I

know—have known since I was five years old, when David Fischer said "Here you go" as he handed me the baseball that had rolled to his feet. Except now his voice sounds so scared and desperate that I scramble up over the frozen snow, and kind of ski down the hillside on Ms. Wilcox's magical snowshoes.

"Sammie?" David says when he sees me.

I nod.

"Sammie?" he says again.

"Yeah," I say. "It's me."

He's half lying down, with his arms wrapped around another kid who I'm pretty sure is Luke, and he's sniffling and hiccuping and kind of panting. The other kid isn't making any sound at all.

"Is that Luke?" I ask.

"I think he might be dead," David says, his voice hoarse and choked. He begins to pant.

"Dead?" I say, which is stupid, because the dead thing is clearly why David is freaking out.

"I think he was here all night," David says. "After what happened at school yesterday. When I found him a little while ago, he was kind of awake, but then he passed out or something and I can't wake him up. Now he's cold all over, and I think he might be—" He makes a hiccuping sound, which I realize is actually that word—"dead." David gives Luke a big shake. Luke just flops a bit but doesn't respond, and David starts panting again.

I stare down at the boy who used to be my best friend, at the two boys who did the meanest thing ever to me—one maybe dead, and the other definitely crazy—and I think about turning around and leaving them here. Just walking away, effortlessly, on top of the snow, wearing these awesome snowshoes. I'll go home and tell Dad, and he can call the police or whatever. It won't be my problem.

But then I remember Haley. The friend I found when David and Luke hurt me. Haley, who listened to me and showed me how to be a true friend. Who didn't walk away.

I turn back to David. "What about your cell phone?"

"I don't have it," he says hoarsely. "I told Pop what was happening at school, and he took my cell phone away and grounded me for the rest of middle school. Maybe forever."

"Oh," I say.

"What about yours?"

"Not working," I say. "It fell into the toilet."

David makes a kind of whimpering sound.

I scan my surroundings. No houses nearby. Just

frozen marsh on this side of the tunnel and frozen marsh on the other. I look up at the sky and then down at my feet. Of course, with my awesome snowshoes, I can walk to the closest house in minutes. I might even be able to run.

"David," I say, trying to sound calm and in control. "I'm going to go get help. I think you should keep doing just what you're doing—" By which I don't mean the whimpering, but just in case, I explain. "Keep your arms around him. Share your body warmth with him. Keep trying to talk to him. He's *definitely* not dead."

David nods, wiping snot off his face with one mittened sleeve.

I nod back and say, "It's going to be okay." I don't actually know that it will be okay, but it seems like the kind thing to say.

I turn and start off, again, walking on top of the snow. In my head, it's like a prayer, I can't stop it: *Don't be dead don't be dead don't be dead.* I skate along the Greenway, through the backyard of the first house I come to, and up onto the porch.

Ring the bell thinking, *Don't be dead don't be dead don't be dead.* Then stand, listening to a little yippy dog barking furiously right on the other side of the door. A quavery voice, somewhere off in the house, keeps saying "Coming" every couple of seconds. After forever, the door squeaks open about three inches, but the old lady keeps the chain lock still on. Her dog's foxy little face pokes out of the door down at shin level. It growls at me, showing its foxy teeth.

"Can you call 9-1-1?" I ask, the chant still in my head: *Don't be dead don't be dead don't be dead.* "There's a boy freezing in the tunnel under the Greenway. He was there all last night, and my friend can't wake him up now."

The old lady looks at me suspiciously, and I ask again. "Can you call 9-1-1? Please," I add because maybe she's one of those old ladies who's constantly complaining about kids these days not having any manners. "It's really important. The boy is maybe freezing to death."

She turns away from the door, and I think she's going to close it and tell herself that the girl on her front porch was all a dream, but she says, "Hold on." She shuffles away from the door, then shuffles back, and through the three-inch gap hands me a cell phone.

"You call," she says. "I don't know how to work that darn thing."

So I call. And explain. And wait, standing on her front porch, for the ambulance to arrive, still with those words—*don't be dead don't be dead don't be dead*—in my head over and over, like maybe I can keep him alive if I just keep saying them.

I wait, listening to the sirens, which start out faint and distant, and grow louder and louder, coming right for me. I keep saying the words *don't be dead don't be dead don't be dead* as an ambulance and an emergency truck come screaming down the street and pull up right in front of me. Two EMTs get out of the ambulance and race-walk over to me. Two more get out of the truck, then go around to the back and open the doors.

"Sammie?" one asks. I nod. *Don't be dead don't be dead don't be dead.*

The two EMTs at the truck pull a stretcher out of the back and the two others grab big black suitcases full of what I figure is EMT equipment.

As I lead them to Luke, they ask me questions about him—do I know how long he's been out here? Are his clothes wet? When was he last conscious? I keep saying, "I don't know, I don't know."

They don't have snowshoes, which is a really big mistake, so by the time we get to Fort Maccabee, the EMTs are all panting and sweating and red-faced. But they don't complain, just follow me down the hill to the tunnel, then set to work.

I stand right outside and watch them, still chanting my chant—*don't be dead don't be dead don't be dead*—as one of the guys kneels down and peels David away from Luke. They lay Luke flat down on the floor of the tunnel, then all crowd around him. One EMT opens Luke's coat and puts a stethoscope against his chest. Still bent over Luke, she calls out, "Pulse is thready but he's got a heartbeat."

Then I know I can stop my chant because Luke's not dead. So instead I start crying, which I would feel really awkward about except David's crying too. And not just crying—bawling, with his mouth wide open and his eyes squeezed shut.

So I figure it's okay if I do it too.

DAVID

Everything happens so fast. One minute I hear them coming toward us on the Greenway and the next there's a crowd of EMTs in the tunnel, and they pull me off Luke, lay him flat on the tunnel floor and crowd around him, with stethoscopes and tubes and an oxygen mask. They wrap him in a silver blanket and lift him onto the stretcher. Luke opens his eyes as they're wrapping him up, and the tears start pouring down my face, but I don't even feel embarrassed. One of the EMTs activates about a dozen instant hot packs and tucks them up against Luke's silver-wrapped mummy body, and then they lift the stretcher and carry him out.

Leaving me and Sammie behind. I look at her, and I

know that there's so much I need to say, but I don't say anything at all. Instead I just wait.

Finally, Sammie says, "I guess we should go home."

"Yeah," I say.

We walk out of the tunnel and start to climb uphill to the Greenway, not saying anything at all. Sammie's got snowshoes, so she can walk on top of the snow, but I sink with every step, feeling stupider and stupider because I can picture the snowshoes that are hanging in the Fischer garage. I don't mention that to Sammie. And she goes slowly, staying right with me as I stumble and slog through the deep, heavy snow.

I wish that she would ask me how I found Luke, so I could at least tell her a story that makes me look good. But she doesn't.

When we reach the top, we stand awkwardly, silently, for a minute.

"It's kind of a miracle that you were walking on the Greenway just then," I finally say.

She nods. "It's kind of a miracle that you found him there. And called for help just when I was walking above you."

I nod. "I was calling for help a lot. I mean, more than once. But still . . ."

"Still . . ."

I look up at the sun and around at the trees.

"I should get home," Sammie says.

"Yeah, me too."

We stand there for another minute, neither of us moving. I think of what Melvin Marbury wrote on my Splish Splash comic strip.

"The truth is," I say, "I was jealous. Of you and Luke. I thought there was something going on between you guys, and I was jealous."

"*I* was jealous of *you* and Luke," Sammie says. "I thought *we* were best friends, and then Luke shows up and it was all 'David and Luke.' And then on the bus . . ." She trails off.

"The bus," I say, and I feel my face flush bright red. I have to look down at the snow because I can't meet Sammie's gaze, but I keep talking because I need to say it all. "It wasn't supposed to be like that. I wanted to show you how I felt because I've had a crush on you for a long time. I was trying to make a move, the way Luke would, cool and smooth, so you'd know how I felt. I'm sorry. For everything." I look up at Sammie, hoping I'll see forgiveness in her eyes, and hoping even more that I'll see us there, the way we used to be. But she's staring down at the snow.

She's silent for a long time. Then she sighs, "Thanks. I should go now."

"Me too."

"See you at school," she says. I look right at her big, beautiful brown eyes, and for a moment they meet mine, and then she turns away from me.

"Okay," I say.

We start walking away from each other, on our separate paths. But I can't help it; I turn and call out to her, "I've been drawing a comic strip about us. About the way we were friends."

She stops and tips her head a little, then half turns towards me. "Like the picture book you stuck in my backpack?"

"Nope. Not a picture book. I'm trying something new. Want to read it sometime?"

Sammie shrugs, then turns away from me and calls over her shoulder, "Maybe. Sometime."

SAMMIE

I walk the rest of the way home hearing David's voice in my head. *I'm sorry. For everything.* They're only words. They can't change what happened. But I feel stronger for hearing them. Surer.

On the back deck, I unstrap Ms. Wilcox's snowshoes. Then I walk in through the sliding glass door, ready to stand up for myself. I will tell my parents who I am. I will tell them what matters to me, and what doesn't. I will speak for myself.

But the house is quiet. Deserted. The kitchen lights are off, and for a moment I think they've forgotten me.

Then I notice my mother, sitting in the dark on the family room sofa.

"Hi, sweetie," she says quietly.

"Where is everyone?"

"Your sisters ganged up on Daddy." She smiles a small smile. "Something about women athletes and taking softball seriously and Title Nine. I heard the name Jennie Finch, and something about Brandi Chastain, and a reference to Venus and Serena. They apparently feel he has to be straightened out about his attitude toward women's sports."

I'm about to ask her to please explain what that means, because the Peas have never been my biggest defenders. But then my mother says, "Actually, I asked the girls to take Daddy out. They plowed our street about an hour ago. Then we heard from the Fischers just a few minutes ago. They said that you'd found Luke, you and David, in one of the drainage tunnels under the Greenway, and that the EMTs left you there when they took Luke to the hospital." She gives me another small smile and pats the space next to her on the couch. "I figured you would walk home along the Greenway. I wanted to have you to myself."

She pats the couch again, and I walk slowly toward her. I want to ask her to explain about the softball paperwork. But when I sit down, she reaches out and puts her hand on my shoulder, then pulls me into her. I feel her begin to shake, and realize that she's crying. We stay like that, her crying into my hair and me holding her, unsure of how to let go, unsure of what to do, until she pushes herself back. Her hair is a mess, and her nose and eyes are red. Her mascara is apparently not waterproof, because it's dripping down her face, leaving thick tracks of black on her cheeks. My beautiful, perfect mother looks awful.

She grabs a tissue out of the box on the coffee table, blows her nose, and wipes beneath her eyes, clearing away the worst of the mascara drips.

"I was so scared," she says. "I'd told Nancy not to interrupt me for anything, so when she told me I had a call, I asked her to take a message. I didn't know it was you until after the clients left. And then I knew it must have been important because you never call me." She smiles a small, sad smile. "You and I don't always . . . our wires seem to get crossed sometimes. I tried to call you back, but it went right to voicemail. I called Daddy and the girls, and no one knew where you were. Then when you didn't come home . . ." Her eyes fill with tears that spill out into the black mascara tracks on her cheeks.

"I knew that you'd reached out to me, and I'd let you down."

"It's okay."

"No," she says, shaking her messy, tangled hair. "It is most definitely not okay. We heard from the Fischers last night. About what's been going on between you and Luke and David. About the way the boys have been ganging up on you. And spreading rumors. Daddy felt awful because you'd tried to talk to him about it, and he completely missed what you were trying to say. He can be so dense sometimes. Me—" She puts her hands on either side of my face and her eyes fill with tears again. "I felt awful because you didn't try to talk to me."

"I didn't know how to," I say.

"Sammie, I may not be the kind of woman that you want to be, and that's okay. There are lots of different ways to be a woman. But I do know what it's like to be a twelve-year-old girl, and to feel responsible for something that is *not* your fault."

She takes a deep breath and tries to smile, but it doesn't stick. "I was twelve too. The boys were strangers. I'd gone to the Y with my best friend, Amy, and we had a wonderful time swimming. We were getting ready to go home, getting out of our suits, and four boys came into the area where we were changing. I was wearing a one-piece and I had it half off. The boys blocked the doorway, watching us. When we tried to get past them, to get away, they let us, but one grabbed me as I passed, touched me"—she hesitates, then grimaces and says quietly, like the words are hard for her to get out—"between my legs."

"Oh," I say, stunned.

She pushes the hair back from her face and takes another deep breath. "We didn't tell anyone. For years I felt like it was my fault, because I was changing in the wrong place, or because I didn't yell at the boy and stand up for myself. I felt like . . . like maybe I deserved it, somehow."

She stops talking, and I'm not sure what to say.

She takes both my hands in hers. "What happened to you. None of it was your fault. You didn't cause any of it."

"I didn't know what to do," I say. "How to make them stop. But I didn't say no."

"You didn't say yes either."

"I felt so scared."

"I know," my mother says. And the amazing thing is, I think she really does.

SATURDAY, MARCH 7

DAVID

Pop probably started telling me how to Be a Man before I could say "man." There's a lot of crap you have to do to Be a Man: own your mistakes, face your problems, treat girls with respect, clean up your own messes, play fair, follow the rules. Sometimes I want to remind Pop that I'm not a man, I'm a twelve-year-old boy, because Being a Man really stinks.

Being a Man is why I end up in the lobby of Memorial Hospital, holding a gift bag with a Yankees fleece blanket in it, asking for Luke Sullivan's room number. Pop wanted me to bring a plant, which would be a totally lame thing for any boy to bring to another boy, and also would *not* be something Luke Sullivan would want, so I suggested a new Nintendo DS game, which made Pop's face turn purple because he immediately thought I was just trying to get around the electronics ban, which I kind of was. Mom had the idea for the Yankees blanket, which I immediately agreed to, mostly because it made Pop's face get less purple. He doesn't look good purple.

Mom and Pop both wanted to go with me to Luke's room, but on that I put my foot down: I would go alone.

Except you can't go alone to a patient's room if you're a minor, even if the patient is a minor, and even if you're the minor who kind of saved the minor patient's life, so Pop agrees to escort me upstairs and then wait in the hall.

We ride the elevator without talking, and then Pop asks the nurse which way to Luke's room, and waits outside while I go in. Luke's dad is sitting next to his bed, and Luke's looking out the window. When I walk in, Mr. Sullivan gets up and holds out his hand, and we shake, but Luke keeps staring out the window.

"David," Mr. Sullivan says. "Great to see you. Super nice of you to stop by. How about your dad and I go grab a cup of coffee and leave you two guys alone?"

"Thanks," I say, watching Luke, who's still staring out the window.

After Luke's dad leaves, I hold out the bag with the Yankees blanket and say, "I brought you something. A get-well gift." Luke doesn't say anything, or even look at me, so I keep talking. "It's from the store, of course. They're a really popular item this year. Made of polar fleece, so they're pretty warm, plus they have this year's lineup printed around the edge. So they're kind of like a collector's item because next year there will be a different lineup."

Luke still won't look at me, and I wonder if he's embarrassed about the way I was hugging him in the tunnel, because I kind of am, but the EMT guys told me that it was the exact right thing to do, because I was sharing my body warmth with Luke, and that I maybe saved his life, plus the doctors told the Sullivans that Luke probably wouldn't remember most of what happened in the tunnel, and Mrs. Sullivan told my mom, who told me.

But since he's still not looking at me, and not talking to me, and I've run out of dumb things to say about the stupid Yankees blanket, I rush on and say the hard thing that I need to:

"I'm sorry about everything. Making up stuff about you and Sammie, and that stupid prank in the stairwell. I was jealous, if you want to know the whole truth. Jealous about you and Sammie, because when you both weren't in the cafeteria I thought you guys were, like, together. When I finally figured out you were with Dr. Ginzburg at lunch . . . well, duh."

I set the gift bag down on the end of Luke's bed and turn to leave.

"You knew where to find me," Luke says quietly. "You told me I was your friend. In the tunnel."

I turn back, and he's looking at me. I nod, and for a moment I want to be the hero of this story. But trying to be the hero is kind of what got me into trouble in the first place, so I say, "Allie saw you in our backyard, and she told me. I guessed that you'd come in to get a coat and boots from the garage, after you ran out of school. Then I found your wet stuff behind my mom's sock bin. That's how I figured out where you'd gone."

"Thanks," he says, and I'm not really sure whether he's thanking me for finding his socks or for telling him he was my friend or for all of it.

But I nod again and say, "No problem. Sammie's really the one who saved you though. She heard me calling for help."

Luke winces. "Sammie," he says quietly. He closes his eyes, and for a moment I worry that maybe he's passed out again like in the Fort. But then he opens them, slowly, not looking at me, and says, "She heard you."

"Yeah. That was some dumb luck," I say. "Crazy dumb luck."

Luke nods again.

I'm not sure whether I should leave or sit down and start talking about basketball scores, so I stand there awkwardly for a long time, neither of us saying anything.

Then Luke says, "They don't think they're going to have to amputate any of my toes."

"Great!" I say.

"They won't know for certain for a couple of weeks, but the doctor said he's pretty confident."

"Good news," I say, sitting down in the chair next to Luke's bed.

"I have blisters all over my feet, and two of my toenails are black, but none of the blisters had blood in them, so that's good."

"Cool," I say.

"Wanna see?"

"Sure," I say, even though I think regular toes are pretty gross-looking, let alone black, blistered ones.

"You can't see much anyway, though. They're all wrapped up." Luke pulls back the covers and reveals two mummy feet, encased in mounds of gauze. "I won't be able to really walk on them for a couple of weeks."

"Wow," I say. "That sucks."

Just then, a nurse walks into the room. "Okay," she says to me, "let's let Luke get some rest now."

"All right," I say, and I get up to leave. "Good news about the toes, though."

"Yeah," Luke says, and one side of his mouth turns up into an almost smile. "Good news."

At the door, I stop, and turn around. "I could come by again, if you want."

"That would be great," Luke says. "Maybe even bring some board games? Like—what was that one we played New Year's Eve?"

"Blokus."

"Yeah. Blokus. Bring that one."

"You got it."

FRIDAY, APRIL 17

SAMMIE

The best thing about girls' softball are the cheers. Okay, maybe not the best thing, actually. But the cheers are really awesome. Because they're not just a bunch of words strung together; they're elaborate, and sometimes even choreographed. The cheers mean that all the time, even when you're in the dugout, and you know you're not going to get up to bat this inning, you're still part of the team. You have a job to do.

I stand on the pitcher's mound, gripping the ball in my right hand, and listen as Savanna, our co-captain, sings from the dugout, "Twenty is her number!" and all the girls repeat, "Twenty is her number!"

"Sammie is her name!" Savanna calls.

"Sammie is her name!" the girls repeat.

I'm concentrating on the plate and the batter and Haley's catcher's glove, but as I wind up and release the ball, I hear Savanna call, "She's one of the reasons—" and my teammates jump in and finish the sentence: "We're gonna win this game."

My pitch is sucked right into Haley's glove. The batter doesn't even move, and the umpire calls, "Strike!"

I didn't plan on being a pitcher. When I showed up for the first official tryout, I was just hoping Coach Wright wouldn't tell me to go back to the baseball team. But both of the girls who pitched last year had moved up to the high school team this year, so Coach tried everyone out. She said I was a natural. She said it was good I'd never pitched in Little League because that would have made it harder for me to switch to underhand. My body would have had to unlearn the feel of baseball pitching first. The stance, and the way you move your arm, and even how you step and when you release the ball—it's all different in softball.

I pitch a second strike. On my third pitch, the batter tries to swing because she knows she has to, but she's too late. She doesn't trust herself.

"Stee-rike three!" the umpire calls.

In the dugout, Savanna has started the cheer over, this time for Haley: "Twelve is her number!"

I look over to the stand of bleachers where the parents sit. Dad's on his feet, clapping and pumping his fist. If he thought he could get away with it, he'd join Savanna's cheer. But the ump keeps the parents on a really short leash.

David's next to Dad, standing and clapping too, but less excitedly. He told me that, since he's not playing baseball anymore, and has gone public with his art club membership, he figured he might as well go all out for King of the Nerds title. So he decided to become the middle school girls' softball team mascot. He calls himself Snerboy, which I don't really understand. He doesn't come to the away games, but if we're playing at home, I know he'll be in the stands. When he sees me looking his way, he gives a big wave.

Next to David, Mom is sitting, but she's clapping too. I never asked her to come to my games, and she never asked me if I wanted her to. She just started showing up. She usually doesn't last the whole game—someone's house needs to be shown, or there are client calls she has to make—but I kind of like it that she comes, even for part of the time.

The next batter is up at bat. In the dugout, Savanna's

starting a new cheer, and everyone's participating, doing their part to send energy and good vibes out to the field. I look at Haley, squatting behind home plate, and she gives a small nod. The batter taps her bat on the plate, then lifts it up over her shoulder. The sun is shining down on all of us, and for a moment, as I set my shoulders and take a deep breath in, I wish I could freeze time. Just stay here, with everything bright and perfect.

But I can't. So I wind up and let the ball go.

SATURDAY, APRIL 18

DAVID

"There's a shipment of baseball caps to unpack," Pop says. "We need to get those out on the floor pronto!" He pats an empty rack right near the front of the store.

I smile and nod because the really awesome thing is that Pop is *not* speaking to me.

"Sure, Mr. Fischer," Luke says.

Who would have guessed. Luke, in possession of all of his toes, and star catcher for the E. C. Adams Middle School baseball team, is also the newest L. H. Fischer Sporting Goods employee. Of course, Pop pays him, which is a better deal than I ever got. And being that Luke is only thirteen, Pop has to keep it off the books, and pays him in cash, which is not entirely legal, and is a new side of Pop that I kind of like.

What am I doing? Well, I'm technically working at the store too—I'm at the register, and ready to ring up any eager customer who wants to buy a new aluminum baseball bat, or a pair of running shorts, or a tennis racket. But it's two o'clock on the first warm spring Saturday and the store is almost empty, so my services are mostly not needed.

So I'm working on my latest comic book, which I'm calling *When We Were Friends*. It's about me and Sammie, disguised as a cat and dog. I've given them names: Chester the dog and Goldie the cat.

I'm using a lot of symbolism, so that no one will know it's me and Sammie, except me and Sammie. Like I'm telling the story of how we first met as being at a dog park, and Goldie knows more about the rules of the dog park than Chester does. She knows how to roll over and how to catch a Frisbee and how to play tug-of-war with another dog. The other dogs and their owners don't even realize that Goldie's a cat because she's so good at all the dog tricks.

Pop strolls over and takes a look at my drawing, chuckling at Goldie's fake dog nose.

Luke hauls the box of baseball caps to the rack where

Pop wants them displayed, opens the box, and starts slapping prices on the tags and hanging the caps on the rack.

"Coach D's got us doing a mandatory practice tomorrow at the batting cages," Luke tells me. "He's really cheesed off about the loss to Briarcliff. Says we all need batting practice."

"Bummer," I say.

"It's okay. Better than Hebrew school." He grins.

"Yeah," I say. "But pretty much everything except a rectal exam would be better than Hebrew school."

Luke laughs.

The truth is, I miss baseball a little. Like on a scale of one to ten, I miss baseball a two. I miss being part of a team, and I miss the way it made me fit in. But honestly, mostly what I miss is being on the team with Sammie, and Sammie's not on the baseball team either, so the team I miss isn't the team that's playing now. It's the team in my memories. The team that used to be.

But sometimes you can't go back to what was. Sometimes you can only go forward, with who you really are right out there for everyone to see. So Sammie's playing softball, and I'm the official girls' softball cheering section at home games. I show her my comics and she gives me great feedback, and we talk on the bus about whether we'd rather be forced to breathe in Mr. Pachelo's fart smells all day or eat horse meat for every school lunch.

But she's best friends with Haley now, and I have Luke and Arnold and Sean. I hang out with the same group of guys at lunch, and they kind of tease me about my comics and kind of don't understand why I'm not playing baseball, but mostly they're okay with it.

I look down at the drawing in front of me, and for just a flash I feel a little bit sad, but then I get back to drawing because it's a story I want to tell, even if I don't always look so good in it. Because it's the truth about when we were friends.

ACKNOWLEDGMENTS

Thank you first to my amazing agent, Saba Sulaiman: Your enthusiastic embrace of Sammie and David, and your certainty that you could find the right editor and house for my manuscript, were beautiful, shining gifts. And you did connect me with the best editor ever in Courtney Stevenson. Courtney, your gentle, thoughtful questions and suggestions have made my characters truer and this book infinitely better; working with you has been a joyous, exciting adventure. Let me also offer a humble and stunned thank you to the entire HarperCollins team; I had no idea you were all there, until you were: Catherine San Juan, Vanessa Nuttry,

Shona McCarthy, Emma Meyer and the entire marketing team, Kristopher Kam, and Andrea Pappenheimer and the amazing sales team. Thank you also to copy editor Jessica White, and to my sensitivity reader, who wants to remain anonymous.

Thank you to my fellow writer's group writers. Some of you read chapters; some of you read larger sections, and some of you read the entire manuscript, more than once even. All of you gave of your hearts, your honesty, and your writerly wisdom: Jennifer Lang, Karen Gershowitz, Liz Burk, Aileen Hewitt, Werner Hengst (of blessed memory), Paul Phillips, Cynthia Ehrenkrantz, and Jean Halperin; and Gerry Hawkins, Ian Berger, Dan Shapiro, Helen Chayefsky, Julie Coraggio, Kimberly Marcus, and Cindy McCraw Dircks. Cindy, thank you is not enough; I owe you flowers and chocolate and maybe even a puppy. Your persistent insistence that my story was ready for the world is the reason I sent it out. What luck I met you at that New York SCBWI conference.

I have relied upon the love and enthusiastic support of my beautiful extended family. To my sisters Amanda, Clara, and Jodie: being with you, your spouses, and your delicious kids is nothing less than magic; it lights me up. Amanda, thank you for talking me down from several ledges; you may be younger, but you are so, so much wiser.

Thank you, Aviva, for the chocolate mousses, front porch evenings, more Shabbat dinners than I can count, and, most important, your steady friendship.

My children, Eli, Noah, and Maggie: Thank you for not telling me I was strange when I gave up a paying job to sit at home and write, for sometimes even seeming a little bit proud of me, and for allowing me to snatch colorful bits of your lives and weave them into the tapestry of my writing.

Peter: Thank you somehow seems like the wrong thing to say to you. I had no idea, when we met in the hall of our apartment building in Park Slope, how deep and total and vital a love could become. I am grateful for you every day, always.